MEMOIRS OF A GARROTER

NEVERMORE BOOKSHOP MYSTERIES, BOOK 4

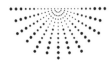

STEFFANIE HOLMES

BACCHANALIA HOUSE

Cover design: Amanda Rose

ISBN: 978-0-9951302-4-1

❀ Created with Vellum

To all the book boyfriends
who keep me up at night.

"I didn't lie. I just created fiction with my mouth!"
  – Homer, *The Iliad*

" h shite, oh shite…"
CRASH.
"Get back here, you bastards!"

I moaned, crawling deeper under my blankets and shoving my pillow over my head. *What's going on now?*

I'd been flatting with my new BFF, Jo Southcombe, for the last six weeks. So far, it had mostly been awesome. Unlike the dingy flat I grew up in, Jo's place had Edwardian features like high ceilings, picture rails, and beautiful fireplaces, as well as decent heating, comfortable furniture that didn't smell faintly like the rubbish tip, and a coffee machine that I would marry if humans and inanimate objects were allowed to wed.

It was also pretty cool to come home at the end of the day to a glass of wine and a friendly face. Especially after all the extra work I'd been doing at Nevermore Bookshop. Not only was looking after my three boyfriends Heathcliff, Morrie, and Quoth a full-time job, but I'd decided to forge ahead with a program of events to bring more business into the shop. I'd lined up the next three months with author visits, art exhibitions, local history talks, and even a ghost hunting tour. It was super exciting and

1

heaps of fun, but also a ton of extra work. Jo was great at listening to my tales of woe and offering advice.

But Jo was also... *unique*. She was the county pathologist, which meant that a) she worked all hours of the day and night, so sometimes she wanted to share that bottle of wine at three a.m., and b) she filled her home with the oddest collection of strange and macabre things. The other day I opened the fridge for a snack and found three Petri dishes of bacteria sitting on the bottom shelf. Then there was the anatomical skeleton behind the shower curtain (The first time I met 'Barry' I got such a fright, I tripped over the edge of the bath and smashed the bottle of Britney Spears' perfume I purchased 'ironically' but secretly loved), and the doorbell that played Monty Python's 'Always Look on the Bright Side of Life' whenever someone called in. Last week, she started a project studying forensic entomology and set up a shelf in the living room containing several jars filled with dead mice and various alive and very disgusting flies, ants, wasps, beetles, and locusts.

Another crash sounded from down the hall. Sighing, I threw off the covers, pulled on an oversized Iron Maiden hoodie, and peeked my head out the door.

"Jo, what's wrong?"

My flatmate danced around the living room, slapping at the air. I squinted into the dim light. *What's she up to now?*

"Are you learning some kind of hunter-gatherer mourning dance off Youtube again, because I think it needs work—" my words died on my lips as I noticed small objects darting around Jo's head. *Are those insects? Don't tell me she let her science experiment escape...*

My gaze fell to the floor at Jo's feet, where pieces of glass scattered across the rug. *Please don't let that be the South American fire ants—*

"Argh!" I yelped and leapt back as something large and black dived at my face. The bug zoomed past me and slammed into the door, where it hung around, admiring the view. "Kill it! Kill it!" Jo screamed.

I grabbed the nearest object – a replica Egyptian canopic jar – and swung. The ceramic vessel shattered into pieces, and the black insect darted down the hallway, completely unscathed.

"What was *that?*" I demanded, watching it flit across her portrait of Sir Bernard Spilsbury (he was the father of forensics, so I discovered in a forty-five minute impromptu lecture after I'd innocently asked Jo about it the other day).

"It's a locust! I accidentally knocked the jar and it smashed and now they're all over the apartment." Jo swung an anatomy textbook at the wall. She left out a satisfied "Yah!" as she connected with her target, leaving an ugly brown smudge along the paint as she drew back and swung again.

"You're telling me the flat is crawling with locusts?" I ducked as another angry insect dove at my head.

"It's less crawling, and more swarming!"

I covered my head with my arms and ducked into the kitchen. Locusts flew around the room like a whirlwind, pinging off the windows and diving at the dirty dishes stacked in the sink. In seconds, they reduced the herb garden on the windowsill to a bare dirt patch.

I fumbled under the sink, barely able to read the labels on the cleaning products. My fingers closed around an aerosol can. *Fly spray.*

By all the goddesses, let this work.

"Go back to Egypt, you poxy bastards!" I yelled, aiming the can at the swarming bugs and slamming my finger down.

A stream of white liquid shot out from the nozzle. I swung my arm around, laughing maniacally as I coated the insects. *Take that, you grotty little wankers—*

"Oh no, that's cooking spray!" Jo yelled.

What? Shite.

I lowered my arm just as a huge jet shot from the nozzle and hit the wall behind the stove. Oily bubbles exploded all over the kitchen, coating the floor and the walls and Jo's Victorian apothecary set and Jo and also me in a layer of slick, sticky oil.

"I'm sorry," I moaned, turning the can around to read the label. How had I missed the words 'Non-Stick Cooking Spray' in huge letters?

Probably because I'm going blind, that's how.

"We've just made them angry." Jo ducked as a dark swarm careened toward her head. She crawled across the floor and grabbed the front door knob. "Hurry, Mina!"

I scrambled after Jo as she yanked open the door and dived down the steps. I slammed the door shut behind us, wincing as locusts dive-bombed the stained glass window.

Icy wind whipped around my bare legs. My feet sank into freezing snow. I hugged my hoodie to my chest. "I'm sorry. I thought it was bug spray."

"Nope," Jo wiped a smear of oil from her cheek. "Definitely not bug spray. If it's any consolation, I'm sorry I broke that jar and set a swarm of locusts free in our flat."

I waved a hand. "I'm sure it happens all the time. What are we going to do?"

Jo raised an eyebrow. "I was thinking of just giving them the house?"

I couldn't feel my feet. "Or we could maybe call an exterminator?"

"I guess that would work." Jo glanced at her watch. "Oh, shite. I have to go. I'm late for work, and Cal will be waiting for me to prep the body." She scrambled in her pocket for her car keys.

"You can't just leave. What if the locusts get out? How am I going to get to my room? I need clothes." I gestured to my bare legs, now turning a bold shade of blue.

Jo shrugged. "I have no idea. I've got some old clothes in the back of the car. You can change while I drive you to the bookshop, if you like. It's not as if those guys aren't used to seeing you without your clothes on."

"But all our stuff—"

She flung open her car door and climbed in behind the wheel. "Forget the flat. We'll raze it to the ground, salt the earth, and get another one. With a hot tub and one of those multi-head showers. Come on, Mina. I've got a dead body to cut up, and you've got three hot guys ready to fan you with palm fronds and serve you peeled grapes. What's it to be?"

Sighing, I pulled the hem of my hoodie down over my arse and climbed into the car beside Jo. "I thought living with you would *save* me from chaos and mayhem, not *invite* it."

"You can't be right all the time," Jo said as she sped off. "Look on the bright side. At least it was locusts and not another dead body."

I groaned. She had no idea how right she was. Just before Christmas, I'd been a guest at the Argleton Jane Austen Experience, where two people were killed. That was on top of the other murders I'd been involved in – my ex-best friend Ashley, and members of the Argleton Banned Book Club. If I never see another dead body, it'll be too soon.

Relax, I told myself as I fumbled in the junk behind Jo's seat for some clothes I could wear. *All I've got to look forward to this week is a book signing, a writer's workshop, and some sexy times with the guys. It's not as if any murderers are going to be in attendance.*

Right?

CHAPTER TWO

"*Y*ou look tired," Morrie said as he held open the door of Nevermore Bookshop for me. "Trouble with your lesbian lover?"

I didn't even dignify him with an answer. Morrie and Jo had been friends for a while now. They both shared a professional interest in the criminal underworld – Jo as an employee of the local coroner, Morrie as a member of aforementioned underworld. He'd been teasing me about being in a lesbian relationship with Jo ever since I moved in with her, just before Christmas. I thought it was rude, considering he knew Jo actually was a lesbian, but that was Morrie for you.

Personally, I think Morrie was a bit hurt that I didn't move into the flat with him and my other two boyfriends, Quoth and Heathcliff. As tempting as it was, I knew being the only girl in a house full of fictional blokes would be a nightmare. Just one whiff of the smell coming from their bathroom reinforced that I made the right decision.

"Come on, gorgeous. Give me something more. How're the new digs?"

"Currently filled with a biblical plague," I replied, shoving past him, tossing my bag into the corner, and collapsing into the velvet chair beside Heathcliff's desk. Quoth fluttered down from the chandelier and perched on the ancient till. He studied me with his deep brown eyes.

You look different, he said inside my mind, tilting his head to the side.

"That's because I'm wearing Jo's clothes. Mine are currently being eaten by locusts," I muttered out loud, pinching the fabric on her red tartan cuffed pants. Jo was curvier than me, so her clothes hung loose, but I had to admit she had great taste. "Luckily, I found one of my bras under the seat in her car, otherwise I'd be sagging today."

Grimalkin darted out of the shadows and leapt onto my lap, purring as she curled herself into a tight ball. I stroked her back, letting her loud purr relax me and bring me to my happy place. Being surrounded by the shelves of Nevermore Bookshop and in the presence of the three men who made me feel all sorts of delightful things could cure any bad mood, even one caused by a plague of locusts.

As if reading my thoughts, Morrie strode across the room. He placed one hand on the arm of the chair, his face inches from mine. A wave of grapefruit-and-vanilla swept over me – Morrie's distinct and expensive shampoo, and a scent that never failed to send my heart into palpitations.

Ice-blue eyes locked with mine. Full lips curled back into a possessive smile. Heat pooled between my legs. *How is this man mine?* I still couldn't believe it.

And he wasn't even my only man, because apparently the universe allowed one lucky girl – me – to hog all the hot guys. Of course, my guys came from fictional books, so they weren't technically supposed to be in this world. It might explain why they were so extra.

"I'm assuming you're not in a mood to elaborate about the biblical infestation. Allow me to direct your mind to other things.

Blasphemous things." Morrie bent down and brushed his lips against mine. All thoughts of Jo's locust experiments flew from my mind as his tongue found its way into my mouth, drawing out a flame of heat that lit up my whole body.

"Meow!" Grimalkin piped up from my lap, annoyed that she was not the one being adored.

Morrie pulled back. "I think your pussy needs some attention," he growled, his cold eyes alerting me that he wasn't talking about Grimalkin.

"Meow!" she butted his arm.

"Sorry, kitty," I shoved her off my lap. "This hug isn't for you."

Grimalkin's claws *clack-clacked* on the wooden floor as she trotted away, howling about the unfairness of it all.

Morrie trailed his fingers along my jaw, pulling my head toward his and claiming my mouth for a long, languid kiss. I forgot all about Grimalkin, losing myself in Morrie's expert touch. This guy was an expert kisser. Locking lips with him was an act of surrender, giving up rational thought and falling headfirst into his psyche. Kissing Morrie was like jumping off the high dive board, like the first dizzying splendor of inebriation.

Slowly, Morrie unwound my scarf from my neck and tossed it on the ground. One by one, he flicked the buttons open on Jo's shirt, the tips of his fingers barely stroking the skin underneath. My breath hitched as he let the fabric fall open, his arms sliding around my waist to undo my bra.

"What about customers..." I murmured.

Relax. I flipped the CLOSED sign.

My eyes swiveled from Morrie to the bust above the door, where Quoth perched still as a statue, his dark eyes boring into mine. He tilted his head to the side, asking permission to stay, to watch, and I nodded. I liked it that he watched; that he *liked* to watch.

Morrie popped the clasp on my bra, and with agonizing slowness, slid the straps off my shoulders, pushing the bra and my shirt fabric down my arms, trapping my hands at my sides. A cold draft blew across my bare nipples, which already stood firm and pert, desperate for his touch.

But Morrie did *so* love to tease. He bent down and kissed my neck, my collarbone, along my forearms. Everywhere but my breasts. I growled at him and he grinned.

"You should know by now that you only have to ask," he purred. "I love it when you beg."

I growled again. My whole body buzzed with electric energy. "Morrie, would you be so kind as to suck on my nipples until I scream for mercy?"

"Why, Ms. Wilde, I thought you'd never ask."

Morrie's lips closed over my nipple. I arched my neck as a cord of fire tore through my body. His tongue rolled me between his lips. Morrie's fingers trailed over the waistband of the tartan pants, slowly tugging at the drawstring knot until I groaned with frustration and undid it myself. Morrie chucked, his musical laugh sending another wave of heat through my body.

With his lips still around my nipple, Morrie slid his hand between my legs, cupping my mound. Heat pooled inside me. I pushed my hips forward, desperate for more.

Morrie slid down my trousers and flung them behind him. They caught on the stuffed armadillo, so his head just poked out from under the tartan. Quoth fluttered down and perched on top of them, his eyes locked with mine.

I raised my legs onto Morrie's shoulders. He slid between my legs, his face lit up like he was unwrapping a present at Christmas. Morrie pressed his lips against my throbbing clit and my whole body shuddered. His tongue moved in slow circles, so I could feel every tiny movement reverberating through my veins. My fingers curled around the arms of the chair as I fought to stop myself melting into a puddle on the floor.

All around me, towers of books stared down in silent disapproval. But I didn't care. Pleasure built inside me as Morrie drew my clit inside his mouth and sucked it lightly. The pressure was so intense I cried out. My nails dug into the chair. Morrie released me and teased tiny, light circles on my clit.

And all the while, Quoth's brown eyes remained locked on mine. At the edges, flecks of gold appeared. Something about his gaze was so intimate, almost more than what Morrie was doing to me.

Mina, Quoth said inside my head. *You're so beautiful. I love you.*

Morrie sucked my clit deep into his mouth and I was gone gone gone, my body shaking in raptures of pleasure. My head lolled to the side, keeping Quoth's gaze even as flickers of blue neon light danced across my eyes.

Morrie stood up. "Less grumpy now?"

"Much." I held out my hand and Morrie helped me to my feet. His ice eyes raked down my body as I pulled on my knickers and Jo's trousers and slumped behind Heathcliff's desk. I knew what he wanted – to slam me up against the bookshelf and bury himself inside me. But Morrie liked his games, and he was playing one now. He wanted me to beg him for it. I wanted to, oh how I wanted to, but I had so much work to do before tonight's event. "Where's Heathcliff? I want to run over the details for the week with him."

Morrie made a face. "His Lord Tetchiness is still in bed. He said that he's not going downstairs while the shop is filled with *writers*. According to him, they're worse than customers."

I groaned. Heathcliff was the only shopkeeper I'd ever met who got grumpy when his shop was popular. And thanks to me, Nevermore Bookshop was doing better than ever.

A month ago I'd wrested free rein from Heathcliff to run the shop however I wanted. I wasted no time in remaking Nevermore Bookshop as a must-visit bibliophile destination. I took new photographs for our website, started an Instagram account, and organized my first ever bookshop event. Famous local crime author Danny Sledge was going to be giving a reading this evening about his latest novel, *The Somerset Strangler*. And tomorrow he'd be running a full-day workshop for crime writers. We had attendees coming from all over the country to learn from this master storyteller.

My stomach fluttered with nervous excitement as I thought about the workshop. Even though I'd never written a book, I would be sitting in on it with the *real* writers. For some reason that excited me more than anything else about the event. I'd filled my whole life with books, and it would be interesting to peer behind the curtain and see how plots and characters really came together.

Or it might be the fact that I'd seen far too many murders in the last few months, giving me enough plots for a whole *series* of crime novels. *Danny Sledge better watch out, or I could boot him off the bestseller list!*

But the event wasn't going to happen if I didn't get the shop ready. I pulled out the list I'd printed in huge letters and inspected everything I had to do. We needed to tidy up the Events room. Danny's publisher, Brian Letterman, would be arriving with a box of books for Danny to sign, and I'd need to enter them into the new digital inventory system Morrie and I set up (against Heathcliff's protests) so we could offer them for sale.

My hand flew to my purse. I kept my father's letter inside my wallet, and I found myself fingering it every time I felt stressed or upset. Right now, I was stressed as fuck about the event tonight. I still didn't have any answers about who my father was or why he'd left me and Mum, but just knowing that somewhere in time he still existed, and he still thought about me, calmed me.

"Right, then." I pointed at Quoth. "You, put on your human suit. I need you to move furniture, set up chairs, and hang your artwork on every spare wall in the Events room."

Quoth fluttered over to perch on the edge of the desk. A moment later, a very naked and harried-looking man leaned over the desk, wiping a strand of shampoo-commercial perfect black hair from his eyes. "You want my artwork—"

"On the walls, yes. This is going to be the most people we've had in the store ever. I want your pieces front and center." Quoth's terrified expression made me pause. I leaned in and brushed my lips against his, trying to assure him that it would be okay. I pointed to Morrie. "You – you're on customer duty. I don't have time to field a single query about how to find the History section or get into an argument about whether J. K. Rowling's best book was *Lord of the Rings*. I've got too much to do—"

"Speaking of time-wasters," Morrie smiled, his eyes on the window. "I see one arriving now, wearing a look of determination that suggests our 'CLOSED' sign will be thoroughly ignored."

Quoth's hot and naked human body disappeared in a cloud of feathers just as the bell tinkled. A moment later, my old high school English teacher Mrs. Ellis appeared in front of the desk. Without a word of greeting, she upturned her purse onto the desk, spilling a stack of brightly-colored travel pamphlets on top of my ledger.

"Mina, help me!" she wailed. "I can't decide what to do!"

CHAPTER THREE

"I'm sorry, Mrs. Ellis. You know I'm always happy to help with your craft projects, but I just don't have time today. I've got so much to do before tonight's event." Guilt flared in my heart, but I pushed it down as I leaned over to jab Morrie in the arm. "Mr. Moriarty will help you with whatever you need."

"Yeah, I can help." Morrie picked up one of the brochures, admiring an image of a tanned Mediterranean man wearing a toothy grin, white Speedos, and about ten gallons of baby oil. "Are you making your own swimsuit calendar again? I've got this computer program that can do photo manipulations. We could scan these and remove the swimming trunks, no problem—"

"Don't tempt me, young man." Mrs. Ellis snatched the brochure from his fingers. "I can't be distracted by the thought of what's under his trunks. I have a time-sensitive issue and it requires a woman's input. Mina, you must help me! There's no one in my life with your level of discerning taste."

I sighed. It was clear that I wasn't going to get rid of Mrs. Ellis until I'd helped her with her problem. I picked up a brochure, admiring yet another picture of a buff Greek man in a Speedo standing on the deck of an enormous cruise ship. The brochure was advertising holidays in the Greek islands.

"Are you going on holiday, Mrs. Ellis?"

"I certainly am! I've always wanted to take a cruise, and there's no time like the present, while England is still all cold and miserable. The only thing is, I need to place a deposit at the travel agent today, and I can't decide where to go!"

"Where do you get the money for a cruise like this?" Morrie asked. "Are you running an underground gambling ring or international Ponzi scheme we don't know about?"

"Not everyone is a criminal mastermind," I shot back. "Mrs. Ellis probably saved her money like a normal person—"

"Heavens, no," Mrs. Ellis clucked, as she opened out a full-page poster of a cruise liner sailing across a superimposed image of a shirtless man. "I've never saved a pound in my life. I spent every last shilling on wine and shoes and gifts for accommodating young men. But just this week I've had a lovely windfall! That nice Mr. Lachlan came to me last week and offered me a vast sum for my tiny flat. I've decided to take him up on it. I'll be able to take my cruise, with enough money left over to buy a smaller house across the village, and some left over after that to stuff into a lucky young gentleman's g-string."

Morrie and I exchanged a glance. Six weeks ago, the developer Grey Lachlan had visited the shop. He made Heathcliff an offer on Nevermore – at least four times what the bookshop was actually worth. Of course, there was no way Heathcliff could sell the shop with a time-traveling room on the third floor and a bunch of unsolved mysteries and the possibility of random fictional characters popping in at any moment, so he'd said no. The whole conversation had been a little weird, actually. Grey didn't like being told no. He kept offering more money and saying the weirdest things – it almost sounded as though he was threatening us.

Grey hadn't returned to the shop since, but it worried me that he purchased Mrs. Ellis' flat across the road. What *really* was his plan for Argleton, and how did Nevermore fit in?

"Since when is Mr. Lachlan a 'nice young man'?" I asked. "According to you and Mrs. Scarlett, he was ruining this village with his King's Cross development."

"Oh, Mina," Mrs. Ellis waved her hand. "Such an old-fashioned attitude. We can't stand in the way of progress, can we?"

Of course we can't, not when we can all get a nice fat cheque and a holiday to Greece out of the deal, I thought but didn't say.

"Are you sure you don't want to think about this? You've lived in that flat for a long time. What would your late husband think if you sold it—"

"Of course I don't want to think about it," Mrs. Ellis scoffed. "And I don't care for Ronald's opinion, not after he upped and died on me, leaving me without a man to remove spiders from the shower or keep me warm at night. The only thing I want to think about is whether I should be cruising around Australia with strapping Crocodile Dundee blokes, or swanning about the Amalfi coast with oiled Greek gods?"

"Okay... well..." I shuffled around the brochures until I came across a particular handsome Greek. I held it under the desk lamp and squinted until I could make out the small print underneath the heading, which specifically stated the cruise was ideal for seniors. I held it up for her. "This looks like the man for you."

"Oooh, hello, gorgeous." Mrs. Ellis kissed the brochure, leaving a smudge of bright blue lipstick across the Greek god's face. "Yes, I think you've cracked it. I knew I could count on you."

"You're welcome. Will you be coming to the reading tonight?"

"I'll drop by with the ladies from my knitting club." Mrs. Ellis skipped toward the door. "I might leave early, though. I've got to pack my bags. I'm leaving in a few days. Oh, and shop for a swimsuit. And learn the Greek for, 'buy me a drink, handsome'."

As the front door slammed shut, Heathcliff's brooding face appeared on the staircase. "I know you think you run this shop now, but that doesn't mean you can open early."

"We aren't open yet. That was Mrs. Ellis. You know how much attention she pays to signage."

Heathcliff grunted, then turned to Morrie, who was sprawled on the leather chair with Quoth perched on the armrest, diligently trying to tear into a packet of dried cranberries with his beak. "Can I talk to Mina alone?"

Morrie stood up. "Fine. I'm going to the shops, because we have nothing except bird food. Anyone need anything?"

"Croak!" Quoth shook his cranberry packet at Morrie.

"Just coffee. Lots and lots of coffee." I held out my empty reusable cup. Morrie slotted it into his expensive leather satchel and headed for the door.

"I want my peaceful shop back," Heathcliff growled. "Failing that, a cheese scone."

"One cheese scone, coming up. You want in, birdie?" Morrie used to use that nickname to belittle Quoth, but now he said it with such tenderness and affection that I no longer told him to stop.

"Croak!" Quoth fluttered after Morrie, still clutching his bag of cranberries in his talons.

Curious, I watched Heathcliff as he stepped into the room, a wave of his achingly beautiful spice-and-moss scent following after him. My pulse raced as his black eyes burned into mine. He must've just come from the shower, because his hair was damp across his head and his clothes were only artfully rumpled as opposed to their usual state resembling the surface of the moon. He carried a heavy leather book, which he set on the velvet chair as he walked past. He placed his hands on the desk and loomed over me, one messy dark curl falling over his intense eyes. I knew Heathcliff was waiting for me to get out of his chair. Well, he may have run things back at Wuthering Heights, but he wasn't the one with a million things to do today. I remained where I was and tapped my to-do list with the end of the pen.

Heathcliff spun the pad around to face him, his frown deepening as he read the items. "You haven't changed your mind about this poxy event, then?"

"Nope. It's happening." I tried to grab my pad back, but Heathcliff slid it out of reach. He jabbed a finger at one of the lines.

"You're not doing a Q&A."

"Of course we are. People will want to ask the writer questions."

"You don't want them to do that."

"Why?"

"Not even the sting of Hindley's whip is more painful than a Q&A at a writer's event," Heathcliff declared, waving the pad around. "There are no actual questions – most are thinly veiled excuses to wax lyrical about their own work, moronic accusations requiring the author to defend their work to insufferable plebs, gushing praise that no one gives a fuck about, or something so utterly unoriginal like 'where do you get your ideas?' that it's a wonder that writers don't expire from boredom on the spot."

I managed to whip my list out of his hands. "Well, you're not helping, so I don't see why you get an opinion."

"Maybe not." Heathcliff picked up the book and slammed it down on the desk between us. "But I have found something about Mr. Simson."

"Oh?" My hand flew to my purse again, fingering the edge of the letter from my father. We'd figured out it was likely my father and Mr. Simson – the shop's proprietor before Heathcliff – knew each other. My father appeared to be hiding somewhere in time, but if we could locate Mr. Simson, then we might be able to get him to tell us who my father was and where we could find him.

I knew it was a long shot. Mr. Simson was an old man who

was nearly completely blind when I knew him as a child. He could be dead or degrading in a wrinkly village somewhere. But as soon as Heathcliff said his name, my heart raced faster. *I have to hope.*

A cloud of dust rose up as Heathcliff cracked open the book and flipped through the pages. "I've been hunting through Simson's old ledgers, invoices, bills, and other documents, hoping to find some information about where he might have gone. I didn't get that lucky, but I did find this."

He turned the book toward me and jabbed a finger at the page. I bent down to inspect it. It was an invoice from another book collector for a small set of occult volumes, made out to Mr. Simson. This time, his first name was printed in full:

Homer.

"His name is Homer. So?" I frowned at Heathcliff. "How is this going to help us?"

"You remember the book that appeared on the floor after we found the Terror of Argleton?"

I smiled at the name the Argleton papers had given to a tiny mouse that had caused havoc in local shops until his untimely death gave us the essential clue we needed to solve a murder. "Yeah, the one with the unpronounceable title about the frogs and mice having a war."

"Right. Simson's first name is the same name as the author of that text, and it's also the same initials as Herman Strepel, who we're pretty sure is your father." Heathcliff jabbed his finger into the ledger. "We've been thinking that Strepel was using the bookshop to give us a message about Mrs. Scarlett's killer with that book, but maybe the book itself was the clue."

"What are you saying?" I asked slowly, not following where his thoughts led.

Heathcliff's lips turned up into a rare smile. "I'm saying that I think our bookshop proprietor and Mr. Strepel the medieval bookbinder are the same person, and that person is your father. "

My mind reeled. I leaned back in the chair, my eyes leaping from the ledger to Heathcliff's face, registering the significance of what he was saying. Grimalkin leaped up on the desk and plonked down on the book. She stared down Heathcliff with a defiant, "meorrw," before lifting her leg in the air and delicately washing her derriere.

"Good. Because I thought for a second there you were going to tell me my dad was a dead epic poet, and then we'd have to get your head examined." I rubbed my temple, reaching out to pat Grimalkin with the other hand. "You're right. It makes perfect sense. Mr. Simson was blind. I inherited my retinitis pigmentosa from my father. Mr. Simson told you that you had to protect me, which also seems to be my father's jam, according to his letter. I mean, I find it hard to believe my mum fell into bed with a doddering old bookstore owner, but..."

"... the time-travel room would mean that the man who impregnated your mother could have come from any point in his own timeline," Heathcliff finished my sentence for me. He'd been doing that a lot recently, as if his thoughts matched mine at every moment. It was a little freaky, but also wonderful.

"Meorw," Grimalkin added, batting my nose.

"Exactly." My mind raced as all the pieces slotted into place. "Perhaps my father came to this time as a younger man, and that's how he seduced my mother. It would also explain why she never told me he was blind – if he had retinitis pigmentosa, then it might not have set in for him yet – and also why she didn't recognize him when she'd come into the shop to collect me. I can't believe I didn't think of it sooner, to be honest."

"At least we figured it out before Morrie," Heathcliff's eyes sparkled with joy. "He's going to be *pissed*."

"Try not to look quite so gleeful when you tell him," I teased. "While this is awesome, it doesn't get us any closer to finding my father. Knowing what we now know, it more than likely he left the bookshop through the room upstairs, making it even less likely we'll find him."

My mind flashed to the note warning of danger, and to the words Victoria Bainbridge spoke to me last time I'd set foot inside the time-travel room. "The next time I see you, you'll be covered in blood."

But whose blood? Whose? My father's? My own? One of the guys... please don't let it be one of the guys.

"You're thinking about the note again," Heathcliff growled.

I nodded.

"And the blood."

"Especially the blood."

"Obviously, she meant the blood of your enemies."

I snorted, mostly because Heathcliff had this fierce look on his face, like he really did believe I'd be walking around wearing my enemies blood. "I don't think so, but that's the problem. I don't *know*, and it's driving me crazy. What if it's your blood? What if it's Morrie's or Quoth's or Mum's or Jo's or—"

"Allow me to relieve your mind of the burden." With one shove of his thick hand, Heathcliff pushed the ledger off the desk, along with my list and all our mail and pens and stamps. Grimalkin howled and leapt out of the way as the book clattered to the floor. She gave Heathcliff a filthy look, turned on her elegant legs, and slunk away.

I'm never going to get anything done today if they keep... Oh, by Isis...

Heathcliff's mouth met mine, hot with need. Fire raced through my veins I tugged on his collar, pulling him closer, molding our bodies together. My hip pressed into our ancient metal till as Heathcliff laid me down on the desk, his hands unlacing the drawstring in Jo's trousers. Dark hunger blazed in his eyes, the kind of hunger that made women in books swoon.

"But I have so much work to do—"

My feeble protests were silenced as literature's greatest gothic hero swept me into his arms and devoured me, body and heart and soul.

CHAPTER FOUR

"*T*hank you so much, Mina. We really appreciate you setting up this event for Danny." Brian Letterman held my hand between his. A pair of sharp grey eyes sparkled as he took in the room.

"Thank you for agreeing to be my guinea pigs. I'm really excited about the potential for this space." I beamed at the publisher as I surveyed my handiwork. We really had worked a miracle.

A week ago, I'd made the executive decision to permanently remove the bookshelves from the World History room and cram them into a small alcove at the back of the shop. Now the light, airy room with its pentagonal bay window was our new event space. I'd cleaned and repainted one wall antique white, and purchased a projector that could be used to show slides or movies against the wall. Quoth and I scoured every junk store in Argleton for enough mismatched chairs to create a small circle around the lectern. Morrie scoured The-Store-That-Shall-Not-Be-Named for product reviews, and based on the internet's recommendations, put together a state-of-the-art sound system, which was at this moment pumping out subdued jazz as our guests filtered in.

Under the window was a buffet of locally-made cheese, crackers, Mrs. Ellis' fruit preserves, and artisan salami. I'd even managed to convince Richard McGreer – the Rose & Wimple pub landlord who'd recently started a boutique cidery – to put on a small bar.

A display of Danny's books stood by the door, mixed with a couple of Quoth's artworks and some props I found in Morrie's bedroom – a magnifying glass, some handcuffs (I had to tear off the black padded lining), and a long black silk scarf knotted around the stand. Danny's latest book, *The Somerset Strangler*, featured a serial killer who garroted his victims. I hoped I'd got the message across without being too morbid.

Our guest list of local reporters, Barchester literati, and members of Danny's fanclub milled around the room, spilling out into the main downstairs room of the bookshop, where they perused the shelves with an appreciative eye. I noticed a woman in the corner had already amassed an impressive stack of volumes on the counter for purchase.

We're going to make a killing tonight.

It was just as well, because we needed all the cash we could get. All this effort wasn't just to inject some life into the place – Heathcliff had finally let me look at his ledger. Things were more dire than I realized. Eight years ago, the roof had been damaged in a bad storm, and Mr Simson – who apparently didn't believe in insurance – had taken out a mortgage on the shop to make the repairs. And that mortgage had been extended over the years as narrowing margins and the dominance of The-Store-That-Shall-Not-Be-Named cut into the shop's already meagre profits. Heathcliff hadn't helped matters – he ran the place the way all landed men of his era ran their estates – with a stubborn refusal to accept that changing times called for a fresh approach. We needed to sort out our mortgage arrears soon, or we'd really be in trouble.

After that, I needed cash to make serious improvements to the shop. If I was going to keep working here after I went blind, then I needed a way to distinguish the books apart when I could no longer see the titles. The absent Mr. Simson was no help – from what I could remember of my childhood, his system seemed to be that he presented people with completely random books and they just accepted them because to say something would be rude, and a British person would rather pay £48 quid for a book on the history of the London sewers than ask for what they actually wanted.

I'd been researching different options – braille labels would be most cost-effective, but an insane amount of work to implement. Plus, even though I'd already started trying to learn braille, it would take me a couple of years to become proficient. However, there was this neat electronic talking tagging system that I could control from my mobile...

"It's great to see this bookshop living up to its potential," Brian said. "I came here a year or so ago, trying to get the proprietor to stock my authors or run an event. He was quite rude. Told me to go shag a goat—"

"Oh yes, well, let's just say he's reformed." I glanced across at Heathcliff, who stood behind the counter, begrudgingly ringing up purchases. I hadn't heard him call anyone an idiot all night, so that was something.

"That's good to hear. You know, you've got a real head for the business side of this industry. I teach a publishing course over in Barchester, and let me tell you that too many naive students come in with the idea that publishing is all about pursuing their dreams of being a bestselling beat poet or bringing the joy of reading to future generations or some such nonsense. They could learn a lot from a woman like you... oh, I'll introduce you to

Danny. He'll want to thank you as well." Brian snapped his fingers. "Danny, come meet Mina. She's the one who put this whole event together."

A tall, handsome figure with vibrant red hair drew away from the circle of admirers who surrounded him and wandered toward us. A shorter man with a sharp suit and thin black hair followed behind him. I recognized the redhead from the jacket of his book. Danny Sledge, in the flesh.

When he reached us, Danny extended a hand and shook mine warmly, flashing me a charismatic smile. He rubbed the line of stubble along his jaw as he gestured to the room. "Fabulous event, Mina. My congratulations at finally talking some sense into that Mr. Earnshaw and turning this bookshop into a success."

I could feel my cheeks warming at his praise. "I'm not sure it's a success yet. But I'm definitely working on it."

Over Danny's shoulder, I noticed Jo enter the room, wearing a red dress that hugged her in all the right places. I guessed she been shopping instead of braving our locust-infested flat. I waved to my flatmate, and she made her way towards our group, grabbing two glasses of cider on her way past the bar.

"—it's so important to support these small independent bookstores," Danny was saying earnestly. "Otherwise they'll go the way of the dinosaurs. Of course, nowadays, readers prefer a screen to an actual book. I make most of my royalties from A—"

I held up a hand as Heathcliff's head jerked up, his black eyes blazing with fury. *Does he have extra-sensory powers or something? How can he hear that all the way from the next room?* "Um, I highly recommend you don't use that word in this shop."

Heathcliff shoved his way into the room.

"What word? Am—"

"Croak?" Quoth fluttered down and settled on Danny's shoulder. Danny immediately reached up and patted him on his head, his previous faux-pas forgotten.

"You're a good wee birdie, aren't you? I saw a cat hanging

around before, too. This place is a regular menagerie. Hey," Danny grinned at Quoth. "I get it now. You're like the shop's mascot. They must've named this place Nevermore after you. 'Once upon a midnight dreary. While I pondered, weak and weary—'"

Panic shot through me. I knew what usually happened when someone recited that poem in Quoth's presence. I squeezed my eyes shut, waiting for the inevitable moment when my carefully-planned event became a disaster—

Don't worry, I'm not going to crap on him, Quoth's voice landed in my head. *I have more self-control than that. I just thought if I flew over here I might distract him from saying the word that makes Heath-cliff go Super Saiyan.*

You're my hero, I thought in return, as my whole body relaxed.

"—each separate dying ember wrought its ghost upon the floor—"

I didn't know it was possible, but the raven beamed. *Anytime. Incidentally, if you could get him to stop reciting that infernal poem, I'd be most obliged.*

Danny was reaching his stride. "—for the rare and radiant maiden whom the angels name Lenore—"

"Danny, um, so..." I frantically searched for a question. "Do you do lots of author events?"

"Not as much as I used to. It's hard to get people to leave their homes and show up. Nowadays I put all my promotional efforts into social media. It's a shame, because it's always great to meet fans in person, hear their stories. I get lots of ideas that way. Tell me, Mina, which of my books was your favorite?"

"Oh, um..." I racked my brain for a title. The truth was, I'd never read one of Danny Sledge's books – commercial crime fiction wasn't really my thing. I'd chosen him for this event because Mrs. Ellis told me he was famous and devilishly hand-some, so she'd be able to convince her entire knitting circle to come along. I'd sold at least twenty tickets to little old ladies who now stood in a group around the bar, tittering every time they caught a glimpse of Danny's arse. I glanced over to the table and caught the name of his latest book. "I really enjoyed *The Somerset Strangler*. I think it's your best work yet."

"Good answer. That's one of my favorites, too." Danny didn't seem to notice where I was looking. "It's always so fascinating getting into the mind of a criminal. As you know, I've made this guy particularly vicious. He likes to get up close and personal with his victims so he can watch the life drain from their faces—"

"Oh, yes, yes." I nodded, only listening with half an ear as I noticed a familiar figure enter the room, wearing an outlandish dress that looked like a Christmas sweater had sex with a raccoon. I glanced at Quoth. *What's Mum doing here?*

You invited her, remember?

Yes, but I didn't expect her to come. I cringed as Mum swung around and I noticed a giant silvery patch attached to her upper arm. *What's that on her arm?*

No idea, but I can see a stack of them sticking out of her purse. My guess is, she's got an exciting new product to sell.

Zing. Panic shot through me again.

"I haven't read your book. What methods does your killer employ?" Jo was asking Danny. "Strangulation? Evisceration? Meat hooks?"

"Death by locust?" I added. Jo stifled a laugh.

"Danny's killer has the garrote as his weapon of choice," the second man piped up. "Garroting is such an unusual method of murder. It was developed by the Chinese as an early form of execution, and was also popular with the Spanish as the death penalty until 1978. Danny's use of this method is part of the reason *The Somerset Strangler* has been so successful. It's a bit different from the usual cannibal serial killer."

Danny peered over his shoulder as if he'd only just remembered the guy was there. "Oh, how rude of me. Mina, this is Angus, my closest friend and first reader. He used to be in law enforcement in Argleton – he nicked me a few times back in my wayward youth. He took early retirement, and his professional input has saved my bacon more than once. Angus, this is Mina, the bird who put this whole event together. Isn't she knockin'?"

Angus offered a firm handshake. He had an open smile and one of those soft faces that made you want to instantly trust him. *I bet he was totally hot when he was younger.* "Nice to meet you, Mina. Thanks for promoting Danny. He's been worried about the reception of *The Somerset Strangler*. It's a lot gorier than his other books, as death by garroting can be a grisly death, especially if described with the level of detail Danny likes to lavish on his victims."

"Tell me about it," Jo said, sipping her drink. "No, seriously, tell me. I've never had a garroting case before. What kind of research do you do, Danny?"

"Don't worry, ma'am. I'm not out knocking off people just to get the details right," Danny grinned. "Angus here fills me in on a lot of the realism from his old cases, an' of course I've got the internet, now don't I? Let me tell you about this strangulation I read about the other day—"

My gaze flicked back to the door. Mum had disappeared into the crowd. Panic rose in my chest as I searched the shadowed faces. *Please don't let her embarrass me—*

Danny slapped Angus on the shoulder. "...so that's how we know our killer used a fabric ligature instead of wire. When it comes to realistic details, I'm not worried about anything. Angus does all the worrying for me. He thinks his professional reputation is on the line with every book I publish. He worked a high profile garroting case back when he was an inspector, but they never caught the killer."

Jo looped her arm in Angus'. "Your drink appears to be empty, good sir. Let me show you to the bar for a refill, and you can tell me more about the history of garroting…"

Angus nodded, and left with Jo. Danny leaned in, giving me a wink. "You'd better tell your friend to watch out. Angus is a bit of a player. The whole reason he hangs out at these parties with me is for a bit of tail."

"He might be so, but he's not Jo's type."

"She not into greying ex-cops?"

"I'm sure the ex-cop is fine. It's more the fact that he's a he."

Danny's eyebrows went way up, and the expression on his face told me that he found the idea that Jo was a lesbian a turn-on. He leaned in close, nudging me with his arm. "And you? Are you guys..."

"I have a boyfriend," I said, suddenly uncomfortable. It was so dumb how guys *still* reacted like that when they heard a girl didn't fancy blokes. Because of course, Jo's sexual preferences were all about *his* enjoyment. A woman tapped Danny's arm to ask him a question, and I managed to slip back into the crowd. I needed to find Mum before she launched into a sales pitch and—

"—all I have to do is wear the Flourish patch, and its transdermal vitamin technology transmits vital nutrients and calorie-burning stimulants directly into my bloodstream, helping me to burn excess fat." Mum's voice carried over the crowd. "Why, right now, as I'm drinking this free Champagne and eating these delicious sausage rolls, I'm burning fifty calories a minute..."

Bloody hell, I'm too late.

"Excuse me, excuse me," I shoved my way through groups of writers and journalists. Finally, I saw her. Mum had cornered three women and was busy patting the silver patch on her arm and giving them her latest spiel.

"... as a Flourish consultant, you'll spread the word about this amazing new technology and help hundreds of people achieve their health and weight loss dreams. Not only that, but you'll be in charge of your own destiny as you build your own business and achieve financial freedom. Just look at me – a month ago I was living on the council estate, now I'm about to be handed the keys to my very own silver Mercedes."

Oh no, what's this about a Mercedes?

"Mum, you came!" I threw my arms around her, hoping to stop the stream of nonsense pouring from her mouth.

"Mina, dear. You look lovely, although I bet you'd look even lovelier with a complete vitamin regimen. I was just telling your friends here about an exciting business opportunity." Mum spun around to show off her patch. "Isn't it amazing? Right now, I'm burning calories while receiving a dose of healthful nutrients through its remarkable transdermal—"

"I'm sure it's wonderful, Mum, but you don't need to wear it here. People came tonight to discuss books, not weight-loss, er, patches…" I flashed the women an apologetic look over my shoulder.

"Oh, it does more than just help you lose weight. The Flourish patch also cures bloating, improve energy, and suppresses appetite, so you don't get those pesky cravings… oh, look, little cupcakes." Mum grabbed two off a tray on the table. "You really have to try it, Mina. It's *remarkable*. I've only been wearing mine for two days and I've already lost weight!"

"You don't look any different to me." I watched Mum pop one cupcake into her mouth.

"Well, of course I don't! It's this lighting. It's terribly unflattering. Maybe I'll go see Morrie about changing it." Mum turned to push her way back across the room, popping the second cupcake into her mouth. "It's great to see you, dear!"

"I really am sorry about her," I told the woman. "She gets sucked into these get-rich-quick-schemes. She's really harmless."

"It's perfectly all right. We've all had friends who've fallen victim to those schemes. They really are criminal, the way they sucker people in. I'm surprised my husband hasn't written about it in one of his books, but I guess it isn't as sexy as *murder*." The woman in the middle scoffed. She had strawberry blonde hair cut in a short, sensible bob and a designer dress that was a couple of years out of date and at least two sizes too small. She extended a hand to me. "I'm Penny Sledge, Danny's wife."

"I didn't realize Danny was married." I shook her hand.

"He doesn't like to advertise it, especially not to pretty young women like yourself." Penny's two friends exchanged a look and shuffled quietly away. "I understand you're the organizer of this event. You've done a fine job, really. An admirable effort, but if I could make a few suggestions…"

"Sure!" I beamed.

"I don't think it will do having all these people crammed into this tiny space. And none of the chairs match! The food is a bit *rustic,* and cider instead of wine?" She tsked. "That won't do. This shop is awfully dusty, isn't it? Much better to rent the ballroom at my friend Cynthia Lachlan's estate. Or even have it down in London at one of the literary salons—"

"I'll make note of that," I said. *Literary salons?* What kind of books did Penny think her husband wrote? As she talked my ear off about the proper temperature to serve wine and why cupcakes and sausage rolls were inappropriate as *hors d'oeuvres,* I cast my eyes around the room, hoping to spot someone who might save me from the dreary conversation.

Penny was right about one thing – the turnout was better than I'd dared to hope. More and more people trickled in, spilling out of the Events space into the shop, and every one of them seemed to have a book or two in their hands. Mrs. Ellis came over with her knitting circle friends, who crowded around me, pushing Penny off to the side (such a shame) as they gushed about the transformation of the shop.

"You're a breath of fresh air to this place, Mina!" said Hazel Barrowly. "I can see Nevermore Bookshop becoming a real asset to the village."

"I'd love to talk to you about running a joint event," Sylvia Blume added. Sylvia ran the local crystal and healing shop where my mum worked sometimes as a tarot reader. "I see you have quite a decent occult section. We could bring in a famous meta-physical thinker for a lecture and then set up a stall in the corner. You mother could even do her readings. It would be *trans-formative.*"

"That sounds like fun." I forced a smile, panic thumping in my chest. I wanted to keep my mother as far away from the financial side of the shop as possible, especially if she kept trying to push a weight-loss patch on my customers. *A change of subject is in order.* "Mrs. Ellis, did you book your holiday?"

"I did!" She swiped a second glass of cider from the bar and brought it to her lips. "I'm leaving in just two more days. It's all very exciting. I was just telling the girls here that—"

"Oh, I *love* your dress," a woman cooed, stepping into the middle of our circle, grabbing at my skirt, and fanning it out.

"Thanks. I made it." I beamed. Since I hadn't wanted to brave our flat for a change of clothes, I'd brushed off my ex-fashion-designer chops and whipped up the dress this afternoon by shredding an old purple prom dress I found at the village junk shop. I'd slashed up the skirt, added black lace panels, and edged the bodice in black ribbon. Worn with my trusty Doc Martens and some gold jewelry, it looked like a stage outfit for the singer of a punk band, which was, of course, why I loved it.

"You're talented. Do you take commissions?" The woman stuck out her lower lip as she jutted out her hip and gestured to her expensive black velvet cocktail dress, shot with threads of silver that caught the light and accentuated her enviable curves. She touched a hand to her ash-blonde hair, perfectly set into a Marilyn Monroe style, and pouted a pair of cherry-red bow-shaped lips. "My husband is always dragging me to these boring book events. Yours is a cut above the rest, because at least you have free booze."

"Who's your husband?"

"Brian, the publisher." She pointed across the room, where Brian stood deep in conversation with Morrie. Looking at his rumpled suit and middle-aged spread, I couldn't imagine him with this vixen, but I guess there was no accounting for love. I wasn't exactly one to make judgments, what with my three boyfriends. "I'm Amanda Letterman. You might have seen me on Youtube. I have my own makeup channel with a hundred thousand subscribers. I wouldn't normally stoop to attending an event in the *provinces*, but Brian says we need to put on a good public face for the business. Of course, I just come along for the talent." She wet her lower lip as her eyes trailed after Danny. Her gaze didn't linger long, as it swept over to devour Angus, and then lingered on Heathcliff. "Mmmm, and what a lot of talent, too. Who is that rugged fox in the doorway? I want to sit on his face and—"

"I've never thought about making clothes for other people," I said, partly to shut her up and partly because the wheels were already turning in my head. If an influencer like Amanda who attended all sorts of industry parties and maybe had an influencer channel online wore one of my designs, I might be able to get some work. It wouldn't be the same as working New York Fashion Week, but at least I'd be able to use my design skills before they became useless...

No. I'm not going to dwell on it. And just like that, I shoved down the fear that threatened to well up inside me whenever I thought of losing my sight. My doctor believed it would happen within the next eighteen months. Last year, thinking about what I wouldn't be able to do made me angry and upset, but ever since the guys had come into my life I found myself feeling more positive about the future. And finding out that with the right technology I could still do most of the things I enjoyed was helping me see that my life wasn't over. In fact, sometimes my life was *too* interesting.

Even though I was feeling better about my eyes, I still occasionally had a moment where the uncertainty and unfairness of it got to me. But I certainly wasn't going to ruin this weekend by dwelling on it, not when Danny's event might help pay for the technology we need to enable me to keep working in the shop.

"Well, I will definitely hire you." Amanda fingered the fabric of the dress. "I must warn you, though, I'm difficult to work with. My husband calls me a right cow. But what would he know, right? He just sells dusty old books."

That's... why did I need to know that? I kept the smile plastered on my face. "I don't have a card or anything. But if you have something I can write on, I'll give you my number."

Amanda grabbed one of Danny's books off the table and indicated that I should scribble my details inside. Danny passed by, raising his eyebrows at us. "Isn't the author supposed to be signing his own books?" he said with a laugh, patting Amanda's hip in what seemed to be an overly familiar way for the wife of his business colleague.

"Oh, Danny!" she giggled, raking her nails over his shoulder. "I'm just getting some details off this sweet girl. She's going to make me a new dress. I'll come for you later. I want a *personalized* signature."

"I look forward to it," he grinned, giving her a look like he might gobble her up. Amanda batted her eyelashes at him, her fingers sliding down his arm. I stepped away, my skin crawling. *Am I imagining it, or is Danny awfully cozy with his publisher's wife? Or is that just how writers are?*

You're not imagining it, a familiar voice said inside my head.

I cast my eyes up to the rafters, where Quoth perched, watching the party from above. I gave him a little wave, which he returned with a nod of his head.

It's obvious to me, and to most of the people here, and especially to Penny Sledge, who is staring daggers at her husband from across the room. Oh, and your mother is sticking Flourish patches on Mrs. Ellis and her friends. She pulled a sign-up sheet from out of her bra.

I rolled my eyes at Quoth. *Of course she has. Can you get over there and maybe try to stop her? Crap on her if you have to.*

37

Mina, I love you, and I'd do anything for you, but I'm not defecating on your mother.

Please. I'd be eternally grateful—

"I'm surprised a bird like that could be domesticated," a voice said beside me. "I expected he'd be crapping everywhere."

Startled, I turned to face Danny's friend Angus. He held a glass of cider in one hand and a plate of food in the other. He held the plate out to me and I accepted a sausage roll.

"Ravens are actually incredibly smart," I said, watching Quoth fly off to rescue the knitting club. "Researchers have had them solve complex puzzles and can even teach them simple vocabulary. Quoth is the smartest raven of them all – he never defecates on anyone unless they deserve it."

Angus laughed. "I love it. He gives this place a bit of personality. Not that it didn't already have buckets of that. But now that the grumpy wanker isn't in charge anymore, I might pop in for my reading material. I only live a few streets away, and read a lot since I retired, especially in hardcopy. No ereader for me. You've got a great selection of crime novels."

"Thank you. Do you come to all of Danny's events?" I asked.

"Not all of them, just when I can. It's exciting to see how well he's doing and how much people love his work. I have a lot of fun working with him, being able to relive some of the highlights of my career. In the case of the new novel, I even got to solve a crime between the pages that I never got to solve in real life."

"That must be a real change from what you used to do. Danny said that he used to be on the wrong side of the law?"

"Oh yes, he was a right ratbag back in his youth. Shoplifting, stealing cars, drugs, getting involved in gangs. I threw him in the clink more times than I can count. Like all young offenders, I hoped he'd straighten out, but it was just the opposite. Danny looked to be heading toward a life of hard crime before he woke up to his talent. It was actually the garroting case that turned him around. He was sweet on the victim, and he might've been stitched up for the crime if he hadn't already had an alibi."

"Wow. And he went straight after that?"

Angus nodded. "He wrote a story about a couple of geezers he met in the clink. Entered it into a national competition and won first prize. Two thousand quid, just like that. Danny said it was the easiest two gs he ever made, much easier than selling drugs or fleecing stolen TVs. He stuck to the writing after that. I followed his career closely – you got to realize, miss, it's rare I got to see a young guy like Danny go straight and stay straight. It warmed my cockles. One day after I retired, I contacted Danny and said I was the copper from back in the day, and how impressed with him I was. He remembered me, an' offered me a decent wage if I came to work as his advisor. Really, I'm just here for him to bounce ideas off, come up with motives and red herrings, fill him in on police procedures and such. Danny's the real genius – he gives me more credit than I'm due since he's such a good bloke."

"He said you read his drafts. I wondered, are you the only person who does? What about his wife?"

Angus laughed. "Oh, no, Penny can't stand Danny's books. She thinks them trashy, not real literature. She's happy enough to take his money, though, and his fame. She loves the literary scene – the parties, the festivals, the expensive cocktails, the pseudo-intellectual twaddle. Danny doesn't want a bit of that wank, but Penny makes him do the festival circuit. He'd much rather do smaller events like this, have a bit of fun. No, no, the only people who read his work before the public are me and Brian. Even then, we'll only get to read something if Danny thinks it's close to perfect. He kept his work under lock and key until the last possible minute."

"I'm so fascinated by his creative process. I'm going to be sitting in on his workshop tomorrow," I said. "I'm looking forward to it."

"Oh, are you a writer, too?"

"No." I waved my hand, gesturing to the piles of books. "I could never do anything like this. I just... I've witnessed some strange things recently. The kind of things that you'd think were too outlandish even for a novel. I was thinking it might be fun to try writing them down or something..."

Morrie tapped me on the shoulder. "We should get started. Someone just asked Heathcliff if they could have an 1837 edition of *The Pickwick Papers* in mint condition for ten quid, and I think his head's going to explode."

I nodded. Morrie went off to speak to Danny and Brian. A few moments later, Danny made his way to the stage. Brian tapped the microphone to get everyone's attention. "Ladies and gentlemen, if you'd like to take your seats. We're blessed tonight to have a true literary genius in our midst. Through his dark and gritty stories, Danny Sledge has allowed us to enter the criminal underbelly without leaving our comfy recliners. I'd like everyone to join me in welcoming Danny to the stage to tell us about his latest book, *The Somerset Strangler!*"

I took a seat in the back row beside Quoth, who must have quickly gone upstairs to change, because he was human and gorgeous in a black silk shirt shot with silver and dark jeans. He looked nervous being in the room with so many people, but he'd chosen a chair near the door so he could run if he felt a shift coming on. I squeezed his hand and he smiled that beautiful sad smile and my heart flip-flopped in my chest.

Even though I could barely see in the dim light, I recognized my mum in the front row by the three silver patches she wore proudly down her arm. *Please don't let her say anything during Danny's talk.*

The whole room burst into applause as Danny leaned against the podium and beamed at the audience. To my surprise, Heathcliff's hulking figure stood in the doorway, even more imposing clad all in black, his dark skin standing out against the mostly white room. He tugged on the collar of his shirt and flashed me an intense stare.

Behind us, Morrie fiddled with knobs on his soundboard. "We should have installed strobe lights," he muttered. "This guy thinks he's a rockstar."

I snorted. It was true that Danny basked in the glow of his audience's love. He held his hands out while the applause rolled over him, blatant in his revelry of their adulation. When the applause died down, he grabbed the mic and launched into a gory reading from his book, followed by a hilarious tale from his days as a petty crook, and then the story of how he got his publishing deal (by getting Brian drunk at the pub and then refusing to pay the tab unless he agreed to read his manuscript). The audience roared with laughter. Even Heathcliff – who leaned in the doorway, his bulk blocking out almost all the light from the bookshop – let out a low chuckle.

Quoth leaned over and squeezed my hand. "Tonight's a real hit."

"I know. And if the guy can write the way he captivates an audience, I think tomorrow will be a hit as well."

Danny finished a short reading of a gruesome garroting scene from his latest book. Brian took the mic and asked if anyone had questions for the author. Fifty hands shot up. Behind me, Morrie waved his arm in the air, a wicked grin on his face.

"Hand down," I warned. "I don't think anyone in this room wants to hear the answer to whatever question you're trying to ask."

Morrie stuck his lower lip out at me, but he lowered his hand. Across the room, I met Heathcliff's steady gaze, remembering what he'd said earlier about all audience questions being terrible. *We'll see*, I thought smugly.

I was proven wrong in the first six minutes, as Danny smiled his way through one gushing fanboy who talked about his own failed crime manuscript and a woman with a fur stole who wanted to know 'where he got his ideas.'

"I get them from the same place I bury the bodies," he told her in his charming way. "But if I told you, I'd have to kill you."

A woman in the front row raised her hand. "Hi, Danny. I'm an author, too, and one thing I really struggle with is removing myself from the narrative. I'm just too connected to the characters, too invested in my role as the auteur. I'm wondering how you make your characters so real, so visceral, while also maintaining narrative distance?"

"Oh yes, well, the skill of a writer is to make you believe all sorts of wild things." Danny grinned. "In my case, I've always been fascinated with the criminal mind – what makes the bad guys do what they do. I like to burrow in like a tick and suck out all the delicious character juices. Also, I have a first reader with real police experience who answers my questions any time, day or night. That true, aye, Angus?"

From his chair in the front row, Angus smiled.

"That there's Angus Donahue, he's a fine fellow. And ladies, he's single." Danny pointed to a hand waving at the side. "Yes?"

"Danny, I wondered if you'd be interested in a remarkable business opportunity to transform the lives of your readers through a revolutionary wellness product—"

"Mother," I yelled. "Sit down!"

Mum harrumphed, but she did take a seat. Danny pointed to another woman.

"Danny, I was wondering if you and perhaps your publisher could comment on the current state of the publishing industry. What do you think about self-publishing?"

I leaned forward. Actually, that was an interesting question. We often had self-published authors come into the shop begging us to stock their books. As a rule, their books were about weird subjects like past-life regression and memoirs of dead relatives who never did anything exciting, and they were only marginally more intelligible than a mossy rock. Heathcliff usually told them to move on. I'd read that self-publishers could do quite well in ebooks, but that was all I knew because Heathcliff wouldn't tolerate any discussion about electronic devices in the shop. Although, I was secretly hoping to change that with a few of the upcoming authors I'd chosen for events.

Brian's lips tightened into a thin line. "Self-publishing is pure vanity. It's the realm of hacks and bludgers – people who want to be authors but don't want to put the real work in. Even writers with a decent amount of talent like Danny here have to go through the process if they want to be discovered. You can't skip the queue."

A skinny bloke with dyed purple hair who I was almost ninety-nine percent positive had been in the shop before trying to get us to stock his terrible erotica novel called out, "But what about all the authors who are doing well on A—"

"Don't use that word in this shop!" Heathcliff bellowed from the door.

The man cowered. "I mean, selling ebooks... I heard about this one author named Steffanie something writing in a genre called reverse harem—"

"The media have made a big deal about a couple of writers who hit it big," Brian scoffed. "But most self-published authors write glorified fanfiction that shouldn't even be called literature. It's an insult to real artists like Danny—"

Quoth leaned over and whispered in my ear. "Can you see Danny's face from here?"

I shook my head.

"He looks super smug, and he's just made a rude gesture behind Brian's back. Brian's wife is tittering. It seems like something's going on."

I stared at Quoth in surprise. "It's not like you to go looking for a mystery to solve."

He flashed me his heart-melting smile. "You're a bad influence on me."

At the front of the room, Danny wrestled the mic back from Brian. "I just have a few things to add. Unlike my dear out-of-date publisher, I'm not one of those snobby writers who think self-publishing is for hacks and wannabes." Danny flashed another of his brilliant smiles. "Here's a little life advice from me to you – don't trust the word of someone who's got skin in this game. Brian here wants to keep the industry the way it is. I believe that self-publishing is just another tool to help authors reach readers, and you should treat it as such. It won't be long now until even big names like me are using it. Next question."

Mrs. Ellis stood up. "Hello, you handsome man. I'd like to know what you'll be writing next. Will it be a sequel to *The Somerset Strangler*? I can't get enough of that buff crime boss."

Danny leaned over the podium, his eyes glittering. "I'm not supposed to say anything. This is going to be a surprise to everyone, even my friend Angus. Only Brian has had a peek so far, but what the hell... you guys are going to be the first to know. I'm actually taking a break from fiction to work on a memoir right now. A completely true and accurate account of my rise to fame out of the criminal underground. There's a lot of mischief and shenanigans and at least three whisky bottles broken over someone's head. I promise you it's wilder than anything Norman Mailer got into."

Excited whispers circled the room as the crowd digested this bombshell, especially when Danny added, "And I'll be self-publishing this memoir. Let's see if I can compete with the hacks and bludgers, aye?"

The crowd broke into enthusiastic chatter. "Brian looks positively *murderous*," Quoth whispered to me, squeezing my hand.

I bet he does.

After a couple more questions, Danny stepped back from the microphone and nodded to me. I stood up and addressed the room. "Thank you so much for coming to the first of many such events here at Nevermore Bookshop. Danny's going to stick around for a bit to sign books. We've got a stack over by the wall you can purchase. All the artwork around the room and of course any other books in the shop are also for sale. Please talk to me or one of my helpers—" I gestured to Quoth and Morrie "—if you need assistance. We've got—"

"Aeeeeeeeee!"

I was cut off by a bloodcurdling scream.

CHAPTER FIVE

"***W***hat happened?" I whirled around, my heart in my throat. *Not another dead body, please... not another victim.*

An older woman with salt-and-pepper hair, wearing a thick gingham coat and clashing red gloves and a leopard-print scarf, stood in front of one of Quoth's paintings, her mouth open in a piercing shriek. Every head turned toward her as her scream carried through the room, bouncing off the high ceiling and ringing in my ears.

I scrambled over the back of my chair and rushed towards her. "Are you okay, ma'am? What happened?"

She cut off her scream abruptly, leaning back against the painting so her hair tangled around the corner of the frame, and glared at me with such blinding hatred that I staggered back in shock. "I'll never be okay again, and it's all *his* fault."

Gasps filled the room as she lifted a finger and pointed it at Danny.

Heathcliff was at my side in a flash. "You can't just start screaming in the middle of an event," he snapped at the woman.

"Especially not this bookshop," Mrs. Ellis piped up. "There's already been one dead body—"

A growl from Heathcliff silenced her. But the woman, emboldened, shoved past me and stepped into the center of the room.

"I screamed because I still have the air to do it – I still have air in my lungs to scream for justice. My daughter Abigail wasn't able to scream when her killer wrapped a scarf around her throat and pulled it tight." The woman's face twisted with hatred as she stared at Danny. "And that man right there may have had something to do with her murder. But he got away scot free and now he's made himself rich off her death. All of you in here lapping up his bullshit – shame on you! Have you forgotten what happened in this very village fifteen years ago?"

Danny sighed. "Please, Beverly, this isn't the time."

"It's never the time, is it, Danny?" Beverly shrieked. "It's never time for justice when there's money to be made off the lives of innocent—"

"All right, that's enough!" Heathcliff bellowed.

The entire room fell silent. I moved to stand beside Heathcliff, letting his bulk and imposing presence strengthen me. *What's going on?*

Heathcliff advanced on the woman. He pointed to the door. "Outside, *now*."

"You can't threaten me," she glared right back.

"It's not a threat. This is my property, and you're disturbing a private event. Now, if you want to say your piece, I'll listen, but you'll be doing it outside."

"I have a ticket. I'm allowed to be here." She folded her arms. "What if I refuse to leave?"

Morrie stepped up beside Heathcliff, and the glint in his eyes was terrifying. "You won't refuse."

The woman glared at them both, but something in Morrie's face must've disturbed her. Her body deflated, the air leaking out of her tirade like a balloon. Her shoulders sagged, and her face collapsed into a look of such utter despair that my heart broke for her.

"Fine," she hissed, storming outside. The shop door slammed so hard it rattled the walls.

"What are we all standing around for?" Danny yelled. "The bar's still open. Let's party."

The crowd shuffled toward the bar and the book table, where Danny shook hands and kissed cheeks and scribbled signatures. Everyone seemed to forget about the screaming woman, even me. I had my hands full trying to stop my mother giving her sales pitch to every person in the room.

Everyone had forgotten except for Brian Letterman. He drowned a glass of cider in one gulp and stormed out. Danny waved at him as he left and said something rude that made Brian's shoulders tighten. The front door slammed again. *I'm surprised the glass doesn't fall out with all this drama.*

I glanced out the window to see Brian and the woman screaming at each other on the sidewalk. The woman pulled her arm back and threw something at Brian, but I couldn't see if it hit him or not. After a few moments, they stormed off in separate directions.

Brian hadn't even waited for his wife. I guessed he was upset about Danny's decision to self-publish his memoirs and he was taking it out on that Beverly woman, but his reaction seemed a little juvenile and dramatic. He had nothing on Beverly, though. Imagine screaming like that to get everyone's attention. And what was she talking about?

"Do you know who that woman was?" I asked Angus, who stood in the large bay window, staring out into the night.

"I'll never forget Beverly Ingram," his voice sounded strange, far away. "I was telling you before about that garroting case that turned Danny straight? The victim was Beverly's daughter, Abigail. We never caught the murderer. It's haunted me these last fifteen years, and Danny, too. That's why he wrote about it, to give the case a conclusion. I think Beverly believes Danny had something to do with her daughter's death, and she doesn't want him profiting off the story, which I can understand. She's been writing letters to Brian for months, threatening legal action if he didn't withdraw the book." Angus laughed, but the sound was hollow. He drew a packet of cigarettes from his pocket. "Publishers don't just pull books because someone objects to it, especially not if it's going to sell like hotcakes, like Danny's books always do. If you'll excuse me, I need a smoke. If Brian's still moping outside, I might be able to talk some sense into him. Hell of a bombshell Danny just dropped tonight."

"I'll join you," Heathcliff said, heading after Angus.

"But the counter?" I wailed.

"Morrie's on it. Someone just asked me if we have a copy of that cookbook where the main ingredient is semen. I'm either having a smoke or sticking a customer through a window. Your choice."

"Fine." I waved him away, just as Mum came running over. She thrust a handful of silver patches into my face.

"Hi, honey, I'm putting these by the counter, so people can add one to their purchases."

"No, you're not."

Mum pouted. "At least let me put one of my pamphlets into each shopping bag? Please, dear, I'm so close to earning my Mercedes…"

"No. And please don't buy a Mercedes before we've had a chat about it. I'm sorry, Mum." I kissed her on the cheek. "I really have to go talk to people. But I promise I'll visit this week."

For the rest of the night, I didn't have a chance to give Beverly Ingram or my mother's new scheme another thought. Morrie schmoozed the crowd while I got busy behind the counter, running up all the purchases through the till. Quoth hung out in the main room, locating books for customers and helping women into their coats. I watched him as he made easy conversation with the guests, even laughing at one of Mrs. Ellis' filthy jokes. A laugh from Quoth was so rare and precious that my stomach tightened just watching it.

He's really doing so well. He's finding it so much easier to hold on to his human form. Maybe a normal life isn't as out of reach as he thought.

As I rung up two copies of Danny's book for that woman in the fur stole, I noticed Heathcliff slinking up the staircase. "You not sticking around?" I called out. "I'm sure there are at least five people who still want to ask you why we don't have an in-store cafe."

Heathcliff made a face and I laughed.

"What happened to your new mate, Angus?"

Heathcliff shrugged. "Dunno. We finished our smoke. He picked up some litter in the street. We went inside. He's around here somewhere."

"What did you talk about? Did he say anything more about that Beverly woman? Did you know Danny was her daughter's boyfriend when she was killed—"

"We said not a word to each other," Heathcliff called down from the top of the stairs. "It's the perfect relationship. I wish more people would follow his excellent example."

There was a hint of tease in his voice, and even though I couldn't see his face from this distance, I knew he was kidding. I blew him a kiss and told him I'd be up to say goodnight after I'd seen Danny out and shut the shop.

Speaking of Danny… it occurred to me that I hadn't seen him in a while. I peeked into the Events room. Richard was packing up the bar, and Jo was deep in conversation with the purple-haired erotica writer about mortality rates among those who practice autoerotic asphyxiation. *Where's Danny?*

A terrible thought occurred to me. If Danny had wandered

upstairs and discovered the Occult room or the time-travel room, he could be in a world of trouble.

Please don't let me lose the guest of honor during our first ever event...

I poked my head into the Children's room and the General Fiction room across the hallway, but couldn't see him anywhere. Panic rose in my chest as I took the stairs two at a time. As I turned toward the Sociology section, a figure barreled out of the darkness and slammed against me.

"Morrie!" I exclaimed. "You scared me."

"Precisely my plan," he murmured, pulling my body against his. "Are you trembling with fear? Because I can make you tremble from—"

"Not now." I wriggled out of his grasp. "I'm looking for Danny. Have you seen him?"

"Actually, yes. Follow me." Morrie led me past the Sociology shelves, and into a dark corner of the Railway History room. Even in the darkness, I could tell the room was completely empty.

I fumbled for the monkey lamp I'd placed on the bookshelf last week and flicked it on. "I'm serious, Morrie. I haven't seen Danny for a while, and if he's upstairs—"

"See that bookshelf – it's actually a secret cupboard." Morrie pointed to a corner next to the window. "Heathcliff uses it to store extra envelopes and the bodies of customers who tell him *50 Shades of Grey* should have won the Man Booker Prize."

I noticed the fan shape on the carpet where the shelf must swing out on its hinges. I jumped as a loud, rhythmic thumping noise came from behind the shelves. "Rats?" I whispered.

"Close," Morrie reached between two books to flick a lever, and the door swung open.

I leaned forward and peered into the dark space. Morrie swung the lamp around, illuminating two bodies curled inside.

I gasped as my eyes resolved Danny and Amanda, locked in a

passionate embrace. He'd pulled her velvet dress up around her waist and his pants and boxers were around his knees. She glared at us over his shoulder as he slammed her into the back wall of the storage cupboard. Without breaking their kiss, Danny reached out, grabbed the inner handle, and slammed the door shut again.

I leaned against the shelf, my chest heaving as I waited for my heart to returned to normal speed. "I guess we found Danny."

Morrie grinned, holding up a copy of *The Somerset Strangler*. "We sure did. Hey, Danny, when you're done in there, can you sign my book?"

CHAPTER SIX

*T*he last cavorting guest left at ten-past-midnight. Quoth and I picked up all the trash, stacked the cider bottles in the recycling, and swept up the Events room. Morrie, of course, refused to help but insisted on following us everywhere, reciting the most grisly passages from Danny's book.

At last, we'd returned the shop to its normal state. I collapsed into Heathcliff's chair, my legs aching and my head swimming from everything that had happened. Our first big event had gone out mostly without a hitch.

And let's not forget the most important fact of all... no one was murdered. Maybe my luck is finally changing.

"Are you leaving now?" Quoth asked softly.

"I can't go back to Jo's place. I fully expect all the water in the taps to turn to blood and hail to pour from the radiators." Quoth's sensuous lips curled up at the corners when I explained about the locusts.

He raised an eyebrow. "So you're kipping here, then? And are you so tired you plan to go straight to bed?"

A ring of orange fire blazed at the edges of his dark eyes. Instantly, my body responded, my sleepy limbs itching to hold him, my blood running hotter. I shook my head and was rewarded with one of Quoth's dazzling smiles.

Quoth took my hand and led me upstairs, his raven hair streaming behind him. This was so unlike him, taking charge like this, asking for what he wanted. *I think we've all been doing some healing over the last couple of months.*

As we stepped into the flat, Heathcliff poked his head out of his room. "Where are the two of you going?"

"To my room," Quoth said.

"My bed's bigger," Heathcliff suggested.

Quoth's fingers closed around his hand. He'd never say anything, but I had a feeling he needed me to himself tonight. "Your bed is covered in the detritus of your life," I told Heathcliff. "I don't want to be shagging and end up with the corner of Sherman's memoirs up my arse."

"Don't say that where Morrie can hear," Heathcliff warned. "He'll get excited."

"Too late!" Morrie's head poked out of the bathroom. "Where do you think you're going, gorgeous?"

I leaned over and pecked Morrie on the cheek. "To Quoth's room. And you're not invited."

Morrie poked his lip out in a mock pout, then he drew me in for a deep kiss that left my legs weak. "You sure you don't want to reconsider?"

I gulped. "I'm sure, but maybe tomorrow…"

He wagged a finger at me. "I'll hold you to that." The bathroom door slammed shut.

I turned to Heathcliff, my hand cupping his cheek. His stubble scratched against my palm. A deep ache formed in my chest as his eyes bore into mine. I was so lucky to have these guys with me. I got to see inside Heathcliff's dark soul, beyond the surly socially-inept arsehole. And what I saw in him was all the hidden parts of myself reflected back at me.

Heathcliff looked like he wanted to say something else.

Instead, he retreated into his room and slammed the door shut. *Great, so I'd have to deal with that later.*

Right now, it was all about my raven boy, my tortured, quiet artist with the hair of spun silk. Quoth kept his hand in mine as we ascended the narrow staircase into the attic. I hadn't been up here since last year. The place was exactly as I remembered it – low ceilings, narrow brass bed, easel set up in front of the tall dormer window looking out over Argleton, every spare corner stacked with paintings and sketches. I stumbled over a pile of art books. Quoth hurried to flick on the lights and lamps so I could see.

I stopped short when a beam of light illuminated the painting on Quoth's easel.

It was a picture of me. Well, I guessed it was meant to be me. The woman in the image had my features, but she looked less like a hot mess in her flatmate's borrowed tartan trousers and more like the heroine from a gothic romance book, all sweeping hair and come-to-bed eyes. The soft colors around her face brought out her delicate features. On her shoulder sat a raven, its head turned toward her. In her hands, she held a stack of books. Quoth had started lettering the titles and authors in gold paint – *Wuthering Heights, The Complete Works of Sherlock Holmes, Poe – Selected Poems.*

"Wow." I touched the edge of the frame. The oil paints were still wet. "Quoth, it's…"

"You don't have to be nice. I know it's not very good."

A lump rose in my throat. "Don't say that. It's breathtaking."

"Really?" His voice caught in his throat.

"I just… I can't believe that's me… it is me, isn't it?"

Quoth laughed, the sound like trickling water. "Of course. Although I can't seem to get you right. I've repainted it going on twenty times now. I was thinking of giving it to you for your birthday. But then I wondered that you might hate it, so I wanted you to see it first. You really like it?"

I flicked on the reading light and directed it at the painting so I could see it better. Light and shadow danced over the canvas. It wasn't just a portrait – Quoth had captured something special, some indefinable element that made my eyes water. There was a strength in my painted face, in the piercing color of my eyes and set of my jaw, but a vulnerability too. It was exactly how I felt these days as I tried to accept what was happening to my vision. The way the raven bent its head toward me, and the landscape framed our faces… Quoth was pouring out his own feelings onto canvas, and the paint bled his hope and his pain and his own journey.

I'll always watch over you.

Those were the words Quoth said to me, again and again. Last month, when I'd been invited to the Jane Austen Experience, Quoth didn't feel he was ready to spend a whole weekend around so many people. While Heathcliff and Morrie attended lectures and high tea and Regency dancing with me, Quoth sat outside in the snow, watching through the windows. Always outside, looking in.

And in the end, he was the one who saved my life. *No one has ever loved me so unconditionally or demanded so little of me.* It made me want to give him more, to give him everything.

Quoth's hand on my hip grew hot. I whirled around and pulled him close to me, drawing his lips to mine for a deep kiss. I poured all of myself into that kiss, trying to show him how good it felt to see this side of him, to be allowed into his heart. My finger traced the scar along his shoulder, left by Christina Hathaway when she attacked him.

He wrapped his arms around me, drawing me against him. His hand snaked beneath my shirt, pressing hot skin against skin. I lost myself in him, wishing that we could close the gap between us, that the atoms dividing us would disintegrate so we could be part of each other.

We fell to the bed, tearing at each other's clothes. This was

Quoth as I'd never seen him before, desperate and shaking with barely contained tension. He touched his lips to my nipple and I cried out, and the shudder that went through his body made me love him more.

Quoth's lips found mine, hungry and hot. His hand thrust between my legs, his fingers plunging inside me, stoking the fire that he'd created. The ache inside me flared into an inferno.

He rolled me onto my side and slid behind me, parting my legs with his knee. When he entered me, colors from the painting bled into the room, soaring across my vision like an aurora. Quoth held me, nails digging into my breast, finger darting over my clit.

Cocooned in his warmth, I'd never felt so protected, so loved, so needed. We fit together so perfectly, our bodies like puzzle pieces that had finally found their mate. Inside me, his cock touched hidden places, building sensation upon sensation until my body could take no more.

We came together in a shower of bright fireworks, our bodies trembling under the stars of our own creation. Bright lights burst across my vision, and I lost myself outside my body, no longer certain where my pleasure stopped and his began.

I sank into his arms, squeezing my eyes shut, relaxing into the hum of release. The colors still danced behind my eyes – Quoth's painting come to life inside my brain. In the stillness of his attic room, in the safety of his arms, I saw the world as he saw it, and it was beautiful.

"Mina..." Quoth shuddered against me. Overwhelming by the rush of emotion, tears spilled over my eyes and rolled down my cheeks.

I grinned. "That was amazing."

"It was." Quoth wiped a finger under my eyes. "You're crying?"

"Not sad tears." I touched my hand over his heart. "I don't think I've ever felt closer to you than right now."

"Good." He swallowed. "There's something I want to ask you."

"Ah." That explained his behavior tonight. He'd been building up toward this moment. I rolled over so I was facing Quoth. I could only just make out the edges of his face. The colors still darted across my vision. I reached out a hand and stroked his cheek. *Even when I'm blind, I'll still be able to feel his soft skin, his warm lips on mine. I'll see the lights and colors and pretend I'm inside one of his paintings. Even when I'm blind, this moment will be perfect.*

"I think I want..." Quoth gulped. "I've been looking at art schools on the internet."

"You have?"

Quoth's cheek moved beneath my hand as he nodded. "I don't even know why. I didn't think I wanted to go. I just wanted to find out... There's a college in Barchester that offers a part-time degree. I would only be in classes a few times per week. The rest of it is independent work. They have this big, bright art studio overlooking a park, and a pottery kiln and metalworking spaces and a photography suite, and all the teachers are professional artists and—"

"I think that sounds amazing," I breathed. My heart just burst for him. Two months ago, Quoth wouldn't even leave the shop. He was invisible, without even a passport or a real name. He barely said a word and wouldn't appear downstairs unless it was in his raven form. Now he was talking not just about being in the world more, but about taking a step toward having a career, a life. "Are you ready for that?"

"I think so." His finger stroked my cheek. "I've realized that if I want to have a future with you, I can't just expect you to hang out in a dusty old attic."

A future with you. By Isis, his words made me feel so good.

"I like your attic, but I like this idea even more."

Quoth's finger paused mid-stroke. "And... I think you should enroll with me."

My body froze. "Um... why?"

"Because you'd love it."

My heart pattered against my chest. "You're right. I would love it. But that doesn't mean it's something I should do."

"I know there's a chance it will make you feel bad about your eyes, but it could also be amazing. Will you at least consider it? You're the only other artist I know. I trust your opinion. They're having an open day next week. Will you come and meet the lecturers with me? Please?"

I sighed, sensing a rat. Quoth's motives were entirely selfless. He probably didn't even intend to go to school himself. He was just trying to get me to find excitement in something since I couldn't do fashion anymore. *Well, two can play at this game.* I'd make him so excited about art school that he signed up on the spot, and it would be his own bloody fault. "Sure, I'll go with you."

"You're amazing." He kissed me again. "Thank you, Mina."

"Yeah, yeah." I reached over and flicked off the lamp. "You won't be thanking me when you're introduced to the reality of student loans. Goodnight, my infuriating bird."

"Goodnight, my rare and radiant maiden, my muse."

I settled my head into the crook of his arm and closed my eyes. Weariness and happiness washed over me in equal waves. "Damn you, yours is much better."

CHAPTER SEVEN

y phone alarm blared an angry guitar solo. I reached over to flick it to snooze, but my arm slapped against warm flesh. I opened one sleepy eye and was met by Quoth's kind face.

"Good morning," I said sleepily.

"It is now." Quoth leaned over and pressed his mouth to mine. My lips parted and his tongue touched mine – tentative at first, then deep and possessive, as if he needed me in order to breathe.

I pulled back, breathless. "You're right. This *is* good. Let's wake up this way every day."

"I'd like that," he smiled. "If you lived here we could wake up like this every day. Well, I'd have to beat off Morrie and Heathcliff."

I laughed at the idea of Quoth beating off the two sword-wielding maniacs of my harem. We'd been jokingly referring to the guys as my 'harem' ever since we got back from Baddesley Hall. I liked it – being the center of attention for not one but three guys was empowering, if not a little overwhelming at times. And it stopped me from feeling sick every time I looked at them and realized I had no idea what the fuck I was doing.

I have three boyfriends. I love them, and they love me.

They also loved each other in their own dysfunctional ways. At the moment, that was enough. If I paused for too long, if I opened my mind wide enough for the doubt to creep in, then thoughts of the future niggled at me. How long could they go on being Mina's harem before it became an issue? What would I do if they needed me to choose?

What will happen to us if I *don't* choose?

One woman with three boyfriends wasn't exactly conventional. I was a punk rocker in my twenties – it was kind of expected that I'd experiment with my sexuality. But what about when I was in my thirties? What about my fifties?

A future without Quoth, Heathcliff and Morrie didn't seem possible. They were a part of me now. But what if the world forced us apart? Perhaps it was because everything about my future was already so uncertain, I wanted to hold on to them tight and never let go. But that wasn't fair – I couldn't ask them to be one of three forever. Eventually, I'd have to let two of them go. The thought turned my heart to ice.

They'd taught me that I was tough enough to handle anything, but I wasn't sure I'd be tough enough to lose them.

I glanced at my alarm clock. *6:15?* Outside, it was still dark – the pale moon hung directly over the window, shining a blue square across the bed. Everything beyond that square was invisible to me.

Why did I set the clock for 6:15? All I have to do is roll downstairs and open the shop at nine. I could sleep in Quoth's arms for another—

Oh, shite. I bolted upright, dropping Quoth like a stone. *Danny's coming around early to set up for the workshop.*

"You just remembered the workshop, didn't you?" Quoth watched from the bed as I scrambled for my clothes. There was a hint of amusement in his voice.

"What gave you that idea?" I muttered as I hopped on one leg, trying to get Jo's cropped tartan pants over my thigh.

"I love that you're so excited about it," Quoth said. "I think you'd make a great writer."

"I'm not going because I want to be a writer," I said. My cheeks flushed with heat, and I was grateful that he wouldn't be able to see my blush in the dark. "I'm just sitting in to make sure it runs smoothly, so I can learn how to run future workshops—"

"You could be a writer if you wanted to," Quoth said. "No one can tell you that you can't write because of your eyes. You have such a unique way of seeing people – you look right into souls. It's why you're so good at solving mysteries. Plus, you'll have plenty of inspiration, what with all the strange happenings around here."

"Stop gushing," I growled. My cheeks stung with heat. I yanked my shirt down and bolted for the door before he could say anything else embarrassing.

"Can you make me a hero in your story?" Quoth called after me. "Every good novel needs a street smart raven shapeshifter with a really huge cock."

"You're becoming more like Morrie every day!" I yelled back as I clattered down the stairs. Figures Quoth had to pick 6:15 in the morning to decide to become a comedian.

The old building creaked and groaned as I snuck past Heathcliff's room. His snores echoed through the door. Downstairs, something thudded. *Probably the hot water cylinder. It always makes that noise.*

In the living room, Morrie was already awake. He stood under the pendant light, buttoning one of his crisp shirts, staring down at the screens on his enormous computer rig with a bemused expression. My breath caught in my throat as I took him in, all his sharp edges and creased trousers and brow furrowed in thought. I'd never been into fastidious men, but Morrie... he made his sharp edges work for him.

He glanced up as I entered. His hands flew from his buttons

to click something on the screen. "You look tired," he said, his usual grin spreading across his face.

"No shit, Sherlock."

Morrie's grin froze, and I recoiled as I remembered who I was speaking to. Just last week, Morrie had confessed a detail about his relationship with the infamous detective that I didn't want him to think I was throwing back in his face. "I'm sorry, I didn't mean that. It's early. I just—"

"You just need coffee?"

I gave him a thumbs up.

"It's already brewing." Morrie stepped toward me. He brushed my nipple with his finger. "Are you sure coffee is *all* you need?"

"Mmmmmm. I wish there was time for that, but I've got to get downstairs and set up for the workshop."

"You're taking this management role way too seriously," Morrie pouted. "If you recall, you made me a promise last night."

"I don't think I actually *promised* jack or shit," I pressed my lips to his. "Luckily, I find you pretty bloody irresistible. I'm all yours tonight, I promise."

"Fine." The coffee machine beeped. Morrie retreated to the kitchen. "I'll make yours extra strong."

"You are my hero. Has Danny arrived yet?" I asked, buttoning my blouse. Downstairs, the hot water cylinder banged again.

"Nope. I hope he's not late. I've got his favorite brand of coffee, but I'm so nervous I'm probably going to drink it all before he gets here." Morrie emerged from the kitchen, clutched two mugs in his hands. I noticed that his knuckles were whiter than usual. He flashed me his brilliant smile as he handed me my coffee, but I noticed it wavered a little at the edges.

Was James Moriarty excited about meeting a *writer*? Or was this about something else?

I heard another thump from downstairs, louder this time, and a sound like someone coughing. *Shite, that's not the cylinder, I bet that's Danny!* I plucked the cup out of his hands. "No more coffee for you. I'm going to need both of these. Come on, let's go downstairs. I gave Danny a key so he could let himself in, and I bet that's him now."

As I descended the stairs, a cold breeze raced up from the ground floor, raising the hairs on my arms. The door banged on its hinges. "See, told you Danny must have snuck in. All those years as a hardened criminal paid off, because he sure was quiet."

"I didn't even hear him," Morrie mused. "As one criminal to another, he's *good*. But then, of course he is. I can tell from his books. In *The Middlesex Murders*, the killer plays a recording of a conversation he taped a few days earlier behind his locked office door in order to give himself an alibi. So clever. I'm noting that for future use."

"Hey, Danny, are you—"

My words died in my throat as the light from the open door illuminated a lumpy shape lying across the rug. A figure on the ground was surrounded by fallen piles of books. Danny's face was turned toward us, his hands frozen at his throat. His eyes bugged out and his features were twisted in a weird sort of smirk.

"Hey, Danny, that's not funny, mate." Morrie nudged him with his boot. "Get up."

But Danny didn't move. Morrie bent down and tipped Danny's head to the side, revealing a dark, ugly mark around his neck, the skin broken in places and blood dribbling from the wounds.

"Well, that's interesting," he said, rising slowly to his feet. His hand reached for mine, and I noticed his fingers trembled. "He's stone dead."

CHAPTER EIGHT

"*C*ause of death is relatively straightforward," Jo announced, leaning over Danny's body and using a small magnifying glass to study his neck. "He most likely died from asphyxiation, caused by the collapsing of his windpipe. These marks and the violent compression of the neck suggest a ligature was used – from the lack of cuts in the skin and this bruising pattern here I'd say it was some kind of fabric – a scarf or rope, rather than a wire. There's no murder weapon on the scene, though. The killer must have taken it with him, which makes things trickier. I'll have to confirm all this in the lab – sometimes these marks can be simulated after death."

I felt sick. Danny's glassy, bugged-out eyes stared up from the floor, condemning me.

Another dead body. Another murder in the bookshop. My mind flashed back to the other times I'd seen the police and forensic teams in here – when my ex-best friend Ashley was the one lying dead with a knife in her back, when the indomitable Gladys Scarlett was brought down at her book club meeting by arsenic poisoning.

This time there was little blood, no knife, no poison, but there was Danny's face, so white and bulbous, so unlike his roguish smile and sparkling eyes.

Who did this to him?

"There is also some bruising here," Jo turned Danny's head and pointed. "As well as hemorrhaging around the strap muscles. This suggests he struggled against his attacker. It might also explain the books strewn everywhere. I believed your victim kicked at the shelves, knocking down the books."

"Time of death?" Hayes asked, jotting notes on his pad.

"This guy is relatively fresh. He's probably been dead about an hour."

An hour. My heart thudded in my chest. That meant that Danny was being murdered while Morrie and I were upstairs discussing coffee and everyone else was sleeping. The murderer had been inside the shop. I thought back to the thumps I'd heard. *I should have run downstairs immediately. We should have called the police. We could have saved him if we—*

DS Wilson ended her phone call. "Guv, I've spoken with the front desk at Danny's hotel. They said he left around five a.m. They're available to let us into his room."

"Good. I'll head over there now." Hayes snapped his notebook shut. "Get the constables to canvas the neighborhood, see if anyone heard or saw Danny or another person around the bookshop this morning at the time of the murder. Start with Mrs. Ellis across the road; she's always first to the post with neighborhood gossip. I'd also like you to interview Ms. Wilde and Mr. Moriarty and anyone else in the house at the time."

Wilson rolled her eyes at me. "Are you sure we shouldn't just have them conduct their own interviews, since they seem determined to play detective?"

"It's not our fault people keep being murdered," I cried. A chill ran down my spine that had nothing to do with the gale-force wind blowing outside.

"What Mina means to say is that we'd be happy to take over your duties," Morrie added, holding me against his chest as Heathcliff and Quoth came down the stairs escorted by one of the uniformed officers. "Since you seem intellectually inferior—"

"That won't be necessary, Mr. Moriarty." Hayes rubbed his eyes. He looked as tired as I felt. "DS Wilson will take your statements shortly."

"So he was garroted." Morrie leaned forward, his eyes sparkling with interest. "Is that unusual?"

"Mr. Moriarty, please remove yourself and Ms. Wilde into another room," Hayes frowned as he stared at the scene. "Let the real detectives deal with this case."

Gladly. I bolted into the main room and collapsed in Heathcliff's chair. The guys followed me – Heathcliff glowering in the doorway, Quoth perched on the corner of the table, Morrie pacing in front of the window, his mind already whirling through possibilities. My stomach churned. Right now, the last thing I wanted to do was think about who was behind this murder. "I can't believe someone would want to hurt Danny. He seemed like such an affable bloke."

"Just because Danny was jovial doesn't mean he didn't have enemies. His wife probably wasn't happy about what was going on in the closet last night," Morrie said.

"Do you think she knew?" I asked.

"Women usually do," Heathcliff said.

I remembered the conversation I'd had with Penny Sledge last night. *Yes, I think she knew.*

"The guy also had a criminal past," Morrie pointed out. He picked up a copy of *The Somerset Strangler* from the stack on the desk and flipped through it. "Maybe something caught up with him. Too bad he didn't get to publish his memoir. I bet that contained all sorts of sordid tales."

"What about that publisher?" Heathcliff asked. "He didn't look too happy about Danny's announcement to self-publish his memoir."

"Oooh, that's a good one. Also, his friend Angus might've decided he deserved more of Danny's money for his contributions," Morrie mused. "Or maybe Amanda wanted Danny to leave his wife for her and he refused."

"Don't forget that batshit woman who screamed bloody murder," Heathcliff added.

I winced. Quoth shot Heathcliff a dirty look. "Poor choice of words. Look at Mina, she's upset."

"I'm fine." I rested my chin in my hands. My head spun. *Keep it together. Don't think about Danny's bugged-out eyes. Don't think about those horrible marks around his neck—*

Jo poked her head in. "Just letting you know that we're taking the body away now, as well as the hall rug. You're safe to wander around. My guys are gonna be here photographing the shelves and collecting trace evidence, but they'll be gone in an hour or so, and then you're free to open up."

"That's great. Thanks, Jo."

"Oh, and I have more good news," Jo's dazzling smile seemed at odds with the somber occasion, but that was Jo – she dealt with grisly deaths every day, so it took a lot to rattle her. "The exterminator came by this morning. No more locusts."

"Locusts?" Morrie raised an eyebrow.

I gave a weak smile. "That is good news. Any serious damage?"

"Apart from the fact that my experiment is ruined? Not really. They've had a nibble on any exposed natural fibers – the cloth shopping bags, the wicker hanging basket, my merino vest on the indoor clothesline. We're going to have to replant the herb garden. Those greedy buggers even ate the linen tablecloth. Can you believe it?"

I leaned back in my chair, my body overcome with weariness. *Can I believe that there's been another murder and a plague of locusts ate our herb garden? I wish I could say I didn't, but the truth is... that sounds like just another day at Nevermore Bookshop.*

~

I slumped between Heathcliff and Quoth, their hands in mine, as Wilson took my statement. She kept glancing between me and the guys, and I could tell she was wondering about the nature of our relationship. When I said Quoth and I had been in bed together this morning, her eyebrows went *way* up.

I guess I have to get used to people reacting like that if I'm going to stay with the three of them.

But I didn't have time to think about my relationship, as Wilson's questions came thick and fast. She'd always been a little suspicious of me. That probably had to do with the fact that dead bodies seemed to stack up wherever I went. And now here we were again, staring at each other from across Heathcliff's desk, while the SOCO team dealt with the third crime scene in the shop in as many months.

We each described as much of the event last night as we could remember, including Danny's talk and the audience questions, the visit from Beverly, and finding Danny and Amanda in the closet. Wilson asked lots of questions about Beverly and Amanda, as well as making detailed notes about our movements. She then asked us to walk her around the Events room and describe the layout while she jotted down a floorplan on her pad.

By the time Wilson finished with us, the SOCO team had left with their evidence. Outside the shop, a crowd of writers had gathered – the participants of Danny's workshop. I noticed our purple-haired erotica writer talking with two ladies from Mrs. Ellis' knitting club. They inched away as he described a sex scene he was working on.

"...and her nipples were hard and round, like the rivets on a steam engine..."

"Excuse me." I cleared my throat. No one looked up.

"...his mouth wet with her delicious vaginal sap..."

Heathcliff stuck two fingers in his mouth and let out a mighty whistle. Our purple-haired friend nearly jumped out of his skin. Mrs. Ellis' friends flashed me relieved smiles.

I cleared my throat. "Hi everyone. I'm Mina, the organizer of today's workshop. Unfortunately, Danny's not going to be able to host the workshop today. He..."

The words died on my tongue. I tried to focus on the people in front of me but all I could see was Danny's bloated face and gaping mouth. I tried again. "Danny is... he is..."

"He's dead as a doornail," Heathcliff finished.

A collective gasp rose through the crowd. I glared at Heathcliff.

"What?" He shrugged his broad shoulders. "That's what he is. He's croaked, expired, popped his clogs, bereft of life, and gone west to meet his maker. He's passed on, cashed in his chips, kicked his oxygen habit, and checked into the Horizontal Hilton for his Hamlet sleep. He's immortality challenged, and will no longer be counted on the census—"

Mrs. Ellis' two friends looked aghast. The erotica writer affixed a solemn expression to his face, but the corner of his mouth tugged up at Heathcliff's description. *Immortality-challenged? I can't believe he just said that.* I jabbed Heathcliff in the side and shot him a warning look, which he ignored.

"It's true?" One of the other writers – a man in a tweed jacket with a pencil tucked behind his ear – asked. "He's really dead?"

"Yes. I'm sorry. So we won't be able to hold the event today. I'll organize refunds for you this week. In the meantime, I know you've come all this way, so why don't you come inside? I've got refreshments arriving shortly, and we could sit in the Events room and discuss writing, maybe read excerpts of your work—"

"What's the point?" growled Tweed-Man. "I've come all the way from Crookshollow to learn from Danny Sledge. I'm not going to discuss my masterpiece with these hacks."

"Who are you calling a hack?" shot back a woman with tortoiseshell glasses. "I'm going to be the next Nora Roberts. I wouldn't want to waste an afternoon with a bunch of literary toffs, I've got a bestselling manuscript to finish."

One by one, the writers turned away, muttering their disappointment. Mrs. Ellis' friends shook their heads sadly as they shuffled away toward the green, nattering loudly about where to get a good cup of tea in the village. I slumped down on the step, my head in my hands.

An arm fell around my shoulders, and a whiff of fresh grass enveloped me. Heathcliff's dark eyes regarded mine with fierce kindness. "I'm sorry, Mina. I knew you were looking forward to that workshop."

"It's fine." Who was I kidding? It didn't feel fine. It felt like things had just started to go right in my life and now everything was falling apart. It felt like no matter what I did I was never going to catch a break. It felt like I'd never get to find out if I could possibly write...

Except that, of course, I wasn't interested in that. I had no talent for writing. No way could I come close to the writers I admire. I was no Emily Brontë or Arthur Conan Doyle. I didn't even think I could manage an E. L. James.

Footsteps sounded on the steps behind me. Quoth slipped down on the other side of me and tipped my head onto his shoulder. His fingers squeezed my skin. He could sense the emotion rising inside me, the flood of melancholy that I'd done so much to temper flaring to life and threatening to overwhelm me.

Heathcliff's eyes bore into mine, their depths unfathomable. "There's a surefire way to cure this malaise."

I sniffed. "How?"

"We'll have our own workshop," Heathcliff tugged me to my

feet. "Morrie has a bottle of expensive French absinthe hidden under the sink. We'll finish it, then test Hemingway's concept that one should write drunk and edit sober. Personally, I think it should be 'write drunk, edit drunker,' but that's why he's the author and I'm the tortured antihero."

CHAPTER NINE

Given my dark mood, it didn't take much convincing
from Heathcliff for me to concede to his plan. I drew
the line at absinthe (I read Poppy Z Brite), but I did
agree to lock up the shop and join the boys at the Rose & Wimple
for an early lunch. Heathcliff and Morrie flanked me as we cut
across the village green. Quoth's talons dug into my shoulder. He
decided that he couldn't face the gossiping villagers after Danny's
murder, but that if we sat in the beer garden he'd come and perch
on the wall beside us.

It looked like the entire village had gathered at the pub. They
spilled out onto the green, talking in furtive whispers. Heads
turned toward us as we made our way down the steps and past
the jaunty iron pig announcing the day's special. *The village gossip
mill must be in full swing with news of Danny's murder. I hope they at
least have the decency to leave us alone—*

As soon as we stepped through the door, the whole place fell
silent. Even though I could barely make out the faces in the
gloomy interior, I could feel their eyes crawling over my body,
their unanswered questions hanging in the air.

"Let's go somewhere else," Heathcliff muttered. *"Tir Na Nog"* in Crookshollow does a decent ploughman's lunch."

"Nope." Fierce determination settled in my gut. This was our village too, and we'd done nothing wrong. If we wanted to eat a four-quid basket of chips and drown our sorrows over a pint, then we had a right to do it. I strode up to the bar and slammed my wallet down. "Hi, Richard. We'll have a pint of lager, one of cider, a glass of your house white, and a couple of menus, please."

The landlord pulled pints for Heathcliff and I. Morrie hopped from foot to foot. From the expression on his face, I could tell he was dying to wrest the cheap wine from Richard's hand and tip it over his head, but even he wasn't prepared to make a scene with the whole village staring us down. All he managed was a weak protest. "Don't you have anything with a more fragrant bouquet? Maybe something from the Napa Valley, or New Zealand…"

"Not for six quid a glass, sorry, mate." Richard set down the wine in front of him. Morrie looked like he'd rather drink toilet water. He picked up the glass and held it up to the light before taking a dainty sip. A choking sound escaped his lips.

"You all right there?" Richard leaned across the bar, his kindly face creased in concern.

"Fine," Morrie croaked.

If I wasn't so wrapped up in Danny's murder and the eerie silence of the pub, I would have cracked up laughing. I quickly paid for our drinks and shuffled away from the bar. "Let's find a table," I muttered.

Chatter picked up in hushed tones, closing behind us like the wake of a boat. Snatches of conversation caught my ears as we maneuvered between the tables.

"That place has always been strange. Remember the old blind man who used to own it? Why did a blind bloke want to spend so much time with books he couldn't read. That's weird."

"I've always said that gypsy was up to no good in the village. He's probably murdering writers to steal their wallets."

"I think that young lady's in charge. She's from the council estate, you know. They don't raise children right out there. I bet you anything she's sleeping with all those blokes. Got them wrapped around her little finger. It ain't right, I tell you."

"One thing's for sure. I'm not setting foot in that shop again. It's too dangerous."

Maybe this was a bad idea, after all.

As we made our way out the back to the beer garden, I caught sight of a hand waving above a table. "Yoohoo, Mina." It was Mrs. Ellis. "Over here!"

I didn't exactly want to spend my drinking time filling Mrs. Ellis in on every gory detail of the murder, but her company couldn't help but improve my mood. Gratefully, we sat down at the end of her table. I glanced around at her companions, recognizing the two writers from her knitting group, as well as local historian Florence Lawton, who I'd roped into giving a history lecture at the shop next week.

"Another spot of trouble at the bookshop, Mina?" asked Dotty.

"Yes." I shuddered. "I don't really want to talk about it, so—"

Mrs. Ellis tsked. "A famous and handsome crime writer, killed in the same manner as the victims in his books! It sounds like the plot of an Agatha Christie novel. You found the body, didn't you Mina? Tell us, was it terribly gory? Was his face all bloated and—"

"Right, I'm having the steak and kidney pie. Mina?" Heathcliff growled, pointedly flinging open the menu in front of my face.

"I bet it was that publisher, Brian Letterman." Dotty leaned forward, her voice conspiratorial. Mrs. Ellis' friends were bound to love a juicy murder just as much as she did. "Did you see his face when Danny announced he was self-publishing his memoir? He looked ready to kill."

"Or it could've been Beverly Ingram. What was she doing, barging in like that!" Mrs. Ellis said. "I know it's a tragedy, but it's not handsome Danny's fault that he happened to use the same murder weapon in his book as Abigail's murderer."

"Beverly's been a bit doddery these last few weeks," added Wenda. "That's what happens when you don't have a husband and when you turn away all the friendly people in the village. Why, just the other week I ran into her at the market. She parked her trolley across the entire aisle, just staring at a rack of cereals. I says to her, I says, 'Beverly, you just have to let it go.' But then she just starts flailing her arms at the shelves. Cereal everywhere! She's been barred from the market for a month."

"Why was she attacking the cereal aisle?" Morrie asked. While Mrs. Ellis turned to elaborate, he swapped her wine glass for his. He sampled the bouquet and decided it was superior, for he took a grateful sip.

"Her daughter Abigail did some modeling back in the day. Abigail's face appeared on a cereal box. She did a commercial for toothpaste, too. Beverly thought her daughter would be in the pictures one day. She was a real looker, was Abigail, and she knew it. She had a trail of boys following her around the village like she was the pied bloody piper. But she could be a vicious trollop – she and Beverly were always going at it about her drinking and partying with the wrong sorts of people. You could hear them screaming at each other halfway across the village."

"I was only young when the murder happened," I said. "I don't remember it, but it must have shaken the whole village."

"It was a terrible tragedy. Beverly was a nurse at Barchester General. She came home from a late shift around two in the morning and found Abigail dead in her room, garroted by her own silk scarf."

My fingers raked at the wooden table. "That's horrible," I breathed.

"It was quite the scandal. There was some drug paraphernalia in the room, and signs of a struggle – a broken mirror, knick-knacks all over the floor. But there wasn't a break-in, so she must have known and trusted her killer, at least initially. The police assumed it was one of her boyfriends, perhaps flying into a jealous rage."

"Boyfriends?" Did Beverly's daughter have a harem, like me? That was chilling.

"Oh yes, at least two they knew about, including Danny Sledge. But they couldn't pin it on any of them since the coppers had nicked them all for dealing drugs that same night. That lovely Angus Donahue was the inspector at the time, wasn't he?"

Dotty nodded. "Poor Angus. He tried so hard to crack that case, and with the media breathing down his neck too, but they couldn't find who did it. I think it haunted him because he left the police force soon after, and he'd only just been promoted. That's maybe why Danny's book has some of the same elements of the crime. It weighs on both Danny and Angus. No wonder Beverly was upset."

"That's not Danny's fault!" Mrs. Ellis cried. "Beverly shouldn't have killed him just because he wrote a book!"

"Who says Beverly was the one who killed him?" Wenda leaned forward. "I heard that Danny wasn't exactly a devoted husband. Had a bit of a wandering eye, didn't he? Maybe that sour wife of his bumped him off in order to put a stop to his philandering. I imagine she stands to inherit a great deal."

"Or maybe it was a crazed fan," Dotty squealed with delight. "That happens, you know. One minute, they're collecting rare first editions, the next minute they're carving their name into your internal organs."

"Only in Stephen King books," Heathcliff muttered, reaching across the table to steal some of their chips.

"Or it could be a serial killer, stalking authors who speak in the bookshop," added Florence. She shuddered.

Panic fluttered in my stomach. "Please don't worry, Florence. I'm sure that's not it. The police are going to catch the killer and everything will be fine in time for your event."

She reached across the table and squeezed my hand. "I'm sorry, Mina. I'm not going to be able to do the event. With the murderer still running loose, I just don't feel comfortable in the shop, especially not after all the other deaths. You understand, don't you?"

"Oh, yes. Sure. Of course, I understand," I said with false brightness, even though I wanted to crawl inside Heathcliff's enormous coat and cry.

The ladies entertained us with more gossip from the village while we ate lunch. I barely touched my roast beef. How could I enjoy a Yorkshire pudding after someone had been killed in the shop?

On our way back to Nevermore, we passed Mike Whitaker, who owned a local distillery and was going to lead a whisky and book club week after next. He strolled across the green in the opposite direction, flicking through today's *Argleton Gazette*.

"Hi, Mike!" I waved. He glanced up and quickened his pace. *Did he not see me? Maybe he's going blind, too...* "Mike!"

He turned around, his eyes wide. "Mina, er… it's nice to see you."

"And you. I'm glad I caught you. I wanted to talk to you about some of the details of your event. I've got the perfect book for us to discuss – it's a history of whisky brewing in England with all these old pictures—"

Mike shifted uncomfortably. "Actually, I'm going to have to pull out. I'm sorry, love. My wife's got a quilting exhibition over in Barchester that night, and I can't upset the missus."

What? Why are you just telling me this now? "No problem," I forced a smile. "I'll ask Richard to fill in. He was such a hit with the cider last night, I'm sure he'd love the opportunity."

"Yes, yes." Mike was already jogging toward the pub. "I'm sure he would. Well, see you."

"Yeah," I watched him scurry away. *Your wife doesn't have a quilting meet. You just don't want to come to Nevermore Bookshop.*

Heathcliff squeezed my hand. I stared across the green at our chimneys jutting above the bakery on the corner, and the little swinging sign that read NEVERMORE BOOKSHOP sticking out beyond the buildings on Butcher Street. I squeezed my eyes shut, trying not to imagine that sign gone, the beautiful old building bordered up... or worse, bulldozed by Grey Lachlan.

"Let's hope the police solve this murder soon," I murmured, fingering my father's note. "Or Nevermore Bookshop is going to be out of business."

CHAPTER TEN

*B*ack at my now locust-less flat, I tossed and turned all night. Danny's bloated, stricken face danced behind my eyelids. *He was alive just yesterday, talking about writing his next book. And now, thanks to me, he's dead.*

I took stock of all the upcoming events I'd booked. Florence and Mike canceled and another author – an amazing romance writer named Bethany Jadin – had called in the afternoon to cancel as well. Unlike Ashley's murder, where villagers crowded into the shop to snoop around the crime scene, Nevermore had remained deserted for the rest of the day. *I guess there is such a thing as* too much *murder in a small English village.*

Morrie pouted when I left the shop – he was heading to London the next day on business and wanted to spend some time alone before he left. But I really needed to be on my own to think. Above my bed, I'd pinned a picture of some guide dog puppies. Their dark eyes peered down at me, begging me to take them in and give them snuggles and let them help me.

Nevermore really will be a menagerie when we add a puppy to the mix... but will it even happen now?

All my plans and ideas for the shop seemed further away than ever.

That night, I slept fitfully, haunted by dreams of living in a cardboard box on the town green while Grey Lachlan turned the bookshop into a casino. "Good!" cried Mrs. Ellis, waving handfuls of money at him. "I like gambling much more than I care for dusty old books!"

In the morning, I hit snooze three times before dragging myself out of bed. It definitely wasn't as much fun waking up without one – or all – of the guys beside me. I pulled on my fluffy dressing gown and headed to the kitchen.

"Coffee," I muttered to myself as I flicked on the lights. I staggered back in terror as my eyes beheld a wretched scene.

No.

An arc of blood splatter started at the coffee machine and curved across the ceiling before dripping down the cabinets to pool on the floor. Something lumpy stuck out of the top of the grinder. It looked like a piece of meat, complete with a knob of bloody bone.

Someone had been dismembered in my kitchen.

CHAPTER ELEVEN

o. No no no no no.

"Jo!" I yelled, my heart in my throat. "JO!"

Where's Jo? Please let her be okay...

My head spun. I whirled around and emptied my stomach across the floor. As I knelt in the filth, my chest heaving, I noticed a large note pinned to the fridge with a skull magnet. It was in Jo's handwriting.

I grabbed the note and held it close to my face to read her scraggly words.

Mina. You weren't awake and I needed to get to the office. I'm sorry to leave the kitchen a mess and the coffee machine out of order. I'm conducting an experiment for one of my other cases about how you might dispose of body parts in the grinder. Don't worry – it's not human blood. It's a pig leg. I won't bore you with the details, but I promise I'll clean everything up and get the machine fixed asap! There's a fiver on the fridge door to cover your morning coffee. XX. Jo.

I lifted another skull magnet on the fridge door and grabbed the money. *Bloody hell, Jo. For the heart attack you just gave me, you should at least leave enough that I can afford a croissant. And about ten years of therapy sessions to get the image of violent death by coffee grinder out of my head.*

~

y day didn't improve. Not a single soul passed through the doors of Nevermore Bookshop, and another author – the fantastic Marie Robinson – called to cancel her appearance. "I just don't think I'll feel safe at your shop," she said. "I'm sorry."

Sorry, my arse. Not even the guys could take the edge off that sting. Although they tried. Quoth brought me a berry cake from the bakery next door that would have been delicious if food had any taste to me right now. Heathcliff added 'Don't murder the authors' to his growing list of shop rules. Before he left for London, Morrie found a company online that printed photographs onto household objects. He ordered me a lamp emblazoned with Heathcliff's scowling face. "You can put it on his desk," he grinned.

No matter how hard they tried to cheer me up, my mind kept returning to those adorable puppies, and to the electronic book tagging system I desperately needed. Every time I had to hold a book up to the light in order to squint at the title or ask for Morrie's help because I couldn't see into a dark corner, my stomach tightened.

"I bet you're loving this," I glowered at Heathcliff, who sat in the window, the picture of gentility with a book open in his lap and a cup of tea on the table beside him. His usual stormy expression had been replaced by something that almost resembled calm and tranquility.

Heathcliff turned the page in his book. Without looking up, he said. "You've got to admit, it's peaceful."

"It's not peaceful, it's *boring*. Not to mention it's not helping us pay the mortgage." I tapped the ledger I'd been poring over for the last hour. "The accounts are in worse shape than I thought. We're behind on all the bills and barely breaking even as it is. If we don't make some sales soon, things are going to be desperate. Forget about ordering that electronic tagging system, we might have to call Grey Lachlan about his offer—"

"Never," Heathcliff growled, throwing his book down. His dark eyes bore into mine with that intensity that made my spine tingle. "Lachlan's not getting his hands on this shop, and you're getting that tagging wossit."

"How? You got some grand plan to instantly make the village not terrified of this bookshop?"

"I do. We're going to solve this murder."

"Wait a second. What happened to Mr. Let-The-Police-Do-Their-Jobs-Heathcliff who was dead against Morrie and I meddling in Professor Hathaway's death?"

"What happened is that his girl's upset, and he wants to make it better." Heathcliff stood up and stalked across the room. He leaned over my chair, a taut, muscled arm on either side of me. Danger flashed in his eyes. "Admit it, you get a kick out of figuring out a murder. You and Morrie are exactly alike, god help us all. And I have no faith in our local constabulary to get this one solved before the bank forecloses. Besides, last time we had a murder in here, this place was gossip central and we had our best month ever. A little bit of murder is good for business, as long as people don't feel as though they're personally in danger. If you solve this murder, you'll be in good with the village again."

"I guess…" I threw up my hands. "But Morrie left for London. He's not back until tomorrow."

"I can help. I know stuff," Heathcliff growled. "What do we do first?"

"Meeorw." Grimalkin leapt onto the desk and tapped my arm with her paw.

"Not now, kitty." I grabbed her around the waist and dropped her on the floor. Heathcliff handed me one of the blank floral notebooks we had on display on the counter. I cracked the spine and wrote 'Danny Sledge Murder' at the top of the page.

"Um... well, usually Morrie and I start by going over everything we know about the crime and the victim. We know Danny was garroted, which is a pretty brutal way to kill someone. It's also the main mode of death for the serial killer in his latest book, and the way an ex-girlfriend of his was killed fifteen years ago. So we can assume the murderer chose garroting to make a point. The first thing we need to do is make a list of his enemies and what we know about them, whether they had motive, opportunity, alibis, that kind of thing."

"Start with that old bint, Beverly," Heathcliff said.

I added her name. "She's the most obvious suspect, which is why I don't think she did it. Danny was a young, fit bloke. I can't see how she'd have had the strength to garrote him, even if she was fueled by adrenaline."

"She's still worth considering." Heathcliff jabbed me. "Who else?"

"His wife, Penny. From what she said to me at the reading, she knew Danny was fooling around on her. Plus, she was obsessed with money and status. Maybe she decided Danny would be worth more to her dead than alive. I'm guessing she is the main beneficiary of his will. But again, did she have the strength or viciousness to garrote him?"

"Add the mistress, too," Heathcliff said. "Maybe she begged Danny to leave his wife for her. He refused. She killed him out of spite."

"Ooh, now you're talking." I jotted down Amanda's name. "And her husband, Brian Letterman. He can't have been happy if he found out his wife was in bed with his top author, especially not when Danny's self-publishing his memoir. And Brian has some decent upper-body strength. So would Angus, the ex-cop. And he's connected to Danny's past. Maybe he found out Danny really did kill Abigail—"

"Meorrw!" Grimalkin leapt up on the desk again, plonking her arse down on the notebook and curling her tail across my suspect list. Heathcliff grumbled and wrapped his arms around her, pulling her against his shoulder. Usually, she nestled into his hair and perched there happily for hours. But today she jumped down immediately to stalk across the desk, howling at the top of her lungs.

Heathcliff plonked her on the floor again. "Anyone else?"

"Those are the ones we know about. I guess we need to figure out if he has any grudges with other authors, or if he's pissed off any stalker fans lately." I eyed Heathcliff's desk warily. "But for that, I'm going to need to use the computer—"

"Forget it." Heathcliff threw up his hands. "I'm not spending a moment of free time on that blasted device—"

"MEEEEOOOORRRWW!"

Grimalkin's shrill cry pierced my ears. She stood in the center of the rug, her back arched, her fur poofed up to twice her size. She shot us both an evil glare, then turned on her heel and trotted toward the hallway.

"I think she wants us to follow her." I stood up.

"So we can admire an eviscerated rodent? Pass." Heathcliff picked up his book.

Grimalkin waited in the doorway, her gaze accusing. As soon as she saw me heading toward her, she trotted away, heading down the entrance hallway to a stack of books by the door. She pawed at something sticking out of the corner of the shelf, sandwiched between two volumes of *The History of the Decline and Fall of the Roman Empire*.

"What have you got there, Grimalkin?" I bent down and pulled out the piece of fabric, holding it up to the light streaming through the stained glass panels either side of the front door. It was a silk scarf, decorated with a pattern of bright leopard spots. Something about it looked familiar.

The scarf had been wound tight around itself. It unfurled as I shook it out. I turned it over in my hands and gasped.

Several small, round stains were dotted across the hem of the scarf.

Drops of blood.

My heart pounded in my chest. I knew where I'd seen it before. It was the night of Danny's book reading, and the scarf had been around Beverly Ingram's neck.

CHAPTER TWELVE

$\mathcal{O}$nly minutes after I spoke to her on the phone, Jo arrived at Nevermore, her clothes soaked in sweat and her breath coming out in sharp gasps.

"I left the autopsy in-progress, but I wasn't about to trust such an important piece of evidence to one of the guys," she huffed as she pulled on her gloves. "Not when they missed it the last time they searched the shop. Let me see it."

So you'll leave an autopsy to come to collect a scarf, but not to clean up the murder scene in our kitchen? I thought but didn't say. I showed Jo where I'd laid out the scarf on the table. Grimalkin scratched at the Events room door, howling about the injustice of being locked away while I claimed her moment of glory for myself. "Sorry, kitty," I called out. "You'll contaminate the evidence."

"Meeeerrrww!" Grimalkin wailed.

Jo smiled. "I hope you gave her a saucer of cream for her troubles. She was the one who found it."

"Meeeerrrww!" Grimalkin concurred, throwing herself at the door.

"I think we can agree that we don't need to encourage any

more amateur sleuths about the place. Besides, cats aren't supposed to have cream. She did get lots of ear scratches, though. Grimalkin was tugging at this corner," I showed Jo where there were a few small teeth marks in the fabric. "I touched the scarf in these top corners when I picked it up. The rest of it, where the blood is, shouldn't have our fingerprints on it."

"Thanks." Jo placed the scarf into a paper bag. (As I'd learned, plastic Ziploc bags looked good on TV, but they were only used for dry items. Anything that contained blood stains, semen, or potential DNA evidence went into paper bags or cardboard containers, as sealing in plastic could degrade the evidence. And yes, I did spend far too much time grilling Jo for crime scene info over wine.) "Now, show me where you found it."

I showed Jo the space on the shelf by the door, between the two books. She photographed the area, then used a magnifying glass and swabs to search for further trace evidence. "This makes sense. We found a couple of blood stains on the carpet here." Jo pointed to a spot on the wooden floor in front of the shelf. "It looks like our killer garroted Danny, then shoved the scarf in here. You said it was Beverly Ingram's scarf?"

"She was wearing it at the reading. If you ask others, they might remember it as well. It's quite distinctive, especially since it clashed with her gingham coat."

"If by 'distinctive,' you mean 'garish beyond belief.'" Jo smiled as she dropped the bag into her crime scene kit. "Did Beverly touch anything in the shop that you remember? I'd like to be able to get some samples to compare DNA."

"I don't think so... wait, yes." I beckoned Jo to follow me into the Events room. Although we'd cleaned the space and arranged the chairs in a circle for the writing workshop that would never be, some of the displays from the reading were still up. I pointed to Quoth's picture on the wall beside the window. "She was leaning against this when she screamed. I think her hair got caught around the corner of the frame."

"That's one of Allan's, isn't it?" Jo peered at the painting. "I recognize his work anywhere. I hope he won't mind if we take this as evidence. I'll make sure we don't damage the image."

I glanced up at the rafters. Only the faintest glint of light revealed Quoth's presence in the gloom. "Croak," he agreed.

I smiled. "He's not here right now, but if it helps catch a killer, I'm sure he'd be happy to help."

"Thanks." Carefully, Jo removed a couple of hair with tweezers, then took down the painting and slipped it into another, larger paper bag.

"Anytime. Listen, Jo, about the kitchen—"

"Yes. Sorry, sorry." Jo picked up her crime scene kit. "I promise I'll clean it all up just as soon as I get home. I'll probably be late tonight, what with all the evidence to process."

"But—"

Jo hurried out the door. "I really am sorry, Mina, but I've got to dash. I have a garroting victim with my name on it!"

I let Grimalkin out of the room. She shot me a filthy look before shooting upstairs, no doubt to eviscerate a mouse in revenge. Heathcliff went back to his book while I read biographies of Danny Sledge online. There were lots of wild stories about his gang days. He'd started writing his first novel in jail, after reading some crime fiction in the prison library and realizing how inaccurate it was. His first book went on to become a New York Times bestseller. Danny negotiated a reduced prison sentence for ratting out his partner in a drug ring, and as soon as he was out, he left crime behind him for good. It looked like he'd been living the high life ever since – Penny's Instagram account was filled with images of the pair of them wearing designer clothes and jetting off to exotic locations. His life had certainly been interesting, but I couldn't see any evidence of crazed stalker fans or criminals returning from his past for revenge—

Wait a second.

I pulled up an image of Danny on the stand at a trial of his partner-in-crime – Jim Mathis, the one Danny ratted out. Young Danny looked smart in his three-piece suit, his hair slicked back, his face as handsome and affable as I remembered from the other night. Behind him, I could make out the face of the accused, glaring at his former partner with dead, soulless eyes.

I'd seen those eyes before.

Jim Mathis was the purple-haired erotica writer. Danny's ex-partner was out of jail and primed for revenge.

CHAPTER THIRTEEN

I emailed the article and image over to Jo, and explained that I'd seen Jim at both the reading and the writers' workshop. It was one thing to stumble upon the answer to a murder, but it was quite another to be involved with mean-looking criminal thugs. If Jim Mathis *was* responsible for Danny's murder, I wanted the police to be the ones going after him.

Unfortunately, that left me without anything to do. I'd packaged up all the online orders, stacked some new books on the shelves, made three pots of tea, *and* turned the paperclips in Heathcliff's desk drawer into a funky necklace. Even Quoth grew bored with the silent shop and went upstairs to paint. Heathcliff didn't move from his spot under the window, but he did finish his book and start another. Not a single customer entered the shop.

Nerves raced along my spine. Another day without a single sale. If this went on for much longer, we wouldn't have any way of paying the mortgage. My fingers drummed against the desk. I couldn't face the silence of the front room any longer. I shoved back my chair. "I'm going upstairs."

"To do what?" Heathcliff asked without looking up.

"To inventory dust mites!" I shot back as I took the stairs two at a time. On the first floor, I paced the length of the Sociology shelves, but that made me think about Ashley's murder.

Murder follows me everywhere.

I solve more crimes than the police, and yet I can't even keep Nevermore Bookshop in the black, or figure out the mystery of my own father.

Wait... when was the last time I'd actually tried to find more clues about my father? Now that I knew he was Herman *and* Mr. Simson, I should take another look at the books they both spent so much energy collecting.

When I first started working for Heathcliff, I'd stumbled upon the shop's hidden Occult collection. Stored in a pentagonal room on this floor, it housed books Mr. Simson had acquired while trying to figure out the mysteries of the bookshop. At least one of them was written by Herman Strepel. Heathcliff always kept the room locked for the safety of everyone in the shop, but now I had his ring of keys in my pocket. I thrust my hand inside, feeling for the small key that would fit perfectly into the lock of the storage room. The metal seemed to hum between my fingers.

Yes, something to take my mind off Danny's murder and all our money woes.

Now that we'd figured out Mr. Simson was my father, certain items in the occult books might make more sense. It was definitely worth a shot.

Before I could change my mind, I inserted the key into the door to the storage room and shoved it open. Grimalkin darted out from beneath a shelf and streaked inside. A cat couldn't stay away from an unlocked door. It was a law of nature.

I followed Grimalkin into the dusty storage room and flicked on the light switch. Heathcliff had stacked several boxes of books in front of the Occult room door. I shoved them aside. As I fumbled through my keyring, looking for the correct key to fit the lock, the door creaked open.

My heart thudded in my chest. *That's right. It did that before, too.* I hovered in the threshold, unsure if I should proceed.

Grimalkin made the decision for me. With a squeak of delight, she trotted into the room and jumped up on the pedestal in the center. I fumbled along the wall for a light switch and flicked it on. The windowless room looked exactly as I remembered it – every wall lined with bookshelves crammed with old leather-bound volumes. Grimalkin purred as she rolled around on top of the open book on the pedestal – the one where every page was mysteriously blank.

I pushed her gently aside and closed the book. My fingers traced the symbol on the cover of the volume – the same symbol I'd seen in other books from Herman Strepel. Now I knew it to be a symbol for my father.

But if this blank book belongs to my father, why did he leave it here?

I flicked absent-mindedly through the pages. Beside me, Grimalkin purred. I cried out in surprise as I glimpsed some words scribbled on a page.

Did I imagine it?

I must have imagined it.

Mustn't I?

This book had been completely empty last time I'd looked at it, of that I was certain. I flipped back several pages, and there it was – the ink on the page faded and smudged in places, as if it had always been there. The writing was made of symbols – Cyrillic, maybe. Or Greek?

Grimalkin wound her way around my arm, purring like a buzz saw. I patted her on the head as I stared at the page. *What does this mean? Why are these words here?*

Morrie will be able to translate this when he gets home. I dug my phone from my pocket and snapped a couple of pictures, texting them to him. I waited a few moments, but he didn't reply. He must really have been busy in a business meeting.

"Mina!" Heathcliff bellowed from downstairs.

I perked up. There could be only one reason Heathcliff was yelling for me. Customers. Finally, we could make a sale, provided Heathcliff hadn't already scared them off.

I slammed the book shut and carried Grimalkin out into the Occult room, locking the door behind me. I took the stairs two at a time and practically vaulted over the balustrade in my eagerness to reach the main room. When I stepped inside, panting to catch my breath, I found the place empty, save Heathcliff and a stuffed armadillo and a thick layer of dust.

"Where are the customers?" I glanced around.

"There are no customers." Heathcliff swung his coat off the back of the chair. "I thought I might take you to lunch."

"You did?" Heathcliff hated going outside, and we'd already been outside once this week.

"It might do you good to get out of the shop." Heathcliff held out his arm. "But don't be getting any fancy ideas. I'm not Morrie. We're going to the pub. There's a two-for-one roast beef special."

"Sounds perfect." I accepted his arm like he was a grand gentleman. Heathcliff called up the stairs for Quoth to mind the shop, not even waiting for an answer. We hiked across the green toward the pub. To my delight, Mrs. Ellis was at the bar when we walked in, dressed in a ridiculous sundress and trying to convince Richard the landlord to make her some exotic cocktail.

"I thought you were leaving on your trip today?" I asked her.

"I've got an hour before the taxi picks me up to take me to the airport." Mrs. Ellis patted the enormous suitcase beside her. "I thought I'd get myself in the holiday mood. Strawberry mojito?"

"Please." Richard shot me a pained expression as he blew the dust off a laminated poster that displayed various cocktail recipes. The Rose & Wimple was definitely not a cocktail bar.

Heathcliff looked at the pink drink like the little decorative umbrella was a weapon of mass destruction. "Scotch for me," he growled.

Once we all had something alcoholic in our hands, Mrs. Ellis bustled us to a table in the corner. So much for a quiet lunch with Heathcliff. Several members of her knitting group were crowded around, all enjoying mojitos. At the table next to them, Cynthia and Grey Lachlan tucked into a ploughman's lunch. I stiffened at their presence, hoping they wouldn't notice me or Heathcliff.

As soon as Mrs. Ellis' friends recognized us, Ethel leaned forward, desperate for more gossip. "Mina, Heathcliff, how are you holding up? You poor dears. Have the police got any suspects for Danny's murder yet?"

"I don't know," I said. "They haven't been keeping me in the loop."

"Why ever not? You solved dear Mrs. Scarlett's murder! And that poor Greer girl."

"*And* she figured out who stabbed Professor Hathaway at my Jane Austen event," Cynthia piped up, gesticulating with such fervor that she sloshed wine over the table. "If anything, they should be coming to you for advice!"

"Careful, dear." Grey set her wine glass back down on the table. "Yes, Mina, we've all heard about your sleuthing powers. It's unfortunate that you seem cursed to stumble over murders at every turn. Your shop seems empty today. Is the murder of a famous local writer bad for business?"

"Things are quiet, but we're not worried." I glared at Grey. He didn't get to make comments like that, not after he'd wheedled and threatened Heathcliff to try and buy the store from us. "I'm sure the police will solve the crime soon, and we'll be back on our feet."

"Oh, that's too bad," Mrs. Ellis tittered. "If only you'd said something sooner, you could have closed for a couple of weeks and come on holiday with me!"

"I don't think I could keep up with you, Mrs. Ellis." I smiled, noting the long line of empty mojito glasses on the table in front of her. Over Heathcliff's shoulder, I noticed Beverly Ingram walk in and slouch into the bar, her head down, hands in her pockets. Today she wore a ghastly mustard-orange jacket over florescent green trousers and a brown paisley scarf. *Does she dress blindfolded or something?*

Mrs. Ellis followed my gaze. Her face softened when she saw Beverly. "Poor thing. She's not coping well. It was the anniversary of her daughter's death last week, which explains why Dotty saw her break down in the supermarket. What unfortunate timing for your event with Danny! And now he's been murdered in the same gruesome way. If anyone could do with cheering up, it's her. Beverly, over here!"

Before I or anyone else could protest, Mrs. Ellis was on her feet, waving at Beverly to join us. The woman scowled, pulling her coat tighter around her face. But Mrs. Ellis was a force to be reckoned with. She grabbed the woman and practically threw her into the chair opposite me. "Richard, another round of strawberry mojitos for us all!"

"Hi, Beverly," I smiled at her. "We didn't get to meet the other night. I'm Mina. I work at the bookshop. I'm so sorry to hear about your daughter. If I'd known it was the anniversary of her death, I would've postponed the event—"

"Don't worry about it." Beverly's cheeks reddened. "I made an awful fuss and embarrassed myself. It wasn't *your* fault. I didn't mean to ruin your event. I just..."

"I understand. You don't have to apologize—"

"I'm not sorry he's dead," she growled, her soft voice suddenly replaced with fierce venom. "The way he wrote that book, it was *exactly* the details of Abigail's murder. Who does that? It's disgusting. And it makes me wonder. The police said Danny couldn't possibly have been there that night, but maybe he had them all fooled."

Mrs. Ellis leaned forward and tapped me on the shoulder. "You know, Mina here has solved all kinds of murders. She's much cleverer than the police. I bet she could figure out who killed poor Abigail."

Beverly's cheeks reddened. "No, I don't think that's necessary—"

But Mrs. Ellis wasn't listening. She'd launched into a long story about how I'd solved the mysterious death of her friend Gladys Scarlett. Cynthia interrupted to gush about how I'd caught Christina Hathaway at her Jane Austen weekend, and soon everyone at the table was telling stories about the recent murders in Argleton. Heathcliff chuckled into his beer as I slunk further into my seat. *How can I get them to stop? What I need is a distraction—*

THUD.

That'll do it.

The pub door swung open, slamming into the wall behind and blowing in a gust of wind and a whiff of impatience as Inspector Hayes and DS Wilson stalked across the room. They marched straight up to my table and flanked Beverly.

"Beverly Ingram, if you could step outside, please."

"Why?" Beverly demanded in that haughty tone of hers.

"We need to speak with you."

"Whatever you have to say, you can say right here." Beverly sipped her strawberry mojito and stared defiantly at Hayes. "I've got no secrets."

"Please step outside." Hayes' face looked pained. "I don't want to have to do this in front of everyone."

Beverly folded her arms across her chest. "I ain't going anywhere."

Hayes sighed, then nodded to Wilson. She held up a pair of handcuffs. "Have it your way. Beverly Ingram, you're under arrest for the murder of Danny Sledge."

CHAPTER FOURTEEN

"*I* just want to see how she's doing," I insisted. "She doesn't have any other family."

The police officer didn't look convinced. I could tell from the way his eyes narrowed that he remembered me from the time I escaped from the cells. Hayes hadn't got me in further trouble because I solved Ashley's murder, but I did totally break out of jail on this guy's shift and that was probably the kind of thing an officer of the law held against you.

"Hey, mate," Heathcliff pointed to the calendar on the wall behind him. "Is that the latest Bentley Mulsanne?"

"It is!" The officer's face lit up. He waved me through, suddenly engrossed in a gearhead conversation with Heathcliff. I fled down the stairs to the cells before he could change his mind.

Past a cell holding a snoring drunk, I found Beverly. She sat on the edge of the narrow bed, her eyes fixed on a spot on the ceiling. I cleared my throat. She didn't turn around.

"What do you want?" she demanded, still focused on the ceiling.

"My name is Mina. We met at the pub the other day."

"I remember. I'm not stupid. What do you want?"

105

"I don't believe you killed Danny Sledge," I said.

"Why not? Everyone else does."

"Because it doesn't make sense to me. You were angry at him, so you came to his reading and yelled. Why do that if you were going to kill him? And why do it with your own scarf? It would only throw suspicion on you, and I don't think you're that stupid."

"So what?" Beverly snapped.

"I think someone is trying to divert attention to you. Which means that the real killer is still out there. I want to stop him before he kills anyone else. And I want you to help me."

"Even if I believed Mabel and the other ladies that you have some talent for solving murders, I can't bloody do anything from in here."

"No, but you can tell me about your movements after the event and on the morning Danny was killed, and about your daughter's death, and I'll try and piece together what happened." The woman's shoulders stiffened. "I'm sorry. I know it must be painful to think about Abigail, but… I think maybe your daughter's murderer is the same person who killed Danny. If we could stop another innocent person getting killed—"

"Danny wasn't innocent." Beverley turned toward me. In the dark, I couldn't make out her face, but there was a strength in her voice that hadn't been there before. "I know I didn't kill him, though. Fat chance of trying to explain it to them coppers. Why do you care? Why are you trying to help me?"

"Because I don't like seeing people go to jail for something they didn't do." I sucked in a breath. Beverly struck me as the kind of woman who needed the whole truth. I bet she'd sense insincerity a mile off. "And… because I've worked really hard to improve things at the bookshop. After this murder, no one will set foot inside. We're going bankrupt. If I can figure out who really did it, then customers will start coming back."

"So your interest in me is purely mercantile?" she scowled.

"No, not purely. I really do care about getting justice for Abigail. But I'm not going to lie to you. If we're going to work together, we've got to have complete honesty."

"And what sort of fee do you charge for your services?"

"No fee. Maybe if I prove to the police you didn't murder Danny, you could come into the shop and buy a book?"

Beverly sighed. "Fine. What do I do?"

I pulled over a metal chair and sat down facing her cell. "First things first, tell me everything you know about your daughter's murder."

CHAPTER FIFTEEN

*B*everly took a shaking breath. "Abigail and I had a fight that afternoon. I was on night shift all week so I was sleeping during the day. I heard the front door open about one p.m. I went up to see who it was, because of course Abigail was supposed to be at school, wasn't she? Only she was in her room, skipping school, pulling on a slutty outfit and tucking a pack of my ciggies into her bra. I had it out with her, told her she needed to stay in school, that she shouldn't be hanging around with those boys all the time, that they were bad news. She told me I couldn't do nothing about it. I threatened to kick her out of the house. She stormed out, slammed the door. Typical teenage behavior, but I did worry about her. I knew she was out there getting drunk, getting high, letting those boys touch her…"

After another ragged breath, Beverly continued. "I went to work, arrived home around two a.m. The light in her bedroom was on. I went in, thought I could apologize for yelling, maybe see if she wanted some ice cream. Instead, I found her…" Beverly's jaw clenched. "She was on the bed, half naked, shirt open across her chest. She had this pretty silk scarf I got her for her sixteenth birthday wrapped around her throat."

My heart went out to her. Even after fifteen years, I could hear the pain in her voice. "What did you do after you saw her?"

"I called the police. I thought they took ages to get to the house, but that might've been because I was holding my daughter's dead body in my arms. They said she hadn't been sexually assaulted, but that she had had sex recently, within an hour of her death. That's what made them think it was a boyfriend, and the fact that there was no break-in, so it must've been someone she trusted. They got DNA from the semen, but it was corrupted in the lab and so they couldn't use it.

"I told the police about Danny and Jim, and they tracked them down right away. Only it turns out, they were already in a police cell. So they couldn't have been at our house the time Abigail was killed, so the police say. They started pursuing another lead – another girl was garroted a couple of years earlier in a nearby village. Inspector Donahue thought the two crimes were linked. Only they didn't get anywhere with that, so they dropped the case."

"Did you know about all of Abigail's boyfriends? Did she have others?"

"If she did, she never brought them home." Beverly's shoulders shook. "They weren't those kind of boys. I saw Danny pick her up a couple of times, and another guy, Jim. That's the only reason I knew about them. Abigail kept a diary – it didn't say much, just scribbles about how much of a cow I was and a list of nicknames, maybe they were lovers. Danny was 'Stallion' and Jim was 'Crow,' but the police never tracked down the rest of the names."

"What happened after that?"

"They couldn't find any other suspects. The killer had been careful – no fingerprints at the scene, no footprints in the mud outside. Every lead they followed came to a dead end, and the media was hanging around every day, hounding them for a result. They camped out in front of my house, making me out as this uncaring, incompetent mother because I couldn't control her! Finally, Inspector Donahue called it. He said he'd never stop trying to find Abigail's killer, but I knew they'd given up."

"Why did you come to Danny's reading?"

"Because I was sick of seeing that smarmy git in the papers, getting rich off all the wrong he's done." She hugged herself. "I heard he was releasing a new book where the victims are strangled, just like Abigail. And in the same month as the anniversary of her death! That's just cruel for cruel's sake. I'd been complaining to his publisher, trying to drum up support online, writing letters to the papers, trying to get someone to pay attention to my story. To Abigail's story. But no one cares because Danny is this hotshot bestseller. So I decided I would go along and give him a piece of my mind."

"Fair enough. Do you have any idea how your scarf ended up in the hands of the murderer?"

"I threw it at that plonker publisher, Brian," she muttered. "He was yelling at me and going on about how it was just business and there were more important things than the death of a made-up character. He said Danny would always do whatever Danny wanted and I couldn't change his mind and neither could he."

I remembered seeing her toss something at Brian. *Did he pick up the scarf?* I didn't see. If he didn't, anyone could have picked it up off the ground outside the shop.

"Thank you so much. It can't have been easy to talk about this—"

"Find the bastard," Beverly's eyes flashed. "If the same person killed Danny that killed my girl, find him and make him pay."

CHAPTER SIXTEEN

J spent the evening at my flat mulling over everything Beverly said. Her pain was evident in every word she'd spoken. I felt absolutely certain that she hadn't killed Danny. If she'd killed Danny, she would have owned it, as the justice her daughter never had.

The next morning I pushed open the door of the bookshop. My back stiffened as I recognized a familiar voice echoing through the empty rooms.

"I've been made aware of your financial situation, Mr. Earnshaw. You can't afford to keep this place open even another month. Your friend may have deep pockets, but much of his funds are frozen in a Cayman bank account."

What? How does Grey Lachlan know about the state of our finances? And what is he saying about Morrie's money?

I peered around the hallway into the main room. Heathcliff stood behind his desk, his fists clenched at his sides. Grey luxuriated in my favorite velvet chair, his shiny wing-tipped shoes crossed on the top of the desk like he already owned the place.

"If you know so much about our finances, perhaps you'd like to enlighten me why a property developer is interested in a rickety house filled with dusty books." Heathcliff was just barely holding back his wild rage.

"My dear Mr. Heathcliff, I'm not here to tell you how to run your business. I'm here to *rescue* you. I'll cut you a cheque for this dump right now, and you could be free. I mean, look at it. There's not a customer in sight!"

"It's our slow period," Heathcliff growled.

"Really? It seems that every day is your slow period lately." Grey planted his feet on the floor and leaned forward. "Listen, between you and me, businessman to businessman, I think your new manager might be the root of your problem. Wherever she goes, murder seems to follow her. Not to mention the fact that she doesn't know the first thing about business. Women always think they can run things like a man, but they just lack that ruthless streak—"

That's enough of that. I stepped into the room, my back straight, my hands on my hips. "Get out."

Behind the desk, Heathcliff smirked. Grey whirled around, his eyebrows rising. "Ms. Wilde, what a pleasure to see you again. My wife would love to see you for dinner at Baddesley Hall—"

"I'll stop you there before you drag Cynthia into this." I folded my arms. "We're not interested. Please leave. Before my feeble female brain explodes and I do something stupid, like call the police or shove a copy of *The Handmaid's Tale* up your arse."

Grey's smile remained plastered on his face, but a flicker of anger flashed in his eyes. He expected us to roll over and thank him for his generosity. *That's not happening.*

"Yes, of course." Grey dropped his card onto Heathcliff's desk. "I'll leave you to think about it. You know where to find me."

"Die in a fire!" Heathcliff yelled at his back. He slumped down behind his desk and picked up Grey's card, crushing it between his fingers and tossing it into the rubbish bin.

"Why did you let him in here?" I demanded. My fingers touched the edge of my father's note.

"He doesn't exactly take no for an answer." Heathcliff rubbed at the scuff marks Grey's shoes had left on the desk. "I was just about to eviscerate him and string his intestines onto the world's tiniest violin when you showed up. Your method was much less messy."

"The world's tiniest violin? Where did you come up with that?"

Heathcliff held up the cover of the book he was reading. *The Somerset Strangler*, of course. "Morrie was right. This is quite good. Those gangsters really have a way with language."

I rubbed my forehead, where a headache was starting to bloom. I got them often now, as my eyesight deteriorated and my eyes strained to focus. This one, I was sure, was more stress-induced. "So how did Grey Lachlan know about our financial situation?"

Heathcliff made a pointed glance around the room. I followed him, taking in the dusty shelves and lack of customers. "A lucky guess?"

"Either that, or he's hacking into our accounts. And what did he mean about Morrie's money being tied up?"

Heathcliff shrugged. "Dunno. He's right about one thing – Morrie hasn't offered up any funds to bail us out. You know how he loves to throw his dirty money at every problem. Well, he hasn't so much as proposed a high-interest loan. I assumed he was just being a greedy prick, but maybe our real estate friend knows more than we do."

Hmmmm. Is that why Morrie's gone down to London? Has something gone wrong with one of his criminal enterprises? I knew very little about the criminal network Morrie claimed to still operate. That was deliberate – I didn't feel good about dating a criminal, and I was hoping one day I could convince Morrie to go straight. I appreciated that he was still respecting my request not to be involved, but I wish he'd told me if he was in trouble.

I picked up a bottle of air freshener I'd left on the corner of the desk and spritzed the chair before collapsing into it. "That horrid man better not ever sit in my chair again, or he'll learn just how ruthless a woman can be."

"I'd like to see that." Heathcliff pulled a bottle of wine from the bottom of his desk and set out two glasses.

"You've been holding out on me," I grinned, accepting a glass.

"You should know by now this desk is a treasure trove of culinary delights." Heathcliff slammed a drawer and held up a crumpled packet. "Jaffa cake? They're only a couple of weeks expired."

"No, thanks." At least wine got better with age. As I sipped my drink, I told Heathcliff about my visit to the station and the horrible story of Beverly's daughter's murder. "Knowing everything that happened, I just can't see her going into that meeting, yelling at Danny, then coming back first thing in the morning and garroting him with that scarf. It would help if we knew for a fact whether Brian picked up her scarf or not."

"Maybe she's just stupid?" Heathcliff leaned over the desk. "Many people are. Or maybe she didn't care if she got caught?"

"I don't think that's it." I flicked through my phone images, scrolling through snapshots from the event. Maybe someone got a shot of Beverly leaving... I squinted at one of the images of Jim, asking his question. I noticed he had the collar of his shirt pulled up over his face. With Jim's purple hair and Morrie's spotlights shining on the lectern, it was definitely possible Danny had never recognized Jim in the crowd. It couldn't be a coincidence that Danny's ex-gang mate come along to the reading. But if Jim killed Danny, why would he show up for the workshop the next day? Did he want to gloat over the murder?

"What's that?" Heathcliff jabbed his finger at my phone screen as I scrolled through images.

"Oh." I blushed. "Um... well, I was going to tell you at lunch, but I guess we got distracted. Remember this morning when I was chasing Grimalkin? We happened to end up in the Occult room..."

Heathcliff's eyebrow shot up. "The Occult room with the locked door."

"Yes, that room. Well, the door just unlocked itself again. And Grimalkin jumped up on the pedestal and was walking around on that book. I happened to flick through the pages—"

"Of course you did." The corner of Heathcliff's mouth twitched. Whether it was from anger or amusement, I couldn't yet discern.

"—and one of the pages had that writing on it. I thought I'd get Morrie to translate it. I texted him, but he hasn't replied. He must have been busy in London because he hasn't texted me since he left."

"Don't you have an app for translations?" Heathcliff glared at my phone.

"Of course not... no wait, I do!" I scrolled through my phone until I found the app I'd downloaded. It was supposed to be able to translate any language, old or new, based on an image.

"Meow?" Grimalkin leaped down from the shelf and landed on the back of my chair, her neck craning over my shoulder as if she was straining to see the screen.

The app dinged. It had sourced a translation. The writing was Greek – Ancient Greek. That didn't surprise me at all. The translation read, "My name is Nobody." It gave me a phonetic pronunciation, as well. I sighed.

"If it's another clue about the shop, it's just as cryptic as all the others. My name is Nobody – what even is that about? Although, the Greek does sound pretty. *To ónomá mou eínai Kanénas.* I wonder if—"

"Meeeeooorw!"

Grimalkin leapt off my knee and rolled on the rug, kicking her feet in the air. I thought she wanted her belly rubbed, but when I reached down, she howled and swiped at my hand before darting away beneath my chair, howling at the top of her lungs.

"What's got her goat?" Heathcliff muttered.

"Here, kitty, kitty." I tipped my head between my legs, trying to see under the chair.

"Belittle me again, honey, and I'll claw out those pretty eyes of yours," a sultry voice simpered from behind my chair.

I whirled around. Where only a moment ago, a black and white cat had been hiding, a tall and beautiful woman with sleek dark hair now leaned against the velvet. A set of perfectly manicured red nails raked along the fabric while her other hand perched on her lithe, very *naked* hip.

For naked she was, from head to red-painted toes. Her hair fell in sleek waves almost to her waist. She ran her tongue along blood-red lips, her lips turning up into a self-satisfied smirk, like a cat who'd got the cream *and* the furry ball toy.

"It's about time you got me out of that infernal fur coat," the woman said. "It's so wretchedly hot, and you two don't spend nearly enough time adoring me. Do pick your jaws off the floor and let me have a seat – I have *so* much to tell you."

CHAPTER SEVENTEEN

"*W*ho... who are you?" I whispered. How had this woman appeared so suddenly, so silently, and so *nakedly?* She'd snuck into the room with all the stealth of a... of a...

...of a *cat*.

"You wouldn't believe me if I told you," the woman purred, sashaying around the room like she was on stage at a burlesque club. She draped herself over the edge of the table – looking every bit the Renaissance woman posing for a piece of provocative art.

"I believe you need to put some clothes on." Heathcliff shrugged off his jacket and tossed it across the room. He stared at some spot on the Science Fiction bookshelf. "It's bloody freezing in here."

The woman grabbed the coat out of the air and swung it over her elegant shoulders. "Yes, it is. It would appear this human form is more susceptible to drafts. So much pasty skin. My name is Critheïs, but you know me by another name."

"I'm pretty sure I don't know you." I stared at her long legs and perfectly-shaped calves.

"Of course you do, dear. I was wrapped around your ankles only a few minutes ago."

"I think I'd remember that. The only one wrapped around my ankles was..." *No. It can't be. Can it?* "You're Grimalkin?"

In reply, the woman flipped her hair over her shoulder, swiped my wine glass from the desk, and lifted it to her lips.

"Quoth!" Heathcliff boomed. "Get your bird arse in here *right now.*"

A few moments later, wings flapped down the stairs as Quoth soared into the room.

Sorry. I've been trying a new impasto technique. It creates a deep texture that's almost tactile—

He did a double take when he saw the woman. She raised her red talons and gave him a wave that looked more like an extension of claws. "Hello, birdie."

Quoth flopped onto the floor. Feathers flew as his body twisted and contorted. A moment later, Quoth knelt on all fours in his human form, a curtain of dark hair falling over his face, the sinuous muscles of his back tensed, as if he might need to take flight at any moment.

"What... what is she?" he gasped, staring up at the woman in a mixture of awe and dread.

"Mmmmmmm," the woman purred, her eyes sweeping along Quoth's body. "So lithe, so fragile, so delicious. If not for the fact that you are a meal for me, I would have you on this table right now."

"No, you wouldn't," I growled.

"What's going on?" Quoth asked again.

"This she-witch claims she's Grimalkin," Heathcliff glowered. "You know anything about this, bird? Shouldn't you shifter types recognize each other?"

Quoth sniffed the air, frowning. "That's Grimalkin, all right. I'd know that smell and those claws anywhere. But how is she a human?" He turned to Grimalkin. "If you're a shapeshifter, then how come I've never sensed your thoughts or seen you shift before?"

"I'm not like you, able to switch between bodies on a whim," Grimalkin frowned, stretching her arms out above her head. "I've been trapped in the feline form for centuries. My thoughts would no longer be recognizable as human. When my granddaughter spoke my son's words, she lifted the spell, and now I am free."

A flare of bright light streaked across my eyes, followed by a sliver of pain through my skull. My headache was worsening. I rubbed my temple as her words registered. "Excuse me, your granddaughter?"

"Why, yes. I thought it was obvious." Grimalkin struck a pose. "Young lady, I'm your grandmother."

CHAPTER EIGHTEEN

"My grandmother is a cat," I said the words slowly, hoping gravitas would somehow make them more believable. It didn't.

"Skepticism doesn't become you, my dear." Grimalkin sat down on the floor, folding her feet beneath her. She certainly did have cat-like movements, and the way she curled her fingers around into claws and said every word in a sensuous purr... "I'm not really a cat, in the same that way your delicious friend here is not really a bird."

I rubbed my temple. The headache circled my head. This time, it had nothing to do with my declining eyesight. "Fine. None of this makes any sense, but fine. If you're my grandmother, then who is my father?"

"Why ask me, when you've already figured that out?"

I thought back to the conversation I had with Heathcliff just this week, when he'd shown me the ledger, and we'd figured out that my dad was both Herman Strepel and Mr. Simson. Grimalkin had been in the room, so she must've heard us talking. "But we haven't. All I said was—"

I thought for a second there you were going to tell me my dad was a dead epic poet, and then we'd have to get your head examined.

That was it. That was what I said.

Holy shiteballs. Isis be damned.

"My father is Homer," I said, slowly, believing and yet not believing.

Grimalkin nodded.

"*Homer*, the ancient Greek poet. Homer."

She nodded again.

Heathcliff whistled.

"I…" My head pounded. "I need to sit down."

"You're already sitting," my grandmother the former cat pointed out.

"Right." My nails dug into the velvet. "Of course. Um… my father is Homer. How is that possible?"

"Don't play the fool, Mina. It doesn't become you. You know all this already. Your father has been traveling through time – from the ancient world to the modern day via this very book-shop, gathering inspiration for his poems. On one of his jour-neys, he copulated with a young woman who, nine months later, gave birth to you. I assume you don't need the actual details of how his seed came to enter her—"

"No thanks." I covered my ears. "I've got a handle on that. Other things, not so much. Why is my father jaunting through time? If he's still writing his poems, then how is it we're reading them now? Isn't that some kind of paradox?"

"Pffft, *paradox*." With a wave of her hand, Grimalkin dismissed two hundred years of theoretical physics. "My dear, we're talking about *literature*. It works because your father needs it to work. For the *story*. How many men do you think they could really fit into the Trojan Horse? Don't you think the Trojans would have been the least bit suspicious of a giant wooden construction that was clearly hollow? How did those men last all that time cramped up inside the wooden belly of the beast without one of them farting or coughing or breaking down into girlish giggles? It doesn't matter how things *actually* work, as long as they make a good story."

Now my head really *was* pounding. A jolt of violent green light danced across my vision. "But... but... why are you a cat? You said you'd been stuck as a cat for centuries, but you don't look a day over forty."

"Forty?" she glared at me. "Have some respect. I am merely twenty-five years of age."

"How can you be twenty-five, and also my grandmother, and *also* centuries old?"

She arched a perfect eyebrow. "Cat years?"

Panic rapidly spread across my chest. My heart hammered so hard I thought it was going to burst out of my skin. My fingers flew to my pocket to finger the corner of my father's note. Quoth must've sensed my distress because he scrambled to kneel beside my chair and take my hands in his.

"I can't deal with this," I said through gritted teeth as starbursts appeared in my vision. "I need answers, and she's making fun of me."

"I think she's been taking lessons from Morrie." Heathcliff leaned over the desk, steepling his fingers.

Quoth turned his eyes toward Grimalkin. His voice was gentle, but firm. "Please explain to us how all of this came to pass. Start at the beginning, while we ponder."

"Very well." Grimalkin crossed her legs, arching back over the desk and tilting her chin toward the ceiling. She indicated her lithe body. "As I have spoken, my name is Critheïs. I am a water nymph, and my territory was the river Meles, which ran by the great city of Smyrna in Asia Minor. I'm reliably informed by a history book Morrie glanced through one day that this land does not exist any longer, and that my river has long since been diverted, broken, and dried up, thus draining away its tremendous power. Even if I could be reunited with Meles, I would never regain my full powers."

"How did you get separated from the river?" Quoth asked.

"Meles was more than just my land. He was my lover. Of our union was born my son, Homer. From the day I first bathed him in the cool waters of my lover, I knew Homer would be special. I took him to the oracle at Delphi, and he was given a prophecy that one day he would write a story that would echo across millennia. The gods, of course, heard of this prophecy and courted Homer's favor, for they each wished to be presented in the best possible light in his tale."

"This is bollocks—" Heathcliff started, but one glare from Grimalkin had him reeling. As a cat, she had mastered the glare.

"Even though he was only a young boy at the time he started writing, my Homer tried to accommodate all the gods' demands, but their needs were fickle and their loyalties changing. The god Poseidon in particular thought he should be the hero of the story, for the seed of Homer's father flowed eventually into his waters. The gods in-fighting turned violent, as it always did. They visited all manner of plagues and misfortunes upon the land in order to force Homer's hand. I knew that if I didn't act, my beloved son would be torn to pieces by the gods. His story would not be made of words, but of his own blood.

"Homer hid in a cave, but the gods found him. They are ever-watchful – there was nowhere in the world where Homer could hide. And so, to protect Homer from the wrath of the gods, I took him to the edge of Meles and bade him swim in the waters of his birth. As my son waded into the river, I worked a spell, asking Meles to carry him away to safety, to a place where the gods couldn't reach him so he could write in peace. Meles sent him through time, to the age where the gods no longer existed save on the pages in storybooks. Wherever and *whenever* the waters of Meles flowed, my son would be able to use them to escape from his enemies.

"Homer circled through time, writing his poems and mingling with the great writers from every era. He came first to medieval England, led by a spring through which the waters of Meles flowed. The gods know why, but he found the oppressive cold of your drab country stimulating to his muse, and so here he stayed, building a small shop atop the Meles spring where he might craft stories and remain close to the written word even as his sight dwindled. As he finished chapters, he sent them back to me in bottles he floated down the river. I gave them to scribes to copy and spread throughout the ancient world."

"But that's a parad—" I started. Quoth shook his head at me, and I clamped my mouth shut.

Grimalkin gestured to the shop. "Here he stayed in relative bliss, frequently making trips through time in order to collect inspiration from the past and the future until his enemy caught up with him."

"What enemy?" I demanded.

Grimalkin waved her hand as if that particular revelation was of no importance. "We'll get to that. You and your mother have caused no end of trouble."

"What's Mum got to do with this?"

Grimalkin's perfect nose twitched with disdain. "*Helen*. She was his muse. And his downfall."

I got the feeling that Grimalkin – sorry, Critheïs – thought *she* should be his muse.

"My mum has nothing to do with any of this. He was the one who left us. *He* broke her heart—"

I stopped as Quoth's head turned up to me, his eyes wide. "Helen," he whispered.

"Yes. That's her name, But I don't see—"

"'Was this the face that launched a thousand ships / And burnt the topless tower of Ilium,'" Quoth quoted Marlowe in his rich, melodic voice. "Mina, your mother was Helen of Troy."

"No, she wasn't. She just inspired the character." Grimalkin tipped her chin forward. "*I* supplied the beauty portion of his imagining."

Helen of Troy – the woman whose beauty started the Trojan war, the figure depicted countless times in medieval and Renaissance art, the muse Salvador Dali believed his wife Gala physically embodied – was modeled on my *mother?*

"Heathcliff," I whispered. "I need a stiff drink. Now."

"Got you covered." Heathcliff yanked a drawer open, pulled out a bottle of Scotch, and poured me a tall glass. I accepted it and took a large gulp, barely feeling the burn as the alcohol slid down my throat. All the while, Grimalkin was still going on about my mum.

"—Homer first came to this modern age in his youth, full of idealism and erotic stirrings. He stayed longer than he should, scribbling illegal copies of documents from our time while your mother seduced him with promises of a life together."

The counterfeiting. Mum had told me last month that my father made knock-off ancient texts to sell to collectors. Little did any of his buyers know they were actually purchasing from Homer the Bard.

"In his love, my son grew careless, desperate to produce more elaborate works in order to give Helen the riches she desired. Together, they contemplated life as parents, as owners of a vast criminal empire and a great fortune, even as the authorities closed in on him. And in his seed, you were given life, with the waters of Meles inside you. You have your father's powers, Mina, and you also carry his curse."

"I'm so confused." Green streaks of light arced across my vision. "What powers? What curse?"

"I'm getting there!" Grimalkin flicked away my questions with her thin wrist. There was no rushing a cat. "As I was saying, you came into the world, and too late Homer saw that if he did not run, he would be locked away forever for his copying, never to return to complete his poem. The world would have lost Helen of

Troy and he would be behind bars, never again able to find the river Meles. And so he left you for the first time."

I knocked back the rest of the Scotch and thrust the glass into Heathcliff's hand. While he refilled it, I drew the letter from my pocket, holding it in trembling fingers. "That's not what my father said. He said he left us because he was in danger."

"That letter was not written when you were born, Mina, it was written a year ago, when your father – now an old, blind man – left Nevermore Bookshop in the hands of Heathcliff Earnshaw and went to do battle with his enemy." She snapped her fingers at Heathcliff, who was busy refilling my glass in between taking swigs from the bottle. "I'll need one of those, too."

"Steady on," Heathcliff frowned. "Apparently, you've been a cat for several centuries. How do you know you can stomach this shite?"

"I've been subsisting on live mice and crickets, and that muck you have the gall to call cat food. My constitution is above reproach." Grimalkin wiggled her glass under his nose. Sighing, Heathcliff topped her up, then leaned back in his chair and skulled the rest of the bottle in one long gulp.

I brought my drink to my lips as Grimalkin continued. "Now that my thirst has been sated, I can continue. News of Homer's epic poems reached the gods, and as Poseidon read what had been written about him, he became incensed. In the *Odyssey*, Poseidon is the enemy – he delays Odysseus' return home from Troy because Odysseus blinds the cyclops Polyphemus, who was Poseidon's son. Incensed that Homer would have his son blinded in the poem and that he'd present the god in such an unflattering light, Poseidon poisoned the waters of Meles. He killed my beloved husband, and now, anyone borne of the waters is also cursed. Here in the future, Homer's eyesight immediately began to fail. This curse, it would seem, he has passed on to you."

Oh, for Isis' sake. She's saying that my retinitis pigmentosa is the curse of a petty Greek god. I was too numb to demonstrate the full brunt of the anger I felt at that moment, at having this essential part of my personage, this part of me that I'd worked so hard to come to terms with, reduced to a line in an epic poem – a foot-note in a fairy tale. I growled in my throat. Quoth's fingers squeezed mine. Grimalkin continued, oblivious.

"He continued his journeys through time, growing older as he established a business in this residence during every decade of history. He yearned for Helen, and for the daughter he couldn't know. He could not return to your time as a youth, for he would be arrested and Helen would never forgive him for abandoning her. So he moved through time and waited out his years in the past, winding back and forth until his years drew long and his hair turned grey. He came back to you only as an old man, so that neither the authorities nor your mother would recognize him. He returned to his spring, and he watched over you from behind this very counter. As more and more book characters showed up at the shop, he explained things to them and sent them on their way as best he could. And he welcomed you with open arms, never telling you who he was but always making sure that you were steeped in the power of story. He hoped one day you might be able to take over his duties, but before he had the chance, his enemy arrived. The rest of the story you know. He left to track his enemy, to keep this creature of evil away from you. In his place, he left Heathcliff Earnshaw with instructions to watch over you when you returned to Nevermore."

"And how do *you* fit into this insane story?" Heathcliff demanded.

"My purgatory is Poseidon's idea of a joke." Grimalkin rolled the 'r' in purgatory, which would have been hilarious if I wasn't completely freaked out. "When he learned of the spell I wove on the waters of Meles to protect my son, he cursed me to live out my days as the one creature terrified of water, to ensure that I would never again find a lover like Meles and regain my powers. The only person who would be able to free me was one who read the words of my son aloud in my presence, in his original language.

She gestured to her sensuous body. "As a nymph, I am already blessed with eternal beauty and long life. Poseidon granted me nine lives – the amount allotted to felines. I have guarded these lives carefully, expending only seven over the centuries I've lived in this form. All those years of waiting, all those dead mice, just waiting for my chance to hold my son in my arms again." Grimalkin paused. "But he has gone, and all I have in his place is an ungrateful granddaughter, a lumbering brigand, a weasely intellectual, a raven I'm not allowed to eat, piles of dusty books, and a looming danger that could end us all."

"All right," I yelled. "I get it. Now we've heard the whole sordid tale, can you *finally* tell me what is this danger my father is protecting me from?"

"The enemy that you should think yourself lucky never to cross," my grandmother folded her arms across her chest. "Count Dracula."

CHAPTER NINETEEN

*J*burst out laughing. "Okay, now I know this is a fucking joke. Dracula is just a character in a book, inspired by Vlad the Impaler but not even historically accurate. He's not real—"

My laughter died in my throat. Because briefly, for a moment, I'd forgotten where I was standing. Nevermore Bookshop had brought my three boyfriends to life – Emily Brontë's Heathcliff, Sir Arthur Conan Doyle's James Moriarty, and Edgar Allan Poe's raven. All flesh and blood and bone, and all borne not from a womb but from the waters of Meles and the mind of a brilliant writer.

If they could be real, then any character could also be real. And if Heathcliff and Morrie and Quoth and Lydia Bennett had walked out of the pages of his book and into the real world through Nevermore Bookshop, then...

...then so too could beasts of myth and horror, like Dracula.

Stoker's words came back to me a flash, as if I'd read them only yesterday. "'...he means to succeed, and a man who has centuries before him can afford to wait and to go slow... water sleeps, and the enemy is sleepless.'" If Dracula came to our world from Bram Stoker's book, then he came with centuries of knowledge and power. No wonder my father – Homer – was worried about my safety. But then, if he was so worried, why did he up and leave? Why did he gift the shop to Heathcliff?

"Where is Dracula now?" Heathcliff growled, obviously wondering the same thing.

"Who knows?" Grimalkin rolled onto her side, stroking the edge of her breast. "Hanging upside down in a cellar somewhere? If my son has his way, he'll be burning in Hades with a stake through his heart."

"What of my father?" I demanded. "Have you heard from him?"

She gave a cat-like shrug. "He has no idea who I am. To him, I was just a stray cat who refused to leave the shop. As soon as he knew that beast was free in the world, he walked out of Nevermore and has never returned. He didn't even have the decency to put out a saucer of cream."

The shop bell tinkled. Heathcliff leaped to his feet. "We're closed!" he boomed. "Can't you read the bloody—"

"Is that any way to treat the person who comes bearing strange delicacies from far-off lands?" Morrie stepped into the room, carrying his laptop bag in one arm and balancing a large bakery box under the other. "I queued for hours to get these cronuts. They're supposed to be the best in England and... oh, we have a visitor."

"Mr. Moriarty." Grimalkin turned her head. Morrie's eyes widened as he took in her... display. A wicked grin spread across his face.

"And to whom do I owe the honor?"

"That's Grimalkin," I said. "And she's my *grandmother*, so maybe stop looking at her like you're the cat the got the cream."

"There's cream?" Grimalkin's long neck extended. "Where?"

For the first time since I'd known him, Morrie was utterly speechless. He stared from Grimalkin to me and back again. I could see the cogs in his mind turning over what I'd said, judging if I was pulling his leg, before accepting that once again, another weird thing had happened in Nevermore Bookshop.

As quickly as they could, Heathcliff, Quoth, and Grimalkin explained what had just transpired. Morrie glided through the room, planted a kiss on my lips that drew me back from the depths of my head, and offered around the box of cronuts. They *were* delicious. There was nothing like sugary baked goods to temper one's anxiety about one's Homeric father taking on Count Dracula and one's cat grandmother being naked in the middle of one's shop.

"This is a fascinating new development," Morrie said, biting into a cronut and dropping crumbs across the rug. Both Quoth and Grimalkin glanced down at the crumbs with forlorn expressions, perhaps intending to return to pick them from the rug later. "Here I was, all ready to tell you that I translated those words from Ancient Greek for you, all ready to dramatically re-enact the blinding of Polyphemus with Heathcliff playing the Cyclops, all ready to accept your everlasting praise and adoration, and you've bloody gone and solved the whole thing without me." He smiled at me, trying to show he was joking, but there was the tiniest waver in his voice that told me something was up.

Again, I wondered what could make the world's foremost criminal mind nervous. Was it learning that *Count Dracula* was somewhere in the world? That sure as fuck made me want to curl up into a ball in the corner.

"We haven't solved anything," I said. "We still need to find my father. And Dracula. Who knows how many people he could kill or… or vampires he could turn. Forget Danny, forget the shop, this is the most important case we'll ever solve."

Morrie reached for another cronut. "Indeed. Luckily, I'm here to lend my expertise. I do have one important question for our former feline."

"Yes?" Grimalkin lifted a perfectly arched eyebrow in a manner that could only be described as cat-like.

"Can you tell us the answer to the Homeric Question? Because I know an awful lot of scholars who'd pay good money for that question—"

The bell tinkled again. Heathcliff rose to his feet, his face thunderous. I shot out an arm but a familiar voice stopped me cold.

"Yoo-hoo, Mina!" Mum called. "I brought over some Champagne to celebrate. You won't believe it – tomorrow, I get the keys to my brand new Mercedes!"

CHAPTER TWENTY

"*S*hite, it's Mum!" I hissed. Any second now, she was going to walk in here and see a very young and mostly naked Grimalkin luxuriating on top of our display table. I leaped to my feet and made a shooing motion. "Get off. You need to hide."

"Why?" Grimalkin glowered at me as she gestured to her languid form. "I'm not Schrodinger's pet. You can't put all of *this* back in the box."

"Just get under the table, or I'll—"

"I'm going to pick it up at the dealer tomorrow, and I'm having a party to celebrate—" Mum stopped short as she entered the room and saw the naked Grimalkin draped over the table. "Mina, what's going on? Who is this woman?"

"Um, right... yes, well..."

How can I possibly explain this?

Quoth grabbed a journal and pencil from Heathcliff's desk. I noticed he'd managed to shrug a throw rug over his shoulders like a shirt, and he crouched down behind the desk so Mum wouldn't get an eyefull of... of all of him. "I'm sorry, Mrs. Wilde.

This is a life drawing session. I'm trying to get into art school, and I need more figure experience for my portfolio. Miss, ah…"

"Grimalkin. Miss Cat Grimalkin," she said pointedly.

"Right… Miss Grimalkin offered to pose for me. She does this sort of thing for a living." He managed to look both charming and sheepish. "It's not anything dodgy, I swear."

Great thinking, Quoth!

Mum wrinkled her nose. "Why are you having this drawing session in the middle of the shop, wearing what looks like a blanket, and why are my daughter and her boyfriend and that *gypsy* watching it?"

I'd tried to explain to Mum several times that she shouldn't use the word gypsy, but these things usually went in one ear and out the other, especially when she was throwing herself into another of her schemes. Right now, I just needed her to believe Quoth's story.

"We're … er, trialing it. For the shop!" I exclaimed. "Yes, that's it. We think local artists might want to run a regular life drawing class here. We were just seeing if the… er… lighting is bright enough."

"What do you think?" Grimalkin stretched one long leg over her head, giving us all a full view of… well, of everything. "Is my skin luminescent? Is my pose pleasing? Have I earned a saucer of cream?"

"A what?" Mum frowned at the woman.

"Yes, sure! I think you'll do nicely. Thanks, Cat. You can go get dressed now." I gave Grimalkin a pointed look. After far too many tense moments, she slid off the table and simpered past Mum, heading for the staircase. As she passed under the door, she tipped her chin at Mum.

"The face that launched a thousand ships looks more like the barnacled belly of a trireme now."

"Huh?" Mum looked confused. "What did she say?"

"Nothing." I glared at Grimalkin, who flashed me an evil smile and flounced upstairs. "Don't worry about it. She's an artist. They're very temperamental. So, what's the story about this Mercedes?"

"I've reached the Prosperity tier in my new business. The company is rewarding me for all my hard work with a brand new car! A Mercedes! Can you believe it?" Mum clasped her hands together, her face bursting with excitement. "Things are finally looking up for me, darling. I've found my calling. I'm creating the life I deserve."

Something crinkled against her skin. I grabbed the corner of her sleeve and rolled it up, exposing a row of shiny Flourish patches dotted all the way from her wrist to her shoulder.

"I thought you only had to wear one of these to receive the benefits of its amazing transdermal technology?" I said wryly.

Mum yanked her sleeve down, glowering at me. "Yes, well, that's what it *says*, but I want to accelerate results. I want to embody the Flourish values of Grow. Nourish. Live. The technology really is miraculous. I feel so invigorated, so alive. I can sense my metabolism working faster, burning away the fat."

I eyed Mum's stomach, which wobbled a little as she drew away. It honestly looked as if she'd gained weight. Which was totally fine, unless you were lying to people in order to convince them to buy silver patches to stick on their arms. "Just how much weight have you lost with these patches?"

"Oh, who's really counting!" Mum flicked her wrist dismissively. A patch peeled off the back of her hand and fluttered to the floor. "The whole point is that I'm *flourishing.* I'm living my truth and changing people's lives for the better. And I'm working with a company who supports me and rewards success. So will you come to my Mercedes party?"

"But how have you sold enough patches to afford a car like that? You've been in business for less than a month!"

"I'm just that brilliant." Mum grinned. "And I didn't even have to *buy* the car. I'm leasing it, and the company is giving me a monthly cash bonus to pay the lease. As long as I continue to keep my status, I'll never have to make a single payment on the car. Isn't that incredible? I got a free car!"

"What?" Of all the things I'd heard so far today, this was *by far* the most ludicrous. "Mum, that's *not* a free car. That's not a gift. It's a fucking trap to keep you buying thousands of those stupid patches every month. This is that smoothie company all over again, and the wobbleators, and what about those high-end baby accessories—"

Mum huffed. "I'd appreciate it if you could be a bit more supportive."

"Yeah, Mina." Morrie stepped up and placed his arm around Mum's shoulders, beaming at her. He flashed me his devil-may-care grin. "Your mother has achieved something remarkable. We should be supporting her, instead of cutting her down."

"See? Morrie respects my dreams. He knows a fellow entrepreneur, a kindred business owner who isn't afraid to take a chance on a revolutionary product—"

"I sure do, Mrs. Wilde." Morrie held out his box. "Cronut?"

"No thank you. With all these healthy nutrients entering my bloodstream, I have no need for processed sugar and gluten..." Mum hesitated for only a moment. "Oh, go on, just one. These patches have been working so well. I've hardly eaten a thing in three days. So one wee cronut won't make a difference. In fact, I can barely taste it! Actually... I'd better have another, just in case. I don't want to completely waste away. Everything in moderation, they say."

"Please, have as many as you like." Morrie grinned.

"You're a treasure, Morrie. Will you please convince my daughter to come along tomorrow night? It's going to be fabulous. I've rented the community hall, and I've got a DJ coming, and Richard's sourced me some lovely Champagne. Of course, my new car will be parked right out the front. Flourish have gifted me five hundred quid's worth of product to give away, and all the healthful smoothies we can drink!"

Oh no, not more smoothies. I sighed. "Of course I'll be there. We'll all come along."

Mum reached over and cupped Morrie's hands, then mine. "Oh, thank you. I think you'll have an amazing time. And maybe once you see my car, you'll rethink this bookshop lark and consider becoming part of my downline. The commission really is generous, and there are so many opportunities to—"

"Is that the time?" Morrie glanced at his phone. He let out a giant yawn. "Helen, I'm so sorry to rush off, but I've spent the night up in London and I had to get up at the crack of dawn to buy cronuts before I caught my train. I'm positively shattered. I need to get off to bed. But I'll see you ladies tomorrow night."

Morrie bent down to kiss my cheek. "Don't run off now," he whispered. His breath against my cheek sent a jolt of heat through my body. Morrie pulled away with a languid smile and disappeared up the staircase. Mum stared after him as if the power of her gaze could force him to run back and beg for my hand in marriage.

Mum sighed. "He really is amazing. You're so lucky, Mina."

Behind her, Heathcliff harrumphed.

"Yes, I am. Actually, I'm really sleepy as well." I did my best fake yawn.

"But it's only just after nine!" Mum pouted. "I thought we could go out for breakfast to celebrate."

"I'm sorry. I've got some important things to do this morning. We'll see you tomorrow, though."

"I'll be the one in the brand new Mercedes." Mum beamed as I shuffled her out the door. As soon as she was outside, I slammed the door shut, drew the bolt across, and glared up at Morrie, who was hiding on the top landing, stifling a laugh.

"Why did you do that?" I yelled. "You're just encouraging her.

This isn't funny. It's a complete *disaster*. Mum can't afford payments on that car—"

"Relax, gorgeous." Morrie was down the stairs in a flash. He spun me around and pressed my back against the shelves. One hand circled my wrist, pinning it above my head. His face hardened with lust as his icicle eyes swept over my body. "I did it because once you get going with Helen, you'll be at it all night trying to convince her to give up her latest business opportunity. I have other plans for you."

"Oh, you do?" I meant it to sound incredulous, but the words came out breathy. Morrie's grapefruit and vanilla scent washed over me, obliterating all my senses.

"I do." Morrie touched his tongue to his bottom lip, his eyes wild with hunger. "I've had designs on this body of yours for days now, but you've been too busy with organized events and chasing murderers and worrying about your father, and I had this stupid trip to take. When is it time for Morrie to defile you? When will a jolly good dicking fit into your busy schedule?"

"Defile me?" I grinned, even as the words sent a delicious shiver down my spine. "I'm not some virgin sacrifice."

"Oh, I know that." Morrie skimmed my cheek with his lips, laying a trail of featherlight kisses against my skin.

"It's not *my* fault you went to London," I added, gasping as he rubbed my nipple through my shirt. It was already hard. His touch sent a warm shiver through my chest that rocketed straight between my legs.

"It's not." Morrie's lips brushed my earlobe. "But the long, lonesome train ride gave me the opportunity to imagine all the filthy things I want to do to you. That *we* want to do to you."

"We?"

I glanced over Morrie's shoulder. Heathcliff and Quoth stood in the doorway. Quoth held up his phone, showing a stream of messages between the two of them. Snatches of words caught my attention… "lick her all over until she screams…" "…you could go down on her while I..." "...two of us inside her at the same time..."

My heart raced so hard I thought I was having a cardiac arrest. But no, it was just the thought of the three of them planning what they wanted to do with me, how they wanted to make me scream...

"He may be an arsehole, but he's very imaginative," Heathcliff added.

"You've been texting?" I glared at Heathcliff in shock. "Or was Quoth reading these to you? I just need to know how—"

In response, Heathcliff swept into the hallway, grabbed my cheek and forced my mouth against his. His kiss stole any chance I had at finding out more about their plans.

Ingrid Bergman once said that a kiss is a lovely trick designed by nature to stop speech when words were superfluous. That was how Heathcliff kissed, as though he had things he needed to say, a desperate compulsion deep within him that couldn't be expressed any other way. His lips never failed to draw me down into that compulsion, until the exchange between our bodies was its own kind of language, rich and lyrical and laced with wild, unquenchable heat.

"Upstairs," Morrie commanded in a tight voice. "All of you. *Now.*"

Heathcliff swept me up into his arms, never breaking the kiss. He lifted me up the staircase, navigating around the low ceilings and rickety bookshelves with ease. Quoth hurried to flip over the CLOSED sign. Morrie followed behind Heathcliff, and the strain on his face as he watched us was almost unbearable. I'd never seen Morrie this desperate. It was exhilarating. It was a huge fucking turn-on.

I do this to him. I make him lose control.

We crashed through the door and into the upstairs flat. Heathcliff set me down on the living room floor. Immediately, Morrie was on me, his lips claiming mine as his hands roamed all over my body. "Heathcliff, stoke the fire," Morrie commanded in his sternest voice.

Oooh, Heathcliff's not going to like that.

"You do it," Heathcliff growled, his lips raising the hairs on the back of my neck as he kissed a trail across my shoulders. "I'm busy."

Tension crackled between them, searing my skin as it caught me in the middle. *Mmmmm, what a delicious place to be.* The two of them could use my body as a battleground any time they liked if it felt this good.

"I'll do it," Quoth – ever the peacemaker – moved across the room. I lost myself as Heathcliff and Morrie kissed and licked and wrestled me between them, their bodies and tongues hot against mine. Heathcliff dragged my shirt over my head. Morrie cupped my breast, squeezing the nipple through the fabric of my bra. Heathcliff's hardness jammed into my thigh as he popped the clasp on my belt, hooking his fingers into the waistband of my jeans and yanking them past my thighs.

"Well, so much for spending a quiet evening in front of the fire."

Grimalkin. Shite. I'd completely forgotten about the cat-turned-grandmother. Our heads all snapped up, but the guys didn't let go of me. Grimalkin peered at us from Heathcliff's chair, an amused expression on her slender features.

"Don't worry about me. I come from the time of Bacchanalian rituals. Nothing about your amorous entanglement disturbs me except for its proximity to my own leisure activities." She set down a bottle of wine and stood up, uncrossing her long legs to reveal a full-length black maxi dress of mine she must've found on Morrie's floor somewhere. *Bugger, I liked that dress, and now I can't wear it again.* "I'm a creature of the night, and there are so many fantasies I've harbored while stuck in that feline body that I desire to have fulfilled. I shall go out and fulfill them. Do not expect me to return for at least three days." With that, she tossed her hair over her shoulder, grabbed a coat from the rack on the wall, and stalked out.

"She stole my favorite jacket," Morrie said.

"I don't care," Heathcliff growled, mashing his lips against mine. Just like that, Grimalkin was forgotten.

The warmth of the fire drew us closer. Heathcliff shoved me forward, heading for a wall. As much as I loved it when he was forceful and swept up in his emotions, I wanted to be in charge this time. I wanted to watch him squirm.

I placed my palms on Heathcliff's shoulders and shoved. It was like shoving a brick wall, but I managed to do it. He stumbled on the edge of the coffee table and collapsed into his chair.

"Exactly where I want you," I said, straddling him, grinding my hips against his crotch. A growl escaped his throat, low and rough like an animal. It rumbled through my chest, dragging up some deep, primal part of me. My lips sought his as my fingers popped the buttons and unzipped his crotch. I reached inside his boxers and drew out his length, wrapping my fingers around his hard shaft.

Heathcliff's eyes bore into mine, his jaw set. He looked like he was fighting for control. I bent down and took his tip in my mouth.

His muscles tensed, then relaxed. He exhaled a ragged breath. I pushed myself up on my knees and took him deeper, wrapping my tongue around his shaft. He tasted so good – heady and masculine and with a hint of his peaty scent. My wild man. My Heathcliff.

His whole body tensed again as I slid his shaft out of my mouth, then took him in again. This time I went deeper, pushing him right back into my throat. He was so long that even when my gag reflex kicked in, I couldn't take all of him. I wrapped my hand around his shaft and pumped him as I circled my tongue around his tip.

Heathcliff's fingers tangled in my hair. Another hand slid up my thigh. Morrie. Of course, it was Morrie. "You're ruining my carefully-laid plans, gorgeous," he whispered against my ear. "I fucking *love* it."

Morrie's teeth bit into my earlobe as he rubbed the head of his cock against my opening, teasing me. We'd all had STI tests when we got back from Baddesley Hall, so we didn't need condoms any longer. The ache inside me begged for more, and I arched my back, rubbing my ass against Morrie's thighs. Morrie trailed his fingers down my back as he pushed his tip in, giving me a little at a time until I was squirming with anticipation. With a sigh, he sank himself inside, touching every secret part of me. I moaned against Heathcliff's cock as the two of them filled me completely.

My mouth around one, another buried inside *This is glorious. But I need one more.*

I searched the room for my third boyfriend but it was so dark, the shaft of light from the fire the only light. I gestured to him with my free hand. In a moment, Quoth emerged from the gloom. He twisted his fingers in my hair, kissing a line down my neck and across my shoulder, making the tiny hairs on my skin stand right on end.

I clamped a hand around Quoth's arm and dragged him closer. My hand circled his cock and I pumped him to the same rhythm as I did Heathcliff. My eyes darted between the two of them as the flickering firelight danced across their faces. My soft-artist, my tortured anti-hero. So different, and yet, so perfect. *So mine.*

With every thrust, Morrie shoved Heathcliff's cock deeper down my throat. It was almost as if he was fucking Heathcliff through me. I could feel the tension stretching between them, as they tossed my body between them. Two forces of nature – one wild and uncontained, the other controlled and careful - battling for supremacy.

Heathcliff broke first. With a cry, he dug his nails into my shoulder. He cock tightened, and I tasted the salt of his orgasm on my tongue. He withdrew, panting, his muscles twitching. His chair groaned as it took his weight.

I turned to Quoth and took him into my mouth. Quoth closed his eyes, his fingers stroking my hair with soft, gentle circles. He made my ministrations feel like a sacred, reverent act.

"Fuck," he moaned as I pumped him hard.

"You like that, birdie," Morrie grunted. He slid his hand underneath me, touching the tip of his finger to my clit. The ache inside me burned, sending sparks shooting through my limbs. With each strong, deep thrust, Morrie slid my lips along Quoth's cock and rubbed my clit with his finger.

So intense. So good. So... ooooooooh.

My lips clamped down on Quoth and I moaned around his cock as an orgasm coursed through me. Quoth's fingers in my hair felt like shafts of heavenly light. Morrie slammed his cock deep inside me, crouching over me and scraping his teeth along my ear. He hummed, enjoying the way my body rocked back against him and the clenching of my muscles around his cock.

Quoth pulled out and shuffled back, his eyes wide. "Mina, you're beautiful," he whispered.

"Sit back on Morrie," Heathcliff ordered from his chair.

As soon as my legs cooperated, I did as he commanded. Morrie stretched his legs out and I sat on his thighs, lowering myself down onto him and feeling him touch new and exciting places inside me. Morrie gripped my thighs, helping me to raised and lower myself.

Heathcliff tore his shirt off and dropped to his knees, crawling forward and resting his head between my thighs. His beard tickled my sensitive skin as he circled my clit with his tongue. Heathcliff licked me with ragged strokes while I rode Morrie's cock in a languid rhythm.

Rich, intoxicating sensations rolled through my body. Pressure built up in my belly. I resisted the urge to close my eyes and let the sensations take over, determined to commit every moment of this night to visual memory. Morrie's fingers circling my nipples, Heathcliff's back muscles tightening as his head bobbed between my legs.

His tongue, so close to Morrie's cock...

A second orgasm slammed into me, more powerful than the first – a hurricane whipping through my body, tossing my limbs about, ravaging my veins with liquid lightning. I felt like I was been torn in two by the power of it. The intensity of having the two guys so close, so in sync with each other, almost as if this wasn't just about me any longer. My legs turned to jelly and I slid off Morrie's cock, collapsing onto the soft rug.

Rough, strong hands lifted my shoulders. Heathcliff tilted his head and pressed his lips to mine. I could taste myself on his lips. His hand slid down to stroke my clit. My veins still buzzed from the last two orgasms – my body could barely handle the touch. I sank back on Morrie's cock and pulled Heathcliff's hand from between my legs, accidentally (not accidentally) placing it on Morrie's thigh.

Heathcliff's eyes darkened. Morrie's breath hitched. I lifted myself and slammed down on Morrie's cock, and a moan escaped my lips. Lightning forked in the air between us as I surrendered myself to the idea of the two of them, faces inches apart, the gap closing, closing... Heathcliff's eyes darting between me and Morrie...

"If you're going to kiss him, just hurry up about it," I joked.

My words shattered the tension, crackling the lightning against my skin. Heathcliff growled and leaned in, mashing his lips against mine, pouring the full force of his strain into his kiss. Behind me, Morrie's teeth dug into my shoulder as he came inside me, his body convulsing with waves of pleasure.

Morrie slunk back, panting. For once he was speechless. Heathcliff pulled away too. I turned to Quoth, my beautiful raven boy, always patient, always understanding. I cupped his face in my hands and pulled his lips to mine.

"I don't know what you've done to them," he murmured. "It's fascinating."

"It's not about them right now," I whispered. "This moment, right here, is for us."

I kissed Quoth with everything I had because he was everything to me. He never demanded anything, always putting everyone else before himself. And I wanted him to feel as though he was the one being worshipped for once.

I crawled on top of him, pressing my body to his as my hand snaked down to grip his cock. Quoth moaned against my lips and the sound was hotter and more intoxicating than my favorite screaming punk singer.

A tap on my shoulder jolted me out of my reverie. "Oh, gorgeous?" Morrie held up the lube he'd been saving since the Jane Austen Experience.

I shook my head.

"Think about it, two of us inside you, filling you up, worshipping you the way you deserve..." his gaze flicked to Heathcliff, and I knew he was imagining it all, their cocks so close inside me, practically touching...

And I wanted it too, my body aching for it. But I knew I wasn't ready. All of this – sharing them – was so new, I needed time to understand what it meant before I let him unleash his full deviant self upon my body.

"I'm not saying no," I said. "But I am saying, 'not tonight.' I'm not ready for that yet."

Morrie looked like he wanted to argue, like he was ready to lay down a series of convincing expostulations he'd prepared ahead of time. He flicked his eyes to Heathcliff again, and when he flicked back, that moment was gone.

"Can I at least make you come again while Quoth is inside you?" he asked.

"Yeah..." I grinned. "You could do that."

Morrie lay on the ground and beckoned me to kneel over

him. I planted my hands beside his hips, on all fours, facing the blazing fire. With a hand on my lower back, Morrie guided me lower, until I was right over his mouth.

"Get in position, birdie," he said, his breath against my swollen clit almost sending me into another release. "Tonight, we're going to make Mina fly."

Quoth slid inside me, filling me completely. As he drew out and buried himself deeper, Morrie's tongue swirled around my clit. Each touch placed perfectly, making my veins sing with music. Morrie could play me like an instrument and when he joined with Quoth – it was like a whole fucking symphony playing inside my body.

As Quoth slammed into me, twisting his hips to drive even deeper, Morrie pushed a finger in alongside him.

"Oh!" I cried out.

It took everything I had just to stop my legs giving out beneath me. The idea of two of them inside me like that, it just… it just… by Isisssssssssss…

Fire consumed me as I came. My body liquified, and I slid off Morrie and puddled on the rug. Heat rolled over my skin, every sensation mapping on my body and inside me, on my soul.

"That was… amazing," I breathed. The guys tucked their bodies in around me, forming a nest. Heathcliff pressed his chest to my back. Morrie lifted my head and rested it on his stomach, while Quoth wrapped himself around my legs, his arm draped protectively across my torso. The four of us slotted perfectly together – puzzle pieces that fit.

"I love you guys so much," I whispered. The truth of it squeezed my heart. "Everything feels less scary when you're around."

"You don't have anything to be afraid of," Heathcliff growled. His chest rumbled.

"No, not at all," I said sarcastically. "Only going blind, losing the shop, seeing an innocent woman go to jail, and having to do battle with Count Dracula. Nope, nothing to be afraid of at all."

"We'll always protect you," Quoth said. He glanced at Heathcliff and Morrie. "Won't we?"

"Always," Heathcliff added.

Morrie's lips parted, but he didn't say anything. Up this close, I could pick out his features in the flickering firelight. Even though he smiled, his eyes were a million miles away.

"You've already proven that you don't need us to protect yourself, gorgeous," he said, averting his gaze. "You're clever and resourceful and creative and if anyone is going to find the murderer, save this shop, and thwart a centuries-old vampire, it's you."

With Count Dracula on the loose, I needed all three of them by my side. I needed Heathcliff's rage and Morrie's cunning and Quoth's kindness. But Morrie was pulling away. Would he be the first to leave the harem? How on earth would I be able to let him go?

CHAPTER TWENTY-ONE

"*H*urry up, Morrie. It's just my mum's stupid fitness patch event. You don't need to dress up."

Morrie descended the stairs, his tailored trousers perfectly pressed, his jacket lapels as sharp as knives, and that familiar evil glint shimmering in his eye.

"Sorry, gorgeous." Morrie ran a hand through his close-cropped hair. "You can't rush perfection."

I shoved him towards the door, where Heathcliff and Quoth already waited, both looking equally gorgeous – Heathcliff in dark jeans and a leather motorcycle jacket, Quoth in dress pants and a blood-red shirt that picked up crimson highlights in his hair, which trailed down his back like a river of spun silk. "Get that perfect arse into the car. We're late. I need to get there before my mother is talked into leasing a yacht."

"Should we leave a key under the mat for Grimalkin?" Quoth asked as I shrugged my coat on over my latest creation – a black sheath dress that I'd artfully shredded around the waist and hem, and added a cascade of glittering rhinestones. It had been another impossibly quiet day in the shop, so I'd made up the dress while Heathcliff finished Danny's book, Quoth painted, and

Morrie fiddled around with something on his computer. It would have been a wonderful day if it wasn't for my lingering worry over… everything.

"No. Serves her right for not deigning to show up," Heathcliff growled. "If she comes home, she can squeeze through the cat door, same as always."

Quoth looked like he wanted to argue, but of course he didn't. Honestly, I agreed with Heathcliff. Who drops the kind of bombshell Grimalkin gave us yesterday, then just ups and leaves for a whole twenty-four hours to stalk through the night doing Athena knows what, instead of helping us try and figure out a solution?

A cat, that's who.

Biting wind hit us as soon as we stepped outside. Heathcliff held me under the protective warmth of his arm as we rushed to the end of the street, where Jo was waiting. She flung the passenger door open and I slid in beside her. The boys piled in back – Quoth in the middle, hunched over as he was hemmed in by broad shoulders on both sides.

"Thanks so much for inviting me out," she grinned, blasting the heater as she pulled away from the curb. "I wasn't sure you still liked me after the kitchen incident."

I shuddered at the memory of it. "I don't think I can ever use the coffee machine again."

"Neither." Jo laughed. "I bought a replacement one. And I promise, no more grinding up body parts. And no more bugs."

"Can I get that in writing?" What is the world coming to, when I need that particular promise from my flatmate?

A few minutes later, we pulled up at the Argleton community hall. Sure enough, a pristine silver Mercedes was parked across three spaces at the hall entrance. No less than ten Flourish stickers were visible on its surface. My stomach churned at the sight of it. *Please, don't let Mum be in trouble.* But I knew my mother too well to have any hope.

I can't believe the same woman who inspired Helen of Troy could fall for such a ridiculous scam.

Clearly, Mum had converted some people to the wonders of transdermal technology. A small crowd milled around the entrance, many of them wearing silver patches on their arms. I walked inside to a soundtrack of pumping bass. An enormous disco ball in the middle of the room splashed colored light on all the walls, and strobes made my eyes strain and blink. In the center of the room, a life-sized silver statue stood on a dais, holding a giant replica of the patch. I guessed it was supposed to be aspirational and inspire us to hit our health and fitness goals, but the sculptor clearly wasn't very skilled because it just looked like a mildly frumpy older woman with knobby knees.

We walked over to a table in the corner that was piled high with platters. On closer inspection, there didn't appear to be any food apart from a box of ninety-nine pence crackers and some processed cheese slices. Instead, the entire table was given over to a range of smoothies and 'nutrient shots' artfully arranged in tiny shot glasses on a tiered stand. We each took one. I sniffed mine.

"A unique bouquet of citrus top notes with a robust body of Worcestershire sauce," I announced, mocking Morrie's wine tastings. No way in hell was I actually putting this thing in my mouth.

"Guacamole and dandelions over here." Morrie tossed his glass straight into the bin.

"I've got peach and... maybe boot polish?" Quoth took a sip, his face wrinkling. "Yup, definitely boot polish."

"You're all a bunch of Nanas. They taste fine to me." Heathcliff snatched Quoth's shot from his hand and tipped it down his throat.

"That's because we haven't destroyed our tastebuds with five-quid-a-bottle whisky," Morrie shot back. "You realize they're not alcoholic?"

Heathcliff immediately set his glass down and reached into his coat for his flask. "Then what's the point?"

As the boys bickered about the merits of various bottom shelf liquors, I glanced around the room, taking in everything I could see. All this must have cost a fortune ... the DJ, the lights, the statue, the ten bottles of mid-range Champagne sitting on the table over there, not to mention that bloody car outside. *How is Mum paying for all this? Surely it's not from selling a couple dozen Flourish patches...*

Where is Mum? I glanced around again, expecting to see her talking and laughing with her guests. When she put her mind to it, she really was quite charming and personable. That was why she made such a good tarot reader – she could sense what a person needed to hear at that exact moment and made sure the cards reflected it. If only she'd give up on these get-rich-quick schemes and actually get a real job, saved some money...

The statue in the center of the room wobbled.

Did I imagine that?

Of course I did. It's the strobe lights playing tricks on my eyes...

No, there it is again. The statue definitely wobbled. And I'm sure it didn't look like it was scratching its nose before...

Oh no.

Please NO.

That's not a statue at all.

CHAPTER TWENTY-TWO

*T*he statue listed heavily to the left. I rushed over and grabbed an arm, steadying it. Warm skin yielded beneath my fingers. Silver paint flaked on the ground and all down the front of my dress as Mum sagged against me.

"Hello, Mina," she slurred. "I'm so glad you could make it. Did you bring your handsome boyfriend?"

"Morrie's around here somewhere. Mum, what's going on? Why are you covered in silver paint? And why do you sound drunk?"

"I'm not drunk! I only drink Flourish smoothies now... oh, except for my celebratory Champagne..." Mum gestured to the table in the corner, but her whole body lurched forward. She slithered to the ground, clutching my legs as if they were the only thing holding me upright. "I was trying to be innovative. Sandy, my mentor, says that you have to stand out from the crowd. She said you have to embody the Flourish brand. So I came up with this idea all on my own. Isn't it genius?"

"Oh, sure, this is absolutely genius." I gestured to Heathcliff, who rushed over with a chair, which I folded Mum into. "I think when Sandy said you need to embody the brand she means, you

157

know, eating healthy and exercising, not literally turning yourself into a Flourish mascot..." my stomach churned as Mum's head lolled to the side. Paint fumes wafted up my nose, and my temples flared with pain. A sickening thought occurred to me. " Mum, did you check that this paint was safe for use on skin?"

"It came from the hardware store. They wouldn't sell it if it wasn't safe!"

Shite. I pressed my fingers through the paint on her cheek and sniffed the pieces that flaked off. My head reeled from the fumes. "Mum... did you cover yourself in *spray paint?*"

"I think I need to lie down," Mum murmured, sliding off the chair.

She's not groggy because she's drunk. She's groggy because she's been inhaling paint for Hathor knows how long. Keep her awake! I pulled Mum upright and slapped her cheeks. "That shit's toxic! You've just spread toxic paint all over your skin. Your body can't get oxygen through your pores. No wonder you're keeling over." I dragged her up again and started trying to rub the paint off. But it was dry now, stuck to her skin like glue. Behind me, Morrie had his phone to his ear, demanding an ambulance.

"Stop fussing, honey," Mum murmured. "You're so stressed out. You need to try the Flourish patch. It will mellow you right out..."

"Out of the way." Heathcliff elbowed past a gathering crowd, holding an armload of smoothie shots, along with a large flag advertising the DJ's services. He upended the shot glasses over Mum, dumping sticky smoothies all over her head, shoulders, and arms.

"Stop that, you gypsy heathen!" Mum screeched. Silver paint ran down her skin in shiny rivers. Heathcliff gritted his teeth as he tossed me the banner.

"That heathen might've just saved your life." I rubbed at her now wet skin with the banner, trying to get rid of as much paint as possible. It came off much easier now, rubbing away onto the banner in big silver splotches, mixed with the multi-colored smoothies. The DJ screamed at Heathcliff that he would have to pay to replace the banner. In the distance, the ambulance siren squealed.

"It could have been worse," Morrie said as he picked up the other end of the banner and rubbed paint off Mum's back.

"How? How could it be worse?"

"Everyone could suddenly turn into a cat." Morrie grinned. "Too soon?"

~

*A*fter Mum left in the ambulance, people milled around, unsure of what to do. I'd wanted to go to the hospital with her, but she'd insisted on me staying on to run the party. Not that there was much of a party now. The DJ left in a huff and there was no one to pop the Champagne or give out the mountain of free Flourish patches and smoothie mixes.

It was Quoth who saved the evening. He went behind the mixing desk, plugged in a set of headphones, and put on some sweet dancing tunes. Mrs. Ellis' friends took to the dance floor, followed by a group of young girls. Heathcliff lobbed free merchandise at anyone who looked like they were about to talk to him. Soon, everyone in the room was affixing silver patches to their arms and gyrating to Lady Gaga.

Morrie popped the corks on the cheap Champagne, and Heathcliff rinsed out shot glasses so we had something to drink with. Jo drove out and returned with a stack of pizzas, which were quickly devoured as the hungry dancers returned to the floor. One thing was for sure – I could wrangle a crew to put on a mean party.

"Fancy a spin?" Morrie held out his hand for me.

I glanced down at his immaculate brogues. "You think your shoes are up to a battering?" I might love music, but I wasn't exactly a demon on the dance floor. More like an uncoordinated rhinoceros.

"I've got plenty of pairs at home. These ones can be sacrificed." Morrie took my hand. Even though the song was fast and pumping, he held me close, his hand resting in the small of my back in a possessive way that made my heart patter.

"So... that bloody cat is your grandmother, Count Dracula wants to suck your blood, and you've agreed to help a suspected murderess clear her name." Morrie swirled me around the edge of the dance floor. "What else did I miss?"

I remembered then that I had something important to ask him. "Grey Lachlan came to the shop yesterday, trying to get Heathcliff to sell."

"Ah. And Heathcliff told him where he could stick it?"

"He certainly did, but not before Grey declared that he knew about the state of the shop's finances. He also said he knew that your funds were frozen in a Cayman Island bank account as they were being investigated."

I watched Morrie's face carefully. In the dim light, it was impossible for me to see, but his right eyebrow might have twitched. "You shouldn't pay any attention to that man. He's all bluster and bollocks."

"I know that, but are you telling me hand-on-heart that there's not a single shred of truth in what he said?"

I waited. Morrie exhaled through his teeth. His fingers pressed into my spine. "There is some truth."

"Is that why you went down to London? And is it also why you haven't offered to bail the shop out of our current financial crisis?"

Morrie didn't answer.

Concern slithered along my spine. "Are you in trouble?"

Morrie opened his mouth to say something, but then his gaze slipped from my face. He was looking at something across the room. "I'll get it sorted, Mina. I experienced a temporary setback, that's all. The only person who could unravel my network is Sherlock Holmes himself, and he's still stuck inside a book, thank the non-existent gods. Everything's fine."

"Don't say 'everything's fine' like that. It makes me concerned that you're plotting something nefarious."

"Me? Never." Morrie's gaze flicked over my shoulder again. His fingers slid down my arm, and I wasn't thinking about his criminal empire anymore. His hands on me, his strong body guiding me around the dance floor... that was all I wanted...

What is he looking at?

I stomped on his toes, a little harder than I was intending. Morrie winced, but his gaze didn't falter. As Heathcliff clomped past, spinning Dotty around in his arms, Morrie leaned over and hissed, "Isn't that Miranda, from the Argleton Arms Hotel?"

I glanced over my shoulder, but I couldn't see with all the shifting lights. Heathcliff didn't even bother to look. "Who cares?"

"We do. I happen to know that she works the front desk most weekdays. It's likely she was working the morning Danny was killed." Morrie craned his neck. "She was probably the last person to see him alive, apart from the murderer. She's heading toward the drinks table. Heathcliff, take our woman. I'm going in."

Heathcliff dropped Dotty like a stone and wrapped his arms around me. We danced closer as Morrie ducked through the crowd and went straight up to Miranda. I could see now Miranda was a leggy blonde with impressive cleavage spilling out of her v-neck sweater. In moments, she was tossing her hair and laughing at something Morrie said. Morrie handed her a glass of Champagne and she touched his arm, smiling up at him while running her tongue along her bottom lip. Watching them laugh and flirt sent a flash of anger through my veins.

Huh. That's weird. I'd never felt like that when the guys talked to other women before. Even though I knew Morrie was over there trying to get information from Miranda by any means necessary, seeing him do it made me feel… not jealous exactly, but possessive. I wanted to go over there, drape my arm across his shoulders, and casually mention that he was mine, mine, mine.

But that's not fair. I was dating all three of the guys, and they were completely fine with it. They bickered about me all the time, but they bickered about everything, so that didn't make me special. They'd happily declared that they'd be exclusive to me, and I… I didn't even want Morrie to pretend-flirt with a hot blonde in order to get some important information?

I didn't like this needling sensation running down my spine. I suspected it had less to do with wanting to keep Morrie all to myself and more to do with my fear that one day they'd make me choose between them, and I wouldn't be able to do it.

I needed something to distract me. Luckily, I had just the something in my arms.

"Did you ever try to date?" I asked Heathcliff, leaning against him and resting my head on his shoulder. Heathcliff couldn't dance the way Morrie could, but he allowed me to stand on his feet while he shuffled awkwardly to and fro. "Before you met me."

He shook his head. "Never wanted to. Morrie made an online dating profile for me."

"No, he didn't!" I couldn't picture it.

"He did. He made me sound like a brooding, soulful artist. I went out with one girl who left me a no-star review."

"I don't believe that."

"It's true. She said I wasn't a tortured bad boy, I was just a dickhead gypsy and it was spending time with me that was the torture."

"It sounds like she was the problem, not you." I tangled my fingers in his tousled hair. "I mean, I can't believe you can give someone a no-star review. Surely you'd get one star for at least showing up."

"Apparently I have that effect on people." Heathcliff's lips brushed the top of my head. The gesture was so uncharacteristically soft that it made my heart skip. For a moment, I forgot all about Morrie and that weird niggling sensation in my spine.

Then I happened to glance over at Morrie and Miranda. They had their heads bent together in deep conversation. The niggling feeling returned with full force.

I spun Heathcliff the other way, so I didn't have to watch. "Do you ever think about what you'd like to do if you didn't run Nevermore?"

He snorted. "Why bother? Your father gave me a job to do. I'm not going to leave. What else would I do, go to the moors and look for my birthright – a house and land and ex-lover that don't exist?"

"I'm serious. Consider for a moment that the upstairs bedroom wasn't a porthole into space and time, and this book magic – whatever it is – didn't randomly bring fictional characters to life, and there wasn't a cache of dangerous occult books hidden in the storage room, and a spring of ancient mystical water somewhere under the foundations. If Nevermore was just a normal bookshop and you were just a normal guy, would you want to run it?"

"Yes."

His answer surprised me. "Why?"

"Because you're there."

"Heathcliff Earnshaw, that's not an answer. I asked what *you* want. You can't stand customers. You don't want to learn how to use the computer. Half the time you're not really even interested in the books."

"I told you. I want to be with you, Mina. And you love the bookshop. Before you came it was just dusty shelves filled with paper, Morrie and Quoth being annoying shits, and customers who seemed sent from hell specifically to torture me. But then you came along, with all your crazy ideas. You make it *fun*."

"Did you just use the word fun unironically? I think I might faint."

"It's true. You make me want to enjoy life, even if I never will use that bloody computer." The hint of a smile played across Heathcliff's mouth. "If what Grimalkin says is true, you, love, may have even brought me here in the first place, brought me to you. Why would I want to leave?" He glowered at me. "Do you want me to go? Is that it?"

"Hell no." I kissed his stubbly cheek. "But it's been crossing my mind lately that we can't just live like this forever. What we have right now – you, me, Morrie, Quoth – it's *amazing*, but it can't be permanent. This world doesn't accept a relationship like ours, and sooner or later it's going to bite us on the arse. Someone will want out."

"Not me." He shook his head. It seemed impossible, but the black of his eyes got even blacker. "You?"

"No. Never. We're like… I never fit in anywhere before, not at school, not in this town, not even really in New York City. I was the puzzle piece in the box that was from the wrong bloody puzzle. But being with the three of you is like slotting the right puzzle pieces together. We all fit, and we make a beautiful, vivid picture. But one of us is bound to get sick of being one of four. And what about marriage? Children? What about power of attorney? What about two-for-one night at the movies? What about how this town will treat us as soon as they figure out we're all dating?"

"I don't care what people think," he growled.

"You might. One day."

"Unlikely."

"Or Quoth might. Or Morrie. We can't exactly do normal things. If we all go out on a date together, people are going to stare. How would we buy a house together? How will we sort out life insurance, or split up the chores? Who cleans the bathroom? How the fuck will we sign our Christmas cards?"

"That's easy. We don't send Christmas cards."

"I'm serious! The world isn't built to accommodate a relationship like ours. We're taking the hardest path, and I just wonder if one day, one of us might wake up and wish things were easier."

"That's not going to happen." Heathcliff narrowed his dark eyes at me. "You know why?"

"Why?"

Hot lips pressed against mine. Heathcliff's kiss drenched me with his need, drowning me in the well of his love. It was a kiss that spoke more eloquently, more passionately, than words ever could.

Heathcliff pulled back, his chest heaving. I gasped for breath. That kiss… it told me that as far as Heathcliff was concerned, all my worries were completely unfounded. The certainty in that kiss steeled me.

Morrie's head popped up between us. "Sorry to break up the party, lovebirds. But I've got news."

"Miranda dumped a smoothie on your head?" I asked, trying not to sound hopeful.

"Of course not. In mere minutes, she succumbed to my not inconsiderable charm and spilled all the details about Danny's last morning. According to Miranda, Brian arrived at the hotel first, by himself, followed by Angus a half-hour later escorting Danny's wife Penny. Danny and Amanda came in after midnight. They sat in the bar for an hour or so before they went up to bed. Miranda said they were flirting hard. She also said they headed upstairs together and it seemed as though they would be… 'shagging all night' was the term she used. Personally, I prefer something more poetic, like bumping uglies or a bit of crumpet, adult naptime, caulking the tub, in the service of Venus, baking the potato, dancing the Paphian jig, groping for trout in a peculiar river, Blitzkrieg mit dem fleischgewehr, bludgeoning the flaps…"

Bludgeoning the flaps? I rolled my eyes. "We get the idea. Where do you even *get* this stuff?"

"I'm a man of many talents. Do you want to hear the rest of my story?"

I sighed. "Yes. Please continue sans poetic euphemisms."

"In the morning, Miranda saw Danny leave the hotel around five a.m. He was in a jovial mood, flirting with her as he asked about the dinner options when he got back. A few minutes after he left, Angus called down to the front desk and asked for some towels to be left in the hall in front of his room. Miranda left the desk and went up with the towels. Angus had the DO NOT DISTURB sign on his door. As she set down the stack outside Angus' room, she couldn't help but overhear the sounds of rather vigorous lovemaking coming from inside."

"Did she recognize the woman's voice?"

"She says it was Amanda Letterman."

I couldn't believe it. "So Amanda was shagging both Danny *and* Angus, on the same night, right under the same roof as Brian? That guy has got to have known about this."

"I agree. And he was the most likely person to have picked up Beverly's scarf. I'm just not sure if he's responsible for Danny's death. If this murder is about infidelity, then why go after Danny? Why not Amanda? What does Brian gain apart from revenge? This murder was premeditated – the killer has gone out of his or her way to choose the manner of death. They're sending a message. Everything about this suggests it was related to the murder of Abigail Ingram. Which means that all the evidence still points towards Beverly."

But my mind was spinning in a completely different direction. "Or maybe all this bludgeoning the flaps was really about creating a distraction. If someone knew Angus and Amanda were shagging…"

Morrie rubbed his chin. "It's possible. It may not have been Angus on the phone. Miranda said he sounded tired and muffled. The killer could have asked Miranda to take the towels upstairs, knowing Angus had the DO NOT DISTURB sign up. With

Miranda gone, the killer could sneak past the front desk to meet Danny at the shop."

"That's elaborate," Heathcliff said. "Wouldn't they be better off just going out a fire exit?"

Morrie shook his head. "All the exits are on alarms, to stop guests sneaking out for a smoke."

"Wouldn't Miranda see which room the call came from on her switchboard? And surely if someone snuck past the front desk, the police would have seen it on CCTV."

"It's the Argleton Arms Hotel, not the Waldorf. They don't have that kind of technology. The CCTV camera over the front door has been broken for months."

"One thing we know for sure," I said. "Angus and Amanda have an alibi – each other. That leaves us with Brian Letterman and Danny's wife, Penny who don't have alibis. Both of them had a reason to hate Danny, and both had ample opportunity to follow him out of the hotel. And that's not to mention Jim Mathis, or any other suspects we haven't come up with."

Heathcliff snorted. "Of course, there's another possibility – that Beverly Ingram really did kill Danny."

I shook my head. "I just can't believe it."

"Fine, fine," Heathcliff muttered. "We'll continue this wild goose chase. How much longer are we going to stay at this party? All the Champagne is gone."

I glanced around. The party looked like it was winding up. The only one still dancing was Quoth, who stood behind the mixing desk, his black hair flying around his face as he head-banged to Blur.

I grinned. "Fine. I guess it's time to wind up. You find Jo. I'll grab Funkmaster Quoth. He needs to get a good sleep tonight because we're going to visit that art school in the morning."

CHAPTER TWENTY-THREE

*N*erves tugged at me as Quoth and I boarded the bus in front of the Argleton Arms Hotel. I wanted so badly for everything to go well for him today. This was the first time he'd ever done something for himself, on his own initiative, and if anything went wrong, he'd retreat back into his shell and that bright smile of his would be even rarer than ever.

Beside me, Quoth burst with excitement. His joy radiated off him, and I felt that every eye on the bus was drawn to him. How could they not, when he was shifting in his seat, tossing his luscious hair?

The bus dropped us off right in front of the campus. Quoth fidgeted with his clothes as we walked through the gates toward the administration building. I reached for his hand and squeezed it.

We walked into a light, airy atrium. An enormous abstract triptych covered one entire wall, the giant panels stretching two stories. Glossy paint had been streaked so thick that it stuck out in sharp ridges, giving the panels a tactile quality that begged to be touched. Students shuffled back and forth, swinging book bags and chatting in loud, excitable voices.

"Hi," I told the woman behind the counter. "We're Mina Wilde and Allan Poe. We're here for a tour of the art department."

"Of course. Mrs. Anders is expecting you. She'll be down in a moment."

A few moments later, a woman with bright pink hair dressed in a flowing multicolored maxi dress and bright purple knitted shawl appeared. She clasped each of our hands in turn. "Welcome. I'm Charlotte Anders and I'm so excited to show you around campus, Allan. I've seen your portfolio. Your work is *arresting*. Not my taste – a bit too dark for me, I'm afraid – but I think you'll fit in well here."

Quoth's features lit up at her words. She turned to me. "Are you also applying, Mina?"

"No, I—"

"Mina's an amazing creative," Quoth cut in. "She made the clothes she's wearing. She studied fashion at the New York Fashion School, and worked for Marcus Ribald."

Now it was my turn to blush. At the mention of Ribald's name, Mrs. Anders face lit up. "Wow, that's amazing. I love Ribald's work. That gown he did at the 2017 New York Fashion Week, made out of nails and screws? Obviously, we're nothing on the Fashion School, but I'd be happy to show you our fashion and textile workshops—"

"Actually, I'm just here to support Quoth— er, Allan," I said. "I might consider returning to school, but it won't be for fashion. I need a career change."

"Well, we have lots of great programs – especially in the arts – and we're a lot closer than New York City. Come, I'll show you the art department." Mrs. Anders ushered us through to a bright, airy studio space. Students worked at individual stations on large canvases or tinkered with steel sculptures. In the far corner, a girl had dabbed her naked body with rainbow paints, then rolled around on a large canvas covering half the floor. Every inch of the walls was covered with paintings and prints and etchings and photographs, each more interesting than the last.

Down another hall were smaller private studios, each one with enormous windows looking out into the park. Quoth's eyes were as large as saucers as he surveyed the beautiful spaces and the storage cabinets filled with art supplies. We saw a wood- and metal-working studio, the pottery kilns, and the photography suite.

"What do you think, Allan?" Mrs. Anders asked as we wandered through the faculty wing, where smaller tutorials were held and lecturers had their offices. "Will we be seeing you next semester?"

Quoth's fingers squeezed mine. "I think so."

"Excellent. I can give you our enrollment forms before you leave... Oh, I'd love for you to meet someone special," Mrs. Anders knocked on a door at the end of the hall. "Marjorie? I've got two prospective students for you."

"New victims?" The woman behind the door cackled like a storybook witch. "Bring them in."

Mrs. Anders pushed the door open and ushered us inside. The first thing I noticed was the round woman with rosy cheeks and glassy eyes swiveling in her chair to greet us. A white walking stick rested against her desk and a black Labrador in a harness napped at her feet.

The room was filled with the most remarkable artwork. Bold slashes of color seemed to leap from the walls. Sculptures sat on every surface – sinuous clay forms, polished driftwood carvings, and lots of beaten metal contraptions that looked like they moved. The window was crowded with chimes and hanging sculptures. Even her wrap dress was loud and vivacious – bright colored squares like a Mondrian painting. Lime green triangles dangled from her ears and a matching bracelet circled her wrist. My eyes reacted to the color and light, dancing their own patterns across my vision.

The woman tapped a button on her keyboard to mute her computer, which was belting out a list of email addresses in a robotic voice. "Welcome, welcome," she said, clasped her hands together and staring at a spot just to the left of Quoth.

It was then that I realized this woman was blind.

CHAPTER TWENTY-FOUR

"*I*'m Marjorie Hansen, the course facilitator, and I'm so happy to have you here," she said, gesturing to a couple of paint-splattered chairs opposite her desk. "Please, sit down. Would you like some tea?"

I nodded, then realized that was stupid. "Yes, please."

I expected Mrs. Anders to leave the room in order to fetch tea, but she sat down beside us. Marjorie turned to a small tea tray beside her desk and flicked on a kettle. She gathered chipped cups in bright colors and arranged them on the tray, asking us each for our preference. I noticed braille labels on her tea tins and a small device next to the teaspoons.

Beside her computer were a sloped drafting table and a flat surface stacked with blocks of clay and sculpting tools. Quoth looked over at me, his eyes wide with concern. He squeezed my fingers, checking I was all right. I squeezed back, more fascinated than triggered. Marjorie was the first blind person I'd met apart from Mr. Simson – my father. "Did you create the artwork on the walls, Marjorie?" I asked.

"Most of it," she replied. "My work is all about movement. I like art that is constantly changing, never static. That's why I took this corner office – I can open the windows and let in the breeze. On a windy day, it sounds like a heavy metal band in here with all the clanging and clattering."

I laughed. "I believe it."

"Tell me, what are your names?"

"I'm Mina."

"And I'm Allan," Quoth said.

"Are you both interested in enrolling in one of our art degrees?"

"I am." Quoth's voice rang like music. He sounded so light and happy, it made my heart soar. "Mina's come along to support me, although I'm hoping to convince her to join, as well. She's incredibly creative."

The kettle boiled. Marjorie attached the small device to the top of a cup and poured the water. When the level reached just below the brim, the device emitted a loud beep, and she set it aside and handed the cup to me.

"We'll let Mina make up her own mind," she said, sitting back and sipping her own cup. "Tell me about your work, Allan."

Quoth reached for his portfolio, but then must've remembered that was pointless. Instead, he described some of his recent pieces, the things he enjoyed to paint, what he felt like with a brush in his hands, and the artists whose work he admired. It was the most words I'd ever heard him speak to anyone who wasn't me. Something about this woman put him at ease.

She put me at ease, too. From the way she moved about her crowded office, picking up pieces of work to show him or finding books on her shelf for him to read, it was obvious she felt completely at home there. She knew where everything was kept in that organized chaos. I had so many questions I wanted to ask her – about the device attached to her computer that was reading the screen to her, about the little tool she used to measure the water level in the tea, about how she chose which colors to paint even when she couldn't see them.

Instead, I watched her. This was a successful, capable woman making a career for herself not only as an artist but as a course facilitator. And she was blind. Majorie was exactly the kind of person I wanted to be. I was desperate to know her story, how she'd found the peace she wore like a perfectly-fitted dress. But I couldn't find the words. I sat, numb and in awe, as Quoth and Marjorie fell into an easy conversation about Mondrian's use of form and geometry.

"Even my guide dog is named after him." Majorie nudged her dog, Mondrian, awake so we could pet him. "I didn't get to name him. People who donate to the charity that trains the dogs give them their names. Each litter is assigned a letter of the alphabet and all the dogs in that litter must have names starting with that letter. Each dog lives with a volunteer for the first year of their life, then they have twenty-six weeks of specialist training before they're paired with an owner. When I was paired with Mondrian I thought, ah, it's fate." Marjorie scratched behind his ears. "And here we are, five years later, and we're each other's family."

Mondrian rolled over so I could scratch his stomach, his tongue lolling out with bliss. I thought about how much fun it would be to have a puppy around the shop, especially if it was as gentle and helpful as Mondrian.

When we left Marjorie's office twenty minutes later, I felt like I was floating. Meeting her had given me a gift I never expected. My mind reeled with ideas, of new things I could do with the bookshop, of ways I could continue to be creative even when I couldn't see.

At the front desk, Mrs. Anders handed up both a thick envelope of enrollment material and a course prospectus. "I hope I'll be seeing both of you back here soon," she said, giving me a meaningful look.

"You never know," I replied.

As soon as we were outside and walking toward the bus stop, I asked Quoth the question that had been nagging me ever since we entered her room. "Did you know about Marjorie when you asked me to come here?"

"I swear I didn't—" Quoth grabbed my arm. "Mina, it's Brian Letterman."

I followed his gaze up ahead, where a man walked along the path in front of us, heading toward the administration building. His hand was to his ear, presumably holding a phone, because I could hear him muttering into it. From this distance, I couldn't recognize him, but if Quoth said it was the publisher, I believed him.

"He said he taught a publishing course here," I remembered. "I bet it's on this same campus. Let's follow him."

If I'd been with Morrie, he'd already have dived into the bushes, his phone ready to record what he heard. But I was with Quoth, who immediately averted his eyes. "It's a private conversation. I don't think we should—"

"Nonsense," I hissed, dragging Quoth into the bushes and digging out my phone to record what we heard. I had learned far too much from James Moriarty. "I'm not going to let this murder destroy the shop. Brian Letterman is one of our suspects, and we could learn some valuable information. Now shhhh."

I held my phone up near the top of the bush just as Brian walked past. "...I realize that, *darling*, but I can't exactly do anything while the police are snooping around." Brian's voice was thick with disdain. He moved toward the bushes, right above our heads. *Excellent, excellent.* "As soon as things calm down, I'll be able to move on Danny's backlist."

He must be talking about Danny's books.

Brian continued. "Exactly, luv... according to the lawyer, he didn't finish the paperwork. Penny would have to begin negotiations all over again, and in the meantime, I can release as many new editions as I like. Thanks to his untimely death, they'll fly off the shelves. Even if we do eventually give the rights back to Penny, we'll make a killing in the meantime. It serves that greedy bastard right for trying to self-publish and keep all the royalties for himself. I'm the reason his career is what it is, and he tried to cut me out? Look where that got him, aye?"

Okay, so that's chilling.

"...our money troubles will be over, but only if we keep our heads screwed on. That means going to the funeral in a black dress that actually covers your tits and not sleeping with anyone for an hour or opening your mouth. Can you manage that, luv?"

The voice on the other end started yelling. Brian cut off the call and shoved the phone into his pocket.

"What does all that mean?" Quoth asked.

"It sounds like Danny was going to revoke his rights to his backlist so he could self publish all his books himself," I whispered. "That would cut Brian out from Danny's royalties. Only, the paperwork wasn't finished before Danny died, which means that Brian will continue to gain from Danny's estate until Penny gets around to reverting them herself..."

"But wouldn't that mean—"

"That Brian had a major financial incentive to kill Danny?" I watched the man walk out into the parking lot with a cold heart. "Yes, yes it does."

CHAPTER TWENTY-FIVE

"You're right." Morrie looked up from his computer. "Brian Letterman is in a world of financial trouble. He's living off credit cards, his business is in the toilet, and his authors are being slammed in the reviews. Add to that, his wife has an addiction to designer handbags and expensive vacations. The only books Brian's making any profit on are Danny's. I bet he was counting on the royalties from Danny's memoir to make things right again, but if Danny self-publishes, Brian gets nothing."

"We have to go to the police," I said.

"We could do that," Morrie said. "It's not enough evidence to convict Brian. Hayes and Wilson probably have this same information, and they've still got Beverly Ingram in custody. In the meantime, the shop will continue to be deserted, and you'll continue to withhold your sexual favors until my entire body turns as blue as my balls—"

"We didn't have sex for *one night* because I had to go to bed early. You'll live. I take it you have a better idea?"

"Of course I do. Every idea I have is naturally superior. Brian's wife is the only other person who knew about his business failing or this case between him and Danny. If anyone could dish the dirt on what might turn a mild-mannered publisher into a cold-hearted killer, it would be her. All we have to do is convince Amanda Letterman to give us information that we can use. I'm willing to bet my considerable fortune of ill-gotten gold bullion that she didn't tell the police the whole truth."

"And how do you intend to do that?" My mind flashed back to Morrie's flirtation with Miranda at Mum's party.

"I'm not going to do it." Morrie grinned. "You saw for yourself at the party. Amanda's taste tends more toward the rugged, unkempt man than a fine specimen like myself. Heathcliff the Desirable is going to do the convincing."

~

"*Y*ou owe me," Heathcliff muttered as I shoved him toward the hotel's ornate double doors.

"I've already agreed to man the shop for the next two weeks," I said. "That's two weeks where you get to lounge around in front of the fireplace upstairs, reading books and stroking my grandmother's back without a single customer in sight. What more do you want from me?"

"You know," Heathcliff growled, his eyes darkening with lust. A deep purr rumbled in my belly.

"Hey, you two, simmer down. Heathcliff needs to save that sexual appetite for our target. Get in there, tiger." Morrie gave him a harder shove. Heathcliff grunted in protest, but he did push his way inside.

"No closets!" I yelled after him, thinking about the last time I'd seen Amanda.

Morrie had downloaded Amanda's calendar from her cloud account and discovered she took tea at the Argleton Arms Hotel every second Tuesday. I booked a table for Heathcliff and then spent a couple of hours schooling him on the correct tea etiquette (apparently a thing Nelly Dean never thought to teach him). Morrie dressed him in what he declared to be a style of passable gentility. Then he ruined it all by trying to shave Heathcliff, and Quoth had to swoop in to break up the ensuing fistfight. It had all been worth it, for Heathcliff sauntered up to the door looking more the gentleman than I'd ever seen him before. In fact, he looked bloody gorgeous, with his hair combed and his clothing fresh and unrumpled—

"Pick your jaw off the footpath, woman," Morrie commanded me as Heathcliff disappeared into the restaurant. "He may look the part, but the poxy bastard refused to wear a wire, so we're just going to have to sit here and wait for him to come back. Hopefully, he remembers everything she tells him because he doesn't have a photographic memory like I do—"

"He'll be fine, and I don't mind sitting here with you." I took his hand. "It gives us a chance to talk."

"What do you want to talk about? I am an expert on several subjects, including bank safe construction, biological warfare, the best places in London to buy a cronut…"

"Biological warfare…" *Nope, I'm just not going to ask.* "Morrie, something's going on with you. Does it have to do with what we talked about that night at Baddesley Hall?"

"Nothing whatsoever." Morrie's ice eyes darted toward the hotel doors.

"It's just that the way you looked at Heathcliff the other night…"

"Oh, that." Morrie turned his head away. "That's been simmering for some time."

"It has?" I knew that Morrie was bi, but I'd never noticed any particular spark between him and Heathcliff. Although come to think of it, their constant bickering did have an air of sexual tension to it.

"For me." Morrie stared at a spot over my shoulder. "When I first ended up in this world, I was reeling from Holmes' betrayal.

And here was this guy who didn't give a fuck what anyone thought of him. He took me in, gave me a room in the shop, allowed me to drink myself into a stupor in front of the fireplace when I found out that I'd never see Holmes again. His nihilism was the perfect antidote to my own rage. I wanted to fall into that scraggly, filthy beard and drown myself. I read *Wuthering Heights* over and over and dreamed that he might one day turn that obsessive devotion to me."

"You didn't," I scoffed.

"Possibly that's a slight exaggeration, but I *do* fancy him. All that barely-concealed rage… it's delicious. I made a move once, when we were both drunk. He nearly tossed me out the upstairs window." Morrie smiled ruefully. "Now that we're naked together on a regular basis, with you, I'm feeling things, stirrings. There's still something unspoken between us."

"So, just Heathcliff, then? Not Quoth?" I hated the idea of Quoth being left out, although that was partly for selfish reasons.

"Quoth is a fucking beautiful specimen of humanity. Don't tell him I said that. But he's far too wholesome for me. Besides, his heart is spoken for. Quoth loves you with a love that is more than love, the kind of love the winged seraphs of heaven must covet. I can't compete with that. But Heathcliff… there's enough of that majestic creature to go around. So yes, I'm debating making a move next time we three are *in flagrante delicto*. Seizing the moment, carpe diem, that sort of thing. You don't mind, do you?"

"Mind that you fancy Heathcliff?" I smiled. "Hell no. I think that's hot as fuck."

Morrie's grin could have melted the polar ice, it was that fucking beautiful.

I held up a hand. "But… I *do* mind that you don't tell me these things. You should have told me this before today. We can't have a relationship if you don't tell me things."

"I do tell you things. I tell you every brilliant thought that enters my head."

"That's true. You talk a lot, but it's mostly bullshit. I want to know about *you*, Morrie. Who you are underneath all the posturing and bravado. Do you understand?"

Morrie nodded, his eyes fixed on the top of his shiny brogues.

"So, with that in mind, is there anything else you want to tell me? Anything at all?"

Morrie looked up at me. The wounded expression had gone from his face, replaced with his usual half-smirk. He studied me, his smirk turning up at the corners as a blush crept along my cheeks.

"What?" I demanded.

"Suspicion isn't a good color on you, gorgeous."

"Don't act innocent. You're up to something. What've you done?"

"I've done everything I needed to, and more than I hoped."

"Oh, that's not cryptic at all."

Morrie sighed. "I was hoping to tell you about it once I'd cracked the entire puzzle. But since you insist, I found out something. About Dracula."

"What? How?"

The ice in Morrie's eyes was hard as flint. Unease flickered in my gut. Whatever Morrie discovered had turned him serious, which I knew from experience was never a good sign. "I wrote an algorithm last night to search through news sites across the world. It identifies specific parameters – namely, the types of crimes that a vampire might commit. Blood-lettings, beheadings, that sort of thing. Then it verifies the stories across multiple sources and creates a map of space and time that might tell us something about his movements."

"That sounds like a pretty complex algorithm to write in a single evening."

"Well, it was *my* creation," Morrie smiled. He could never ever miss an opportunity to show off. "Besides, I've had a lot of time on my hands lately. The only thing I haven't had nearly enough of is your body, which is a shame, because I think another orgasm or ten might do you good, eliminate all this suspicion and negativity."

"If I want to eliminate negativity, I'll go to Sylvia's shop for some banishing incense. What did this algorithm tell you?"

"Look for yourself." Morrie handed me his phone.

I swiped across the screen, viewing a complex timeline of events. The trail started over a year ago, around the time Heathcliff first appeared at the shop. There was a single newspaper clipping from the *Argleton Gazette*, reporting a Barchester arboretum was broken into. The thieves made off with three large cartons containing rare orchids from the Carpathian mountains encased in their natural soil.

"I remember this from the novel. Dracula was trying to move from Transylvania to England, in order to find new blood and spread his curse. To regenerate his powers, he transported fifty boxes of Transylvanian earth." My hands trembled as I swiped to the next entry in Morrie's program. "If he found himself already here in England, all he needs is the dirt from his homeland to regain his strength and regenerative powers."

"Precisely why he stole only three specimens, all brought from Romania," Morrie said. "He's starting small."

After a few months of no activity, the timeline expanded rapidly, with locations popping up all over the map. More articles revealed thefts from private gardens, rare plant displays, anywhere with plants transported from Romania. No one seemed to have connected the crimes, and there were few clues and no arrests. 'It's as if the burglars flew over the fence, like a bird or a bat,' one reporter said.

But the burglaries weren't what made me gasp. Notices of strange deaths, missing people, bodies found in the woods, blood smeared on the door of a church. When looked at individually, it was all business as usual given Britain's high crime rate. But put together like this and connected with the dirt burglaries...

It's him. Count Dracula. He's repeating the story from his novel. Which means that as soon as he's powerful enough... he won't stop until the rivers run red with innocent blood.

"What are these dotted lines?" I asked, pointing to the map.

"Those connect real estate sales in the areas where the dirt was stolen. I figured that if Dracula is following the plan from his book, he'll be acquiring property in England to house his graves. I've been tracing property sales in the areas around where the deaths and burglaries are happening, but so far I haven't found a convincing pattern that will point conclusively to any particular addresses. It would help if I knew whether his tastes ran to Victorian semi-detached or modernist apartments."

I threw my arms around Morrie's neck. "This *is* genius. You've done half the work, Morrie. With this map, we can trace Dracula's movements. It looks as if he's moving through the Midlands and up the country. It will only take a bit of sleuthing to figure out which properties he's purchasing. If I remember rightly from the book, to destroy him we simply have to find all his graves and destroy them. Then, if we injure him he won't be able to heal."

"I *am* a genius." Morrie leaned in for a kiss. "Why don't you show me just how clever you think I am?"

I kissed him, because he was indeed very clever, and also because there was the tiniest hint of vulnerability in his voice. Morrie tasted like... like deception and desperation. I pushed down my doubts and lost myself in his lips, his fingers trailing across my cheek, his other hand brushing over my nipple...

"Stop canoodling and get me out of here." Heathcliff barreled through us, tearing my lips from Morrie's. He stalked down the street toward the green. Morrie and I scrambled to our feet and rushed after him.

I jogged alongside him as he stalked across the green, heading to Butcher Street like his life depended on it. "How'd it go?"

"That woman is a weapon of mass destruction," Heathcliff said. He reached up and rubbed a stain on his collar.

"Is that... lipstick?" I said.

"You told me to be convincing," he growled. "I couldn't exactly tell her to get off me."

Did I want to know what happened in there? My mind flashed back to Danny and Amanda in the closet at Nevermore. *Nope, I definitely don't want to know.*

"So, did you find out anything?"

"I've confirmed what we already knew. Brian was deep in debt. Danny was taking him to court to get his rights reverted on his books so he could self-publish them. If Danny won, Brian would be ruined. It sounds as if Danny's announcement about his memoirs was the icing on the cake." Heathcliff rubbed at another lipstick stain on his cuff. "What's more, Amanda was helping Danny with his case, by giving him documents showing Brian hadn't been paying all his royalties. Apparently Amanda was convinced Danny was going to leave Penny so the two of them could run off together. She was showing off a diamond necklace Danny gave her."

"Wow. Anything else?"

"Yes. Amanda does a bit of admin work for her husband at the publishing house. She said that the woman, Beverly, contacted her a few days ago, pretending to be a literary agent scouting for new talent. She asked lots of questions about Danny's schedule. Amanda sent her a free ticket to the event and the draft of Danny's memoir she found on Brian's hard drive. I think she was trying to stir up trouble."

"Interesting. Beverly said she'd seen the posters of the event around town and purchased the ticket herself," Morrie said.

"Exactly." Heathcliff glowered. "So if she's so innocent, why did she lie?"

CHAPTER TWENTY-SIX

"*W*hy didn't you tell me Amanda gave you a free ticket?" I asked.

Beverly paced the length of her cell, wringing her hands. "Because I thought it would make me look more guilty, okay? Like I'd been stalking Danny for weeks, waiting for the perfect chance to strike."

"And were you?"

She nodded grimly. "Ever since his new book came out. I can't explain it – it made me crazy. Seeing him on TV or Youtube videos talking about it, reading passages about garroting, taking gleeful pleasure in what he put his character through. All I wanted to do was write to the venues and request they cancel the events. I know it's bloody pointless, but the media already made it clear they're not interested and I had to try *something*. It was her who encouraged me to go along and stir up a fuss."

"Amanda? How come?"

"How should I know?" Beverly shrugged. "She said she'd give me the ticket and Danny's manuscript if I went and said my piece and made sure everyone was looking. As if I'd want to read a memoir that was full of lifes! I deleted the file right away."

"But you decided to go to the event?"

Beverly nodded. "Amanda said if I should yell at anyone, it should be her husband the publisher – he was the one who put the book out. She even said I should say that to the TV cameras if I saw any. Well, I hardly got the chance before your lug of a colleague kicked me out, but I had a right go at him outside. That's all I can tell you. Now, get out of here. They're about to serve breakfast and I don't want to eat the medieval gruel that passes for food in here in front of you."

~

*A*s soon as I walked through the door to the flat, Jo thrust a wine glass into my hand. "Wow, it's as if you have magical mind-reading powers," I smiled as I took a sip. After the day I had, I needed wine in an IV.

"I've got to try and make up for the biblical plague," Jo smiled back. "And I've made Bolognese, too."

A delicious tomatoey, garlicky smell wafted from the kitchen. "You're forgiven."

I slid into the table while Jo bustled around, piling generous servings of pasta and Bolognese sauce onto plates and setting out garlic bread and parmesan. "What did you get up to today?"

I shrugged. "Oh, you know… the usual."

"Shelving books, sticking your nose in police business, shagging your hot boyfriends, that kind of thing?"

"Exactly. Boring stuff, unlike your day. You did the autopsy on Danny Sledge," I said nonchalantly. "Find anything interesting?"

"Mina Wilde, you're not using me to get confidential information on a murder victim in order to further your own ends."

I smiled sweetly. "I'm just chatting with my flatmate about her day, trying to show an interest in her work."

"Sure." Sarcasm dripped from Jo's voice. She set down her

wine glass and steepled her fingers. "However, I'm a sucker, because I'm *dying* to talk to someone about it."

I sprinkled a generous handful of parmesan over my Bolognese and dug in. It tasted even more delicious than it smelled. "Go on, spill."

"Well, as you know, Danny was garroted. The evidence on the body suggested that someone snuck up behind him and wrapped the piece of material around his throat. But he didn't die from asphyxiation as I'd first thought. The killer used the murder weapon to lift Danny off his feet, and the pressure was enough to sever his carotid artery. He died from bleeding internally."

I shuddered. "That sounds brutal."

"It is. The person who did it would have to be relatively strong. We don't like to make assumptions these days, but it's most likely we're looking at a male assailant."

"So Mrs. Ingram is free, then?"

Jo shook her head. "The scarf you found was the murder weapon, all right. Numerous witnesses claimed to have seen that scarf around Beverly's neck at the reading the night before, including me. And it also happened to be the same scarf used to kill Beverly's daughter all those years ago. I found traces of Abigail's blood that match her file, and the description of the scarf is the same – it was leopard-print."

"What did Beverly say to that?" *I can't believe she didn't mention this to me.*

"She said she had no idea where that scarf came from. She admitted she wore a leopard-print scarf, but it wasn't her daughter's. As far as she knew, the police still had that. She said she purchased hers from the charity store a week ago, in the hope it would make Danny remember."

"But that can't be true. Was there a mix-up somehow? How else would the scarf have got out?"

"Nope. According to their records, Beverly checked that scarf out along with some of Abigail's other belongings fifteen years ago."

Shit. This was sounding worse and worse. "And there's no way to prove the murder weapon was the same scarf Beverly wore that night."

"She says she threw it at Brian Letterman at the party. When Hayes questioned him, he said that it dropped on the ground and he didn't pick it up. We've got officers emptying rubbish bins in case some well-meaning citizen tossed it out, but more likely than not it's lost forever, or…"

I finished. "…or, Beverly Ingram is lying, and she went back early that morning with Abigail's scarf and killed Danny Sledge."

CHAPTER TWENTY-SEVEN

"*I* just don't believe it," I said.

In what felt like a way too common occurrence, the four of us were slumped around the empty bookshop, discussing a murder. I sat behind the desk, a ledger open in front of me as if the very presence of our dwindling accounts might somehow miraculously will a customer to show up. Morrie perched on the edge of the velvet chair, his body trembling with nervous energy. Heathcliff paced between the shelves, unsure of what to do with himself now that I'd all but usurped his chair. Quoth perched on the chandelier, chewing on a stash of cranberries he'd secreted away up there.

"What's not to believe?" Heathcliff grumbled. "She killed the guy with her daughter's scarf in revenge for her murder."

"But if you're going to kill someone, why show off the murder weapon to a hundred people the night before? And besides, Beverly knows Danny couldn't have done it. He was in a jail cell at the time."

"Then she did it because he wrote *The Somerset Strangler*," Morrie piped up. "She said so herself – Danny got rich off Abigail's death, and Beverly couldn't abide it."

"How could he get rich off that guff?" Heathcliff picked up a copy of Danny's book and slammed it down on the counter. "Its ineptitudes are so many in number that to account for them would produce a tome more than double its size. And I only read the first page. How anyone could finish the thing is a mystery to me."

But he said he liked it the other day, I remembered. Heathcliff was *trying* to pick a fight with Morrie.

"Actually, *I* read it on the train down to London." Morrie held up his phone. "It's good, though brutal as hell. It won't help us much because in it the coroner was the murderer, and we know Jo's no killer. I was looking forward to discussing it with you all but it appears no one else is as dedicated to solving this murder as I am."

"You read that on your *phone?*" Heathcliff glowered, his hands balled into fists.

"Yeah, I did." Morrie rose to his feet and waved the phone in Heathcliff's face. "I made the text nice and large, held it in one hand, and scrolled with my finger while sipping my espresso in the other."

Okay, *now* I was picking up on the sexual tension. Heathcliff's nostrils flared and his shoulders tensed as he stared down Morrie, who met his simmering rage with his signature smirk. As the two of them faced off against each other, the whole room sizzled, like the air between them might burst into flames at any moment.

I leaned forward, my heart leaping into my chest even as heat pooled in my belly. *I should break them up before Heathcliff punches Morrie.*

But I didn't move.

"You didn't buy a copy from the bookshop," Heathcliff boomed. "The bookshop that's housed you and your criminal activities when you had nowhere else to go. The bookshop that you could save in a heartbeat just by writing a cheque but are too selfish to do so. No, instead you betray us all by purchasing from The-Store-That-Shall-Not-Be-Named and then come back here to rub it in my face—"

"At least you're not over-dramatic about it." Morrie patted his shoulder. "I read a book. It's not a crime. Calm down, mate. Don't burst a blood vessel."

Heathcliff's already dark skin burned a deeper shade. I thought I could see steam coming out of his ears.

Shouldn't you be breaking this up? Quoth asked inside my head.

Not this time.

"You don't take anything seriously," Heathcliff growled, this time. "Everything is a bloody joke to you. I know you don't give a fuck about me or Quoth, but this is Mina's life and it's about to be taken away from her and you don't care—"

"I *do* care. I just don't see how moping and raging will actually fix things. Your problem is that you're too serious." Morrie grinned. "Lighten up, mate. Have some fun. Here, I'll show you."

And he leaned forward and kissed Heathcliff square on the lips.

CHAPTER TWENTY-EIGHT

"*C*roak?" Quoth quipped, transfixed by the sight of them.

I froze, my body locked in a rage of lust as Morrie's lips teased Heathcliff with a featherlight touch. Heathcliff's eyes narrowed, and he raised his fist. I forced myself from my chair, thinking that he was going to punch Morrie.

Instead, he wrapped his huge hand around the back of Morrie's head and pushed his face hard against his. Their tongues twined together, their mouths smashing together in a hot, violent, punishing kiss.

Well, well, well, Quoth said.

You don't sound surprised, I thought.

Oh, I've seen it for a long time. Honestly, I thought it would happen much sooner. You okay with it?

Better than okay. An ache rose between my legs as I watched those two powerful men fight their battle with tongues and lips, laying bare something that had gone unspoken for so long.

With a gasp, Heathcliff broke free of whatever spell Morrie had him under. He planted his hands on Morrie's shoulders and shoved him. Hard.

Morrie sailed across the room and slammed into the Classical

Studies shelves. He crashed to the floor, and a cascade of hard-cover volumes poured over him. He winced as Thucydides smashed into the side of his face.

"Get out," Heathcliff growled, pointing to the door.

"But—"

"I said, *get out*. I don't want to see your fucking face right now."

"Heathcliff—" I reached for him, but he yanked his arm away.

"Don't anyone fucking touch me," he yelled, storming upstairs.

My chest tightened. I rushed to Morrie's side, but he was already scrambling to his feet, shoving the books aside as he fled for the hallway. His face was bone white. "I… I'd better go."

"Wait, we should talk about this." I glanced up at the staircase, but Heathcliff had already disappeared. "I'm sure when Heathcliff calms down he'll realize—"

"No," Morrie said. "I can't be here with him. Not now. I have to—"

The front door slammed on its hinges. "Hello, pitiful humans. Did you miss me?"

Grimalkin strode into the shop like she expected a string quartet to announce her presence. She wore a figure-hugging dress in a slinky fabric that I could tell from the cut was a designer piece. Under one arm, she had a series of totes from expensive brands and under the other, she clutched a brown paper bag from The Third Wheel, Argleton's super expensive artisan cheesemaker. The corner of a carton of artisanal heavy cream jabbed into my thigh as she shoved her way between us, heading for the main room.

"I'm not sure 'missed' is the correct word." I grabbed Morrie's hand and yanked him after me. "What is all this stuff?"

"Essentials. Now that I have opposable thumbs again, I intend to indulge myself in the manner to which I intend to become accustomed." Grimalkin set her bags down on the floor. She dug around in the cheese bag and pulled out a wheel of Camembert, which she proceeded to unwrap with gusto.

"But... you're a cat. You don't have a bank account. How did you afford all this?"

She pulled a credit card out of her cleavage and tossed it to Morrie. "I've seen him use that many times to obtain items he wanted. I figured he wouldn't mind if I borrowed it to do the same."

The expression on Morrie's face suggested that he did in fact mind, very much. "H-h-how much did you spend?"

"I didn't really look," Grimalkin said sweetly as she took an enormous bite out of the cheese wheel. "Currency has little meaning to a cat."

"You sure you don't want some crackers with that?" Quoth asked. He'd come down from the chandelier and was now sitting in all his naked glory on the edge of the table. "Perhaps a bit of quince paste?"

"Hardly." Grimalkin took another enormous bite, her eyes closed in bliss. A ring of red lipstick stained the cheese rind.

"You're not a cat anymore," I reminded her, but then something occurred to me. "So you can't transform between your human and cat forms the way Quoth can? You're stuck as a human now, forever?"

"I tried transforming several times upon my prowlings, and it didn't seem to work. No matter how hard I concentrate, I cannot—"

Her words cut off into a shriek of surprise as whiskers sprouted from her cheeks. She dropped the cheese as her lithe fingers sprouted fur and pads to form a paw. Her knees cracked against the floor as she toppled forward, her body contorting, her back arching and dark fur sprouting from her smooth skin.

A moment later, a familiar mottled cat stepped out of a rumpled designer dress and strutted across the floor to nibble the cheese. Quoth burst out laughing.

In a flash, Grimalkin the woman appeared again. She shook out her hair and tested her fingers, curling them over and scraping her long fingernails through thin air.

"Hmmm," she purred. "It appears that I can shift forms, after all. Likely, the shifting is tied to proximity to the spring that delivers the waters of Meles."

"Where is this spring?" I asked. "If it's under the house, how come we've never had drainage issues?"

"Oh, Homer took care of that decades ago." She waved her hand. "If you go down to the basement, you'll see where it's been diverted. Just don't expect me to show up. It's damp down there. I don't do damp."

"How do you know all this stuff? About the spring and my father's comings and goings, and about Dracula?"

Ignoring my question, Grimalkin picked a volume off the table and opened its pages. "Books have a magic of their own. Did you know that? Especially when the tales inside are woven by a master writer. You have felt that all your life, dear. That's why you spent your youth in this very shop. You were drawn to the waters of Meles and to the magic of words and stories, as was your father before you. But stories can play their own tricks. Certain books... certain characters... they have a magic of their own. And when your father passed his seed to you, he diluted his own magic, weakening the barrier between this world and the world of books. If a character is strong enough – if he or she has been so damaged that they wish to leave their story, to cut it off before it has come to its full conclusion – they can fall through the barrier and become real."

I blanched, reeling at her words. "Are you saying that the reason fictional characters come to life in this shop is because of *me?*"

Grimalkin took another bite of cheese, and didn't reply. My hand flew to my pocket, touching my father's letter. This time, it didn't do much to calm my beating heart.

"How do I know you're not lying?" I said. "You've been a cat for several thousand years. You haven't had a conversation with Homer since Poseidon cursed you. So how could you possibly know all these things? "

"Because people, especially lonely people who own bookshops and watch their loved ones from a distance instead of actually telling them the truth, tend to get chatty around cats." Grimalkin stretched out along the sofa under the window and took another bite out of her cheese. "My son was no exception. Even though I *had* spent centuries looking for him, I did wish he'd just shut up sometimes. Cheese?" she held out a crescent of white rind to me. I shook my head. Grimalkin tossed the rind on the ground and cracked open a carton of cream.

Morrie tugged at me. I tightened my grip on his arm. "Don't leave."

"He wants me to go," Morrie said. "I need to go."

"I'm sorry." My heart ached for him. He looked so vulnerable, so dejected.

"What do you have to be sorry about?"

"I should have split you two up sooner. But after our conversation, I wanted to see..."

Morrie sighed. "I'm the one fucking things up here, gorgeous. Don't you worry your clever wee head about me. I'll be fine. Heathcliff will calm down. Things will go back to normal. You'll see. I have a plan."

As he swung his lanky body toward the front door, his shoulders sagged. I had a sinking feeling in my stomach that whatever Morrie was planning, I wasn't going to like it. At all.

❦

*T*hree hours later, I was slumped over the desk, playing chess with Quoth, drinking my third wine of the day, and trying not to think about the fact I might be responsible for

Count Dracula walking the earth, when Heathcliff stomped down the stairs. He watched us from the doorway. I could feel his glower creeping over my skin. It took all of my self-control to ignore him, but I had to. Heathcliff needed to come to terms with things in his own time. If I pushed him, he'd kick me out of the shop next, and I couldn't handle that right now.

"Check," Quoth said, sliding his queen across the board to threaten my king.

"Mina, I'm going out to price a book collection," Heathcliff muttered. "Want to come?"

"Hell yes." I stood up. Acquiring stock from estate collections was a part of the business I hadn't learned much about. At least it would be a welcome distraction from the empty shop, the Dracula fears, the kiss, and just... argh, *everything*. "Quoth's kicking my arse. I could use a distraction."

"Quitting while you're behind?" Quoth grinned, cracking his knuckles. "Smart move. I've been taking lessons from Morrie. I was about to stop going easy on you."

At the mention of Morrie's name, Heathcliff stiffened. I hurriedly grabbed my coat. "Are you okay to mind the shop for us? Remind people that the books on that display table are half-off and—"

"Don't bother." Heathcliff threw open the front door. It slammed against the wall behind, rattling the ancient frame. "No one's coming."

Don't remind me, I thought sourly as I flipped the sign to CLOSED and shut the door behind us. At the rate our accounts were deteriorating, we'd be out of business within the month.

Heathcliff shoved his hands in his pockets and rushed off down the street. I had to jog to catch up with him. A bitter wind rubbed my face raw. I looped my arm around his and jammed my hand in his pocket, which felt super-warm but forced me to keep up with his grueling pace.

"Shouldn't we call a rideshare?"

"Nope. The call is local. It's four blocks this way."

"How will we get the boxes back to the shop?" I asked.

"We make a couple of trips."

My arms already ached with the thought of it. "I think you've overestimated how much I can carry. You should buy a van or something, then you can make trips whenever you need to."

"I don't want a car," he muttered. "I hate that no one goes anywhere on foot anymore."

Heathcliff spent his youth rambling over the moors. He felt most at home in wild places, cloaking himself in mists as he ducked along sough and beck, clambered over rocky crags, and skirted the edges of the deadly mires. Foul weather like this was his jam.

Not mine, though. I wished I'd thought to bring my phone. "Good. That's four blocks where we can talk about what happened."

Heathcliff said nothing.

"You didn't really kick Morrie out of the shop, did you? Like, not forever?"

Heathcliff grunted.

"You've got to give me something. He kissed you. You kissed him back. What are you feeling right now? I'm dying here."

"I feel like I betrayed you, that's how I feel."

"That's not true."

"It is true. I promised my heart to you, Mina. To you and you alone. Morrie had no right to force me to—"

"But you must have some feelings for him. Or you wouldn't have kissed him back."

"It shut him up for five minutes," Heathcliff growled. "You can't say that's not worthwhile."

I laughed. Heathcliff didn't. "I want you to know that if you and Morrie want to try out this thing, see where it leads, I support you, as long as we discuss it first."

"There's no discussion because it's not happening."

"Tell that to the hottest fucking kiss I've ever had the honor to witness," I said. "You sound like you're telling yourself how to feel, instead of acknowledging what's between you and Morrie—"

"You sound like you been hanging out in the self-help section," Heathcliff shot back. "There's nothing between me and Morrie except a rapidly deteriorating friendship. Morrie didn't mean it, he was just trying to distract us all from the fact that he's a selfish tit. I don't want to discuss it."

"You can't just shut down and ignore your feelings—"

"Thank fuck, we're here," Heathcliff muttered, slamming open a white wooden gate with such force I heard the wood splinter. He stormed up the path ahead of me, not waiting for me to catch up.

The house was a beautiful Victorian gothic with a white lattice porch and freshly painted weatherboards. I noticed a real estate sign on the front lawn with a giant SOLD sticker across it. Shame to leave such a beautiful house. I hoped it was because the owners were going on to a new opportunity and not because of... other reasons.

Heathcliff rapped on the door. A smiling old lady wrapped in a black shawl answered and ushered us inside. "The books are through here," she said. "Both Edward and I are terribly fond of the collection, but of course we can't fit them all on the houseboat."

"Houseboat?"

"Yes!" She was practically bouncing with excitement. It was adorable. "Edward and I never had much money. This big old house took all our savings to maintain. But then along comes Grey Lachlan, offering four times the worth of the property. Well, it was too good a deal to resist."

"Grey Lachlan?" My mouth dropped open in horror. "You know that he's a big developer. He's going to knock this beautiful old house down and build a bunch of modern townhouses."

"Oh, heavens no! We would never have sold if that was the case. Grey has purchased the house for his wife. He said that she was interested in building a hospitality business, and since her Jane Austen Experience ended up blighted by those nasty murders, she thought she might run it out of here. Apparently, there will be themed teas and a ball and all sorts of fancies. It sounds wonderful, and it's nice to know the house will be on proud display while we enjoy our retirement. Well, here are the books." She gestured into a large room with a bay window overlooking the front garden. "I'll bring through the tea things for you."

I stared at the floor-to-ceiling bookshelves with dread. How did Heathcliff possibly imagine we'd carry all these back to the shop? There must've been at least two thousand books stacked on these shelves.

Seemingly undaunted, Heathcliff started removing books from the shelves. With just a glance at the covers, he sorted them into two piles.

"Which pile is the books we're keeping?" I asked him.

"That one." He pointed to the smaller pile, which mostly contained railway books. "Anything about planes, trains, local history, or whisky-tasting goes in this pile. Anything that you wouldn't be caught dead reading on the bus goes in the trash pile. Start in that corner and work your way toward me."

I grabbed books off the shelves and sorted them into three piles. Books to keep, books to leave behind (I couldn't bear to think of any books as 'trash'), books to ask Heathcliff about. The third pile was by far the largest.

By the time we'd finished, we had every book off the shelves, and two small cartons of books to bring back to the shop.

The woman looked disappointed. "Is that all?"

"Yes," Heathcliff said. He opened his wallet and peeled out three twenty-quid notes, which he handed to the lady. "Call the charity shop in Barchester. They'll come to pick up the rest."

"Okay. But what's their number—" But Heathcliff was already heading down the path with one carton of books.

"I'll call them for you if you like." I smiled at the lady. She beamed back. "Thank you so much for letting us take a look at your collection. Enjoy your houseboat!"

"I will. Thank you, dearie." The woman slipped one of Heathcliff's notes into my pocket. "You're much more friendly than that horrid man."

He's not horrid. He's just been kissed by his best friend and doesn't know how to deal with it. But I smiled and accepted the money.

I wanted to try to talk to Heathcliff about Morrie again, but he was so far ahead of me and the books were so heavy that I had to focus all my energy on putting one foot in front of the other. With every step, the weight of everything dragged against my body.

Halfway there, I dropped my box on the side of the road and slumped down beside it. A moment later, Heathcliff was standing over me, frowning.

"Why are you doing? It's freezing out here."

"Yes, it is." I rubbed my hands together under my hoodie. "I've decided I'm just going to sit here and wait for erosion to pull me safely back to the shop's entrance."

"Mina."

"The box is heavy. I'm taking a break. I'll be fine as soon as I can feel my fingers again."

Heathcliff set down his own box, dragged mine on top of his, and hefted both of them into his arms. "Erosion waits for no one," he called out as he took off toward the shop in a brisk pace.

I caught up with him just as he set the boxes down in the hall. "You okay?" he asked.

No, I'm not okay. My life was finally coming together and everything was falling into place and then Danny Sledge and my cat grandmother and Dracula and you and Morrie and fucking Grey Lachlan had to go and throw a spanner in the works. "Why is Grey buying up the town?" I asked.

Heathcliff shrugged.

"I don't like it. Something about it doesn't sit right. He can't get his hands on Nevermore, can he?"

Again, Heathcliff shrugged. "You've seen the accounts. How much longer can we hold on?"

I winced. I'd been hoping he had some magic plan up his sleeve, some secret deal with the bank he was going to pull out at the last minute. But of course, that was more Morrie's style. "Maybe we ask Morrie to bail us out, just this once—"

"I'm not begging Morrie for his money," Heathcliff snapped.

"*All right.* I'm sorry."

"I thought you didn't want to use his coin, anyway, seems as how it undoubtedly comes from the profits of criminal activity?"

"I don't." I buried my hand deeper into his pocket. "I also don't want to lose the shop."

As Heathcliff moved the empty boxes, I noticed a small square of paper laying on the welcome mat. 'To the residents of Nevermore Bookshop' was written in an elegant script. My heart beat faster, and my hand flew to my pocket, where I still kept my father's letter.

But this wasn't my father's handwriting. "Heathcliff, did you see this?"

I handed the envelope to Heathcliff. Frowning, he ran his finger along the seal to break it, unfolding a small square of paper and a newspaper article. He handed the article to me.

I held it up to the light and scanned it. It was an article from the *Argleton Gazette*, dated fifteen years ago. It showed the headline, 'Local teen sentenced on drug charges.' This seventeen-year-old girl, whoever she was, had been in deep trouble after being caught selling to local kids. Because she was still underage, the paper didn't print her name or show her picture, so I had no idea who it was. Abigail? Or someone else?

Weird. Someone wanted us to have this. But who. And why? Is it connected to the drug dealing Danny and Jim used to do? I turned to Heathcliff, who was frowning at the note.

"What's it say?" I asked.

Heathcliff lowered the paper. "It says, 'you've got a date with a funeral.'"

CHAPTER TWENTY-NINE

*D*anny's funeral attracted hundreds of mourners. He was the closest Argleton had to a real celebrity, so everyone wanted to be seen as his close personal friend. As Morrie and I entered the church, heads turned to watch us. My skin prickled from all the eyes on me. I grabbed Morrie and yanked him into the back pew.

"You can't see from back here," Morrie pointed out.

"It's a funeral. I know how it ends," I whispered back. "I just don't think we should sit up the front when Danny was killed in our shop and everyone thinks Nevermore is cursed or whatever. Plus, from back here we can people watch."

"True that." Morrie nodded across the aisle as more people filed into the church. "There's Brian and Amanda. My, they are the picture of marital bliss, aren't they?"

I squinted, but in the dark church filled with black-clad mourners, I couldn't distinguish anyone. "I can't see."

"Brian's shirt is rumpled and he's wearing mismatched socks. Amanda's tits are spilling out of her dress, and she's got on that grotesque necklace Danny bought her. She's also recording something on her phone for her Youtube channel. And look,"

Morrie flipped over the program, which was printed with a full page ad for *The Somerset Strangler*. "Brian's trying to drum up sales."

"Gross. Do you see Penny Sledge anywhere?"

"Yes, she's sitting down the front with Angus. She's the perfect mourning widow, complete with black veil and everything. That purple-haired guy, Jim Mathis, is a couple of rows back, looking very dapper in a 20s cut suit. I might ask him for the name of his tailor."

The service got underway. Instead of hymns, they played a Metallica song. The priest made a vile face as the congregation stood to bow their heads during the guitar solo. Despite myself, I nodded my head along with the drums. Danny may have been a philandering tosser, but he did have excellent taste in music.

After the priest spoke a prayer and made his usual speech about the journey of the immortal soul, Angus got up. He spoke with eloquence about Danny's career, and what it meant to him to have seen Danny turn his life around and share his stories with the world. He even teared up a little toward the end. "I didn't just lose an inspiration. I've lost a dear friend."

Next was Penny. "Danny was a complete wanker with no sense of propriety or decorum. I don't miss his stupid face or his crass jokes or the way he couldn't keep his dick in his pants. I will, however, miss his money. But the proceeds from his estate will buy me a respectable home amongst respectable people in London, and that's as good a legacy as he can hope for."

Wowsers. Danny was a dick, but that was a pretty harsh thing to say at his funeral. I reminded myself that although Angus and Amanda both had alibis for Danny's death, Brian, Penny, and Jim were still unaccounted for, and all three had pretty strong motives for wanting to see Danny dead.

Angus and Brian joined the pallbearers to carry the coffin out. Morrie and I waited until most of the mourners had followed them outside. Even so, when we stood up to join the throng waiting to place flowers on Danny's coffin, I overheard the villagers whispering about us.

"They're from the bookshop where he was murdered, aren't they?"

"It's a bit sick, them showing up like this. They must be raking it in by being the place where the famous author Danny Sledge met his grisly end."

I wish, I thought with annoyance.

"Hmmph. It would be just like that new girl to do that. She's been trying to commercialize the place with events and whisky tastings and such. *Whisky tastings?* At a *bookshop?* I've never heard of anything so crass. Apparently, she's from the estate, which isn't a surprise, now, is it? Those girls are always hungry for money. I've told everyone I know not to set foot in that place. It's despicable."

"No class! I'll tell the ladies at church. We'll boycott."

Great. Just great.

After the service was complete, guests milled around the parking lot in front of the church, drifting into the Sunday School room where tea, coffee, and a spread of food had been set out. I made a beeline for the food, figuring that if I was going to get gossiped about for being a money-grubbing poor girl, I would at least get a free meal out of it.

"Look who Penny's talking to," Morrie nudged me, his hands filled with sausage rolls.

He gestured to the other end of the room, but I couldn't see. "Let's get closer." I touched Morrie's hand and we made our way down the food table. I knocked back three sausage rolls as I shuffled forward. Finally, I was close enough to identify Penny, her head hunched as she talked with a tall, weedy fellow I instantly recognized. Jim Mathis.

Did the two of them know each other? Interesting. I didn't think Danny would have anything to do with Jim after he sold him down the river. So how did Penny know him?

After a few minutes of conversation, Jim held up his phone and indicated he had to make a call. Penny nodded, and Jim disappeared outside.

"Wait here," I said to Morrie, pulling on my coat. "Keep an eye on Penny."

If Heathcliff had been with me today, he'd never have let me go after a criminal like Jim on my own. But Heathcliff wasn't here. He refused to be in the same room as Morrie, so he'd stayed at the shop. Quoth was up in the trees somewhere, but he wouldn't know what was going on. Morrie nodded and inched closer to Penny. I slipped away and followed Jim as he made his way down the side of the church. He paused at the end of a short concrete path, resting his elbow on a stone gatepost. I pressed my back against a pillar, hoping like hell I was invisible behind it.

I dared a look around the corner. Jim was looking away from me. He lit up a cigarette, sucking the smoke into his lungs as he pressed the phone to his ear. "Yes, I'm at the service. Didn't you see me? It was Danny this, Danny that, blah blah blah."

The person on the other end spoke for a while.

"We've got to wait for the right time," Jim said. "There's too much press around. Too much attention. Everyone thinks Danny's a fucking hero. I think we should wait—"

The person on the end was speaking again. I wished like hell I could hear what they were saying.

"Yes, fine. We'll do it your way. I've got to get back." Jim stubbed out the cigarette with his toe. "Don't get your knickers in a twist. You know I always come through. I'll do what needs to be done."

He whirled around and headed toward me. I bent down, muttering to myself under my breath as I scrabbled through the garden. "I think I dropped it here somewhere," I said in a louder voice as he wandered past. He didn't offer any assistance.

I met up with Morrie across the road, and we watched as Danny's coffin was lowered into the ground. I scanned the crowd for Jim, but couldn't see him anywhere in the massive crowd. Refreshments were being served in the Sunday School room. Mourners dawdled in the cemetery, not wanting to appear too eager for free sausage rolls and cream scones on what was supposed to be a somber occasion.

"I hope you discovered something sordid," Morrie said, taking my arm and leading me away from the crowd so we could talk. "I listened to Penny Sledge discuss *ad nauseam* how she'll be revitalizing Danny's backlist now that she has ownership of it. New covers, classier branding. She said she may even hire a ghostwriter to produce 'a more literary series' under his name. The woman is deluded if she thinks Danny's fans want his crime thrillers to turn into introspective bollocks—"

Morrie was cut short by a bloodcurdling scream.

"What was that?" someone cried.

"It came from the Bible Study room!"

Morrie and I rushed toward the entrance of the Sunday School, shoving our way through the confused mourners. Angus and Jim emerged from a second room toward the back of the hall, their faces grave. They blocked the doorway to this room with their bodies.

"Please, everyone step back," Angus said, striding forward and waving his arms in an attempt to drive the crowd back further. "Something horrible has happened. The police are on their way and we don't want anyone to panic—"

I ducked under Angus' arm and stumbled into the room. My own scream froze in my throat.

Brian Letterman lay on the carpet, his body completely still. His hands clasped around his neck, and his glassy eyes bugged out from his contorted face. Around his neck, a gauzy black scarf had been twisted tight.

CHAPTER THIRTY

"He was dragged into the Sunday School room and garroted," Jo explained as she flopped down into a pew at the front of the church, where I and the other main witnesses were gathered while Hayes and Wilson questioned us. "Exactly the same pattern as the last murder, except this time the material was left at the scene." She held up a black, gauzy cloth with a pair of tweezers and slid it into a paper bag. Something about it looked familiar to me, but I couldn't place what it was.

"I've seen that cloth before," I said, touching my father's letter in my pocket. A headache bloomed across my temples. "I just wish I could remember where."

I glanced over to the next pew, where Hayes and Wilson were interviewing Angus Donahue. I strained to listen – as an ex-cop and the first person on the scene after the tea-lady found Brian's body and screamed, Angus probably had some insight.

"As we were all heading across the road to the cemetery, I happened to notice Brian walking into the Sunday school with Jim Mathis. I didn't think much of it at the time. I know Jim's been working as a ghostwriter for Brian's wife."

He has?

"This is the same Amanda you spent the night with at the Argleton Arms?" Hayes said, while Wilson furiously made notes.

"That was just a bit of fun," Angus said. "Amanda's reputation is no secret in our circle, not even from her husband. Brian knew all about it. I think he almost preferred it when she was out with other blokes. It meant she was spending their money, not his."

"And was she sleeping with this Jim Mathis?"

Angus shrugged. "Probably. He was helping her write a trashy erotic novel. My guess is, they were doing practical research for one of the scenes."

Gross.

"You saw Brian and Jim enter the Sunday School," Hayes pressed. "Then what happened?"

"Then I went across the road to the cemetery with the rest of the guests. They should be able to confirm I was by the graveside. I was the first to throw dirt into the grave. I didn't see Brian or Jim again until..." he shrugged again. "Well, you saw."

"Did you notice anything out of the ordinary in the cemetery?" Hayes asked.

"Apart from Penny Sledge gleefully kicking a clot of dirt on top of the coffin, nope. Seemed a normal funeral for me." Angus hung his head. "As normal as it ever feels to lose your best mate."

"Thank you, Angus." Hayes snapped his pad shut and headed over to Jo. "Has your team found anything else?"

"Unfortunately, all those people stomping around in the Sunday School room ruined what little physical evidence there might have been." Jo patted the small box of evidence bags she was labeling in preparation for transport to her lab. "I'll know more once I've processed the body, but I'd say it's obvious the crimes are related."

"If the murderer is the same person who killed Danny, it means Beverly Ingram has to be innocent," I piped up. Hayes frowned.

"Agreed, it does," Jo said. "But I didn't say they were the same person."

"But you said they were related. You think it could be two separate killers?" I asked.

Jo shrugged. "It's not up to me to do the thinking. That's Hayes' job. I just supply the data."

"Correct." Hayes tapped his pad with his pen, frowning at Jo. "And you also shouldn't be sharing private information about our cases with a civilian, especially not a nosy one like Miss Wilde."

I let that dig slide. "Did Wilson tell you I heard Jim Mathis on the phone earlier? He was saying to someone 'we've got to wait for the right time. There's too much press around. I'll do what has to be done,' which sounds a little sinister if you ask me. It sounds like someone put him up to murdering Brian."

"Thank you for the information, Miss Wilde, but no one asked you for your interpretation. In fact, you've been specifically warned to stay out of police investigations—"

"Jim was also the guy that Danny snitched on in order to get a shorter jail sentence," I shot back. "Why would he show up at Danny's funeral, unless it was to cause trouble? I think you've got the wrong person in jail, and Brian's death proves it."

Hayes tapped his phone. "This phone call Jim made... it would have taken place around quarter-past-two?"

"Yeah, that sounds about right."

"The exact same time Beverly Ingram received a phone call at the station?"

Oh. Shite.

"I don't think it was her! Jim made it sound as if the person on the other end was at the funeral. Besides, even if it was Beverly, that doesn't mean anything! All I really heard was them talking about Danny's funeral. It could have been about something completely unrelated."

"Miss Wilde." Hayes' voice was stern. "It sounds to me as if you're trying to insert yourself into official police business."

"No, but I—"

"We're currently very busy interviewing witnesses. DS Wilson has already taken your statement, so you're free to go."

"But—"

Hayes pointed outside. "If you have any further information for us, please speak with DS Wilson."

I glared at him as I collected my things. "You're making a big mistake!" I yelled as Morrie and I left the church. "And I'll prove it!"

~

"*I* can't believe they've still got Beverly in prison!" I cried.

"You have to admit, that phone call does link Beverly and Jim Mathis," Heathcliff said.

"I don't think so. The person Jim was talking to was at the funeral, but wanted to discuss something in private, without anyone overhearing. But even if it was Beverly talking to Jim, why would she want to kill Brian? If she murdered Danny, then surely she got her revenge? And wouldn't she hate Jim because he was also dating Abigail? He could have just as easily been her killer."

"Brian published the book," Heathcliff said. "Beverly was outside at the reading having a spat with him. She wrote him all those letters demanding he pull the book and he refused. She sees him as equally culpable."

Damn. That's a convincing case. No wonder the police still have Beverly in custody. "So Beverly hired Jim Mathis to kill Brian? Even if Jim was motivated by money, I just can't see it..."

"You can't see it because you want that woman to be innocent," Heathcliff pointed out annoyingly.

"You're no use. Where's Morrie? I want to rant to him."

Heathcliff stared at the page. "He's upstairs, at his computer."

I lifted an eyebrow. "Oh really? You allowed him back in the shop?"

"He was scratching on the window. I couldn't concentrate. He's so fucking annoying."

I grinned. "You let him back in the shop."

"He's on probation. One wrong move and he's out on his arse." Heathcliff slammed his book shut and regarded me with his stormy eyes. "Even if he is a fucking majestic kisser."

I grinned from ear to ear as I climbed the staircase to the flat. I found Morrie not at his computer as I expected, but risking life and limb by sitting in Heathcliff's chair, hunched over a scuffed laptop with what looked like tomato sauce smeared across the screen. "What's that? It doesn't look like yours."

"It's not." Morrie didn't even look up from the screen. "This, my dear, is Danny Sledge's laptop."

I slid in beside him. "How did you get that? Isn't that in evidence lockup at the police station?"

"Don't worry about the hows or whys. I'm going to get it back to the precinct tonight." Morrie pounded away on the keys with gloved hands. "In the meantime, I thought we should have a poke around Danny's files."

"What have you found so far?"

"Nothing much. The guy has a search history so sordid it could rival mine, but I put that down to being a crime writer. There are lots of notes, and of course his manuscripts... the only thing I haven't been able to find is the manuscript he was working on."

"His memoir?"

Morrie nodded. "There's a folder for it, but nothing inside the folder. At the reading, Danny said he'd already started working on it, so there should be *something* here. I'm checking back through the logs to see... hmmm, this is interesting."

"What is?" I leaned in close to look at the screen, but all I could see were lines of code.

Morrie pointed to some unintelligible twaddle. "According to this log, Danny had been working on a document in this folder. He also had several PDFs – possibly research material. However, he deleted everything."

"When did Danny delete the files?"

Morrie frowned at the screen. "That doesn't make any sense. According to the log, the deletion occurred on Wednesday, a full day *after* Danny was murdered."

CHAPTER THIRTY-ONE

I stared at the screen, my mind ticking over this latest piece of information. "What you're saying is that either Danny's ghost did it, or someone else accessed Danny's computer."

"They'd have to know Danny's passwords," Morrie said. "They've logged in as Danny. I can't detect any hacking attempts. It had to be someone he trusted."

"And someone who'd have access to his computer in his suite at the Argleton Arms," I added.

Morrie and I turned to each other. "Penny Sledge," we both said at exactly the same time.

"We know there was no love lost between them," Morrie ticked off the facts, his face lighting up with excitement. "Danny's infidelities and other shameless deeds had been well documented in the media. Penny put up with it in order to share in his money, but perhaps when Beverly Ingram walked into the reading, she saw a way that she could finally be rid of him. She knew that Danny was trying to get his rights back and that he stood to make a huge profit from self-publishing. But she didn't know the reversion hadn't gone through yet."

"Yes," I cried. "She watched Beverly throw her scarf at Brian and grabbed it off the street on the way home. She called down to the front desk pretending to be Angus, and snuck out of the hotel. But then, how did she overpower him? Jo said that the killer was most likely a man…"

"Jim Mathis," Morrie said, his eyes glinting. "She hired Jim Mathis, a crook-turned-assassin."

"That's it! She probably met up with Jim that morning, gave him the scarf, and told him to catch up with Danny. But how did she know Jim? Wouldn't he hate her if she was Danny's wife? And it doesn't explain how she could call him at the funeral if you were watching her the whole time."

"She went to the kitchen!" Morrie cried. "While you were gone, she ducked into the kitchen to check the brand of the coffee they used. Apparently, it didn't meet her standards. I couldn't follow her without arousing suspicions. She was only gone a few moments, but it was long enough to make a quick phone call."

"So that's it. Jim called Penny. He was having second thoughts because of the attention on Danny. But she insisted. So Jim came back, lured Brian into the Bible Study room, and garroted him."

"I bet Jim took great pleasure in garroting Danny," Morrie exclaimed, relishing the gory details of the case. "And then turning up to the writer's workshop afterward to gloat over his deed."

"But what's her motive for Brian?"

"He read the manuscript, so he knew the truth about her," I said. "She intended to silence him."

"You're so hot when you're unraveling a sordid murder," Morrie's lips grazed mine. I collapsed against him, allowing the kiss to deepen.

The air around us charged with electricity. Reluctantly, I pulled away and turned back to the computer. "If all this is true, then why delete the memoir? There must've been something in it

Penny didn't want anyone to see. Some evidence that will convict her. Can you retrieve any of it?"

"Doesn't look like it..." Morrie pounded the keys. "No, wait... I can restore an earlier version. It won't have some of his recent edits, but there might be something."

I waited with my heart pounding as Morrie pounded at the keys. His leg jiggled with excitement. A few minutes later, he yelled in triumph. His eyes flickered across the page. "It's a memoir, all right... I can't wait to devour this. Danny Sledge has had a sordid life of criminal misdeeds, just my kind of fella... hang on. I've found something."

Morrie tapped the screen. "Danny's describing a girlfriend of his. 'I met Penny in the summer of that year, what was to be one of the most important years of my life. She was sixteen, but she dressed and talked like she was twenty-five. I was utterly smitten with her airs and graces. Jim was, too. We fought over her, like we fought over all the girls. Unlike Abigail, who didn't want to choose, Penny chose me. I won, haha. Take that, Jimmy!'"

"So Penny met Danny back when he was a crook," I breathed. Suddenly, it came to me. I reached into my pocket for the newspaper article, but it wasn't there. I remembered that I'd read it downstairs yesterday. I'd probably left it on Heathcliff's desk. "I bet you anything that article was about her. And she knew Jimmy, too. She would have recognized him at the event, even if Danny was too distracted to notice—"

Morrie nodded as he kept reading. "It's all here. All about Penny going down for dealing drugs. When she came out of the young offenders institution, Danny had turned over Jim and was going straight. He says Penny's parents were rich toffs who paid a lot of money to keep her name out of the papers and make sure her crime didn't end up on her permanent record."

"That's what was going on here," I breathed. "Penny must've read Danny's memoirs. She knew that if he published it, her secret would be out. You've seen how much she cares about the 'airs and graces.' She'd be mortified if all her literati London friends knew she used to be a drug dealing delinquent. She killed Danny to stop the memoir, and Brian, because he had read it."

"Danny said that he usually showed his work to Angus, as well," Morrie pointed out.

"That means that Angus is in danger, too." I grabbed up my coat and tote bag. Morrie stood up, but I was already running for the door. "Call the police," I cried.

"And where do you think you're going?"

"I've got to go see a woman about a scarf."

CHAPTER THIRTY-TWO

"*I* need that newspaper article," I called out as I clattered down the stairs.

"Hello to you, too." Heathcliff shot back as I rushed into the main room.

"No time for hellos." I shuffled through the stack of papers and paperbacks on the desk. *Where is it?* "I need to find that article and get it to the police."

"It's not here. Someone called for you. About an hour ago."

"Who?"

Heathcliff shrugged. "Dunno. They didn't leave a name. It was a woman."

"Was it Mum?" She'd come home from the hospital yesterday with a bit of a headache but otherwise fine. I'd been intending to go and visit her after work. Hopefully, she hadn't got herself into more trouble, but I knew that was too much to wish for.

Heathcliff shrugged again.

"You're no bloody help." I was searching under the desk when I remembered, I'd taken it home last night to look at, but then Jo and I hit the wine and I'd forgotten about it. Sighing with annoyance, I fished my keys out of my purse.

"I'm going over to the flat," I said. "We know Penny Sledge committed the murders, and the article proves it. Morrie's heading out to watch her, make sure she doesn't murder anyone else. I need you to find Jim Mathis – we think she's hired him to do her killing for her. Or find Angus Donahue – he's going to be the next victim."

Heathcliff stood up. "I'm not leaving your side when there's a murderer out there."

"I'm just going from my flat to the police station. I'll be fine. I'll take Quoth with me if it's really important."

Heathcliff shook his head. "Quoth left to take his application over to the art school. This is the problem when he gets ideas above his station. He's not here when we need him."

"Don't say that! Quoth deserves this." I peered in the corner, where Grimalkin sat on the velvet chair in cat form, delicately washing her anus. "Grimalkin will come with me."

"Meeeow." Grimalkin stretched her neck up and shot me a look that clearly said, 'don't bother me. I'm busy with Important Cat Business.'

Heathcliff frowned at the cat. "What's she going to do if someone comes at you with a garrote?"

"Scratch their eyes out, hopefully." I picked up a protesting Grimalkin and dumped her in my oversized tote bag. "Besides, I'm hardly unprotected if you and Morrie are watching the two murderers. Now, get going! Morrie's hacking Jim's phone right now. He'll come down as soon as he has a location for you."

"I don't like this!" Heathcliff yelled after me as I fled the shop.

"Get Morrie to kiss it better!" I yelled back, slamming the door behind me.

~

a s I jogged toward the flat, Grimalkin howling in protest and swiping at my arm, I dialed Jo's number. "Hey, Jo. Are you busy?"

"Just about to start some analysis on the murder weapon."

"I might be able to save you some time. I remember where I've seen that black cloth before. It's Penny Sledge's mourning veil."

"Really?"

"Yes, really. She was wearing it during the service. Morrie noticed it, and I saw it on her as she walked past me. But when she was giving her statement to Hayes, she wasn't wearing it."

"Hmmmm." Jo said. "That's interesting. Thanks, Mina. I'll tell Hayes."

"Tell him that Penny's the murderer, and I have something that'll prove it. I'm heading home to get it now, and I'll bring it right over to the station," I said.

"Oooh, intrigue. Just don't touch anything on the second shelf down in the fridge. I'm doing an experiment on flesh-eating microbes and if you eat the Cornish pastie, you'll die a terrible, painful death."

"Duly noted."

"Oh, according to the desk sergeant, Beverly was asking about you," Jo said. "I think she really wants to talk to you. Apparently, she used her phone call to ring the bookshop, but I'm guessing Heathcliff answered."

I groaned. That would have been the call Heathcliff got earlier. "I'll see her at the station. It'll be good if someone's there when they let her out, see if she needs any help at home. I don't think she has anyone in her life."

"You're a good person, Mina."

"I try. I'm here now. Got to go." I jogged up the steps and inserted my key into the lock. Last night when I'd come home, I'd set down the newspaper article on the kitchen table. Something about it had been bugging me, but I couldn't put my finger on what it was. Until now.

I rushed through the flat. Ah, yes. There it was, exactly as I remembered it. As I picked up the article and tucked it into my purse, my gaze caught movement out of the corner of my eye.

What's that?

I stepped in front of the fireplace. Instead of the taxidermy monkey and shrunken heads that usually decorated the mantle, someone had placed a row of large bell jars. Each one contained swarms of large, disgusting bugs, all fighting over various lumps of meat and fabric.

Ants, spiders, beetles and...

Yup... those are definitely locusts.

Anger surged inside me. Jo *promised* no more creepy crawlies. Why would she have locusts again after what happened last time?

"That's it." I muttered, shoving the jars of bugs into my tote bag. They clanged against each other. I hoped they wouldn't smash. I'd take them to Jo's lab, which was near the station, and tell her they either had to move, or I would.

"Meoorrrrw!" Grimalkin complained as she batted at the jars.

I locked up and jogged over to the police station. I was surprised to see the duty officer slumped over the counter, sound asleep. I rang the bell in an attempt to wake him, but he didn't stir.

"Sorry, mate, this won't take long. I don't want to hang around with these little critters in my bag." I scribbled my name and details down on the visitor's sheet, so he wouldn't get in trouble, and slipped past him to head to Inspector Hayes' office.

When I poked my head in, I discovered it was empty. They must've been out chasing a lead. I tried Hayes' cell, but it went straight to voicemail. I set the article down on the desk, but it felt weird to just leave it. In fact, the whole station felt weird. It was eerily quiet. *Must be a busy day for crime in Argleton.*

I know. I'll go down to the cells to see Beverly. I'll tell her the good news that I've cleared her name. If Hayes or another officer hasn't returned by the time I get back, I'll leave the article with a note.

I knew my way around the precinct from that one horrible night I was sent to the cells under suspicion of Ashley's murder. I headed down the staircase and along the dank corridor between the cells. The whole place reeked of piss.

"Beverly?" I called out. "It's Mina Wilde. You wanted to talk to me? I've got good news for you. I—"

She stepped toward me, her eyes wide with panic. "Mina, get out of here!"

"But, I have to—"

"Look out!" she cried. "He's right—"

Beverley's cry cut off into a sob as something cold and slippery wrapped around my neck. A raspy voice whispered in my ear. "Hello, Miss Wilde."

CHAPTER THIRTY-THREE

"*D*on't move a muscle, Mina. Or I'll twist this scarf and you'll be a dead woman."

The smooth voice echoed in my ears, impossibly loud, impossible in all ways because... he couldn't be the killer. He had an alibi... *an alibi...*

Morrie read one of Danny's earlier books. He said it was a great story where the killer used a recording to fake an alibi, and Danny got his ideas from...

"Let go of her, Angus." Beverly hissed. "She hasn't done anything. It's me you really want."

"No can do." Angus' voice was calm. "I need to tie up all the loose ends. When Danny told me I couldn't read the memoir, I knew he'd figured out I was the killer. I had to stop him. Brian knew the truth too, so he had to go. And you Bev... you're right. I did come here to finish you off. You're a thorn in my side and you won't stop harping on about that dead daughter of yours! How fortunate that Mina happened to be here as well. Now I'll be able to kill two birds with one stone. Or one scarf, as it were. I've got this one that I picked up from the ground on the night of Danny's reading. That will do nicely. It looks exactly like

Abigail's scarf from back in the day. I'll make it look as though Mina broke you out of jail, and you turned on her, garroting her to death before hanging yourself in your own cell."

His words slipped through the fog in my mind as I struggled for air, but they made no sense. *Angus can't be the killer. He can't...*

Of course. My frenzied mind pulled up all the information we'd uncovered about Abigail's murder. I'd never even thought to suspect Angus because he was a cop... but that put him in the perfect position to try to pin the murder on Danny, and when that hadn't worked because Danny had an alibi, to declare the case unsolved, and *oh Isis...*

Beverly said that DNA evidence had been inconclusive, that Angus had tried his best to find the killer, but there wasn't enough evidence. What if there wasn't enough evidence because Angus was covering his own tracks?

The scarf. Abigail's scarf that the killer used to garrote Danny... Angus must've taken it from the police inventory. He'd kept it as a memento all these years. But why befriend Danny... and why kill Danny now... and Brian and Beverly...

Angus tightened the scarf around my throat. All my thoughts cut off as panic surged through me. My hands scrambled, searching for something, anything. Red welts appeared in front of my eyes, growing larger and punctuated by sparks of flourescent light. My head screamed.

My tote clanked against the bars as Angus lifted me. My fingers closed around something smooth and cold. Glass. The jars!

I tightened my grip. My muscles howled in protest. Even as my mind closed off and my vision blanked, I swung my arm up and slammed the glass jar into Angus' face.

"Aaaaargh!" He screamed, releasing me. I fell to my knees, gasping for air. Angus staggered back, slapping at his skin. In the darkness, I could just make out a trail of red dots marching over his skin.

"Get them off! Get them off!" he yelled, falling to his knees. "It burns!"

"Meeeorrw!" Grimalkin strode over to him, stepping daintily over the bugs, and swiped him across the face with her claws.

My ears rung. I knew I had only moments before I passed out. I fumbled in my bag, trying to get to my phone, but I couldn't find it amongst all the jars. "Grimalkin, get help... find Morrie..." I gasped, every word tearing at my throat. I leaned my cheek against the bars as tiny baby birds danced in circles inside my head.

Everything went black.

CHAPTER THIRTY-FOUR

"*I* can't believe our killer was brought down by fire ants." Morrie leaned over and planted a languid kiss on my cheek. "You really are something, Mina Wilde."

"Don't crowd her!" Heathcliff boomed, shoving Morrie back into the wall.

Morrie brushed himself off and flashed Heathcliff his signature pout. "Such rough treatment from the man who's been hovering over her like a bad smell for the last two days."

"Can you two just hurry up and kiss again," Quoth rolled his eyes. "It'll cheer Mina up."

"I agree with Quoth's suggestion," I said, even though the words tore at my throat. Angus had done some damage to my vocal cords, and I was supposed to be taking it easy for the next few weeks. It was going to be a difficult feat with this lot constantly in my face.

Morrie leaned forward and puckered his lips. Heathcliff tore himself away, flattening his back against the wall. Morrie's mock-hurt expression was so adorable that I burst out laughing, which *really* hurt my throat.

After two days in this hospital I was going a little stir-crazy.

We all were. Heathcliff, Morrie, and Quoth hadn't left my side, taking turns to fall asleep in the hard plastic chair beside my bed while someone stayed on duty at the shop. When visiting hours were over, Quoth hid under my bed and then flew up to perch above the door, watching over me all night.

A nurse poked her head into the room and rolled her eyes at me. "Mina Wilde, you have *another* guest."

I grinned. I had been pretty popular. My room was filled with bouquets from all over the village. Mum had been in every day, covering my arms in Flourish patches which the nurses removed as soon as she left. Beverly had come in to thank me for clearing her name, and brought with her several hideous scarves from the charity shop which I would never ever wear (because they are a) hideous and b) after being nearly garroted to death no way was I wearing a scarf again). Jo came by with a giant chocolate cake made in the shape of a locust. Several villagers had stopped by to thank me for finding the murderer. Richard left me an entire case of cider (which Heathcliff insisted on taking back to the shop 'for safekeeping'). Even Penny Sledge had been in to thank me stiffly for finding her husband's killer. I was glad that I wasn't supposed to talk, so I didn't have to tell her I'd mistakenly convinced myself she was the murderer.

"You're already over the limit," the nurse frowned at the guys and Grimalkin hovering around my bed. "Rules are rules. I'm not letting her in until—"

"Young lady!" A familiar voice barked from the hallway. "I'll have you know I left a rather nubile young Greek god in my hotel room on Santorini in order to visit my friend. I don't care one whit for your rules!"

The door slammed open and Mrs. Ellis bustled inside. The nurse made a 'hrrrmph' noise, but retreated from the room, pulling the door shut behind her.

"Mina, dear." Mrs. Ellis leaned over the bed and planted a

hundred wet kisses on my face. "I'm so glad you're all right. How do you always get yourself into these pickles?"

I smiled at her and managed to croak out, "I think I've learned a few tricks from a certain old lady."

Mrs. Ellis grinned back, then turned to the three guys. "You boys should be watching out for her. You can't just let her run around getting strangled."

"No, we shouldn't," Heathcliff growled. "We should wrap her in cotton and lock her in the shop. It's the only way she'll learn."

"That's true." Mrs. Ellis stepped forward to embrace Heathcliff and Morrie. As she moved toward Quoth, she noticed Grimalkin in human form luxuriating on the one comfortable chair in the corner of the room. "Who's this?"

"I'm Mina's grandmother," Grimalkin simpered.

"Grandmother?" Mrs. Ellis peered at Grimalkin's perfect skin. "Would you care to join my knitting group? The ladies and I would love to hear about your skincare secrets."

Grimalkin looked like she'd rather take a bath with a puppy than endure Mrs. Ellis' knitting group. She stood up and ducked under Mrs. Ellis' outstretched arms. "If you'll excuse me, I think I hear a mouse in the hallway that needs attending to."

Mrs. Ellis settled into Grimalkin's vacated chair. "I had to take two separate flights to get here, and I left behind a distraught Greek pool boy. So I expect a grand tale. Tell me all about the murders."

"It was Angus Donahue, Danny's friend," Morrie explained. "It turns out that he's a bit of a serial killer nutjob. All those years ago, Angus killed Beverly's daughter, as well as another girl in Barchester, and two more a couple of years before that in Stoke-on-Trent where he did his police training. He confessed everything to the police."

"Please, Mr. Moriarty," Mrs. Ellis beckoned for him to continue. "I demand every sordid detail."

"With pleasure," Morrie grinned. "Angus was dating Abigail,

but he didn't like her seeing other guys. He confronted her about it, and she laughed in his face. So he took the leopard-print scarf from her bed, wrapped it around her neck, and squeezed the life out of her. He figured he could pin it on Danny or Jim, so he left the room in a mess and the door open. Only he found out later that another cop had arrested them earlier that night, and they were in the cells at the time. They took DNA from Abigail – evidence from the sexual intercourse she'd had an hour before her death. Only Angus tampered with that evidence, corrupting the results so it wouldn't point to him. Any of his fingerprints at the scene were discounted because he was the lead investigator. He got away with it for all those years.

"When Danny reformed and was looking for a cop to consult with for his books, he met up with Angus. Our killer supplied sordid stories from his past cases, and Danny twisted them into best-selling novels. That is, until Danny pressed Angus for details on the garrotings for his latest novel. Angus, figuring he was safe by now, helped Danny concoct a story that was so clever it could never be true – the story of a coroner who framed a crook for the murders by tampering with evidence. While Danny wrote *The Somerset Strangler*, it occurred to him that details of the story rang a little too true, and that there was one person who absolutely *could* have killed Abigail – Angus.

"When Danny announced he was writing a memoir but that Angus wasn't allowed to read it until it was published, Angus grew worried. He was safe as long as Danny stuck to fiction, but with non-fiction… Danny could be on to him. At the party, he found out Danny had given a copy of the memoir to Brian, but not to him, and his suspicions were confirmed.

"Amanda told him that night how she'd conspired to get Beverly Ingram to come to the event, and that she'd also leaked a copy of the memoir to her. Angus knew Beverly would be reading the book with a fine-toothed comb, looking for evidence to convict a killer. He had to silence them all. And when he saw

Beverly at the party wearing that scarf, he realized this was the perfect chance. That night he picked up Beverly's scarf from the footpath outside the shop, went back to the hotel with Amanda, then pretended to fall asleep until she got annoyed and snuck off to Danny's room, where she was when Danny left in the morning.

"Just after five a.m., Angus rang the front office, put the tape on play, and then snuck out the front of the hotel while Miranda was delivering the towels. Later, he told Amanda he'd corroborate her alibi and say she was with him, so the police wouldn't suspect her as the last person to see Danny alive. In fact, she was the one corroborating *his* alibi.

"Angus then used a tape recording of their lovemaking to create a false alibi and get Miranda away from the front desk so he could sneak out after Danny. He still had the scarf from Abigail's murder, which he'd stolen from the evidence room years ago. He snuck up behind Danny, garroted him, then stole away when he heard us coming down the stairs."

"Impressive," Mrs. Ellis said.

"That is next level genius," Morrie said. "I'll be remembering that one. It was a trick Danny used in one of his books. That's how I figured that out."

"And Brian Letterman?"

"Angus had already deleted the manuscript off Danny's computer before the police searched his room. But he know that Brian had received that early copy. He knew that if he read it, Brian would know Angus murdered Danny, so he garroted Brian before he could talk. It was inconvenient that Beverly Ingram wasn't there to take the blame, but he tried to pin the murder on Jim by claiming he'd seen him walking into the Sunday School room with Brian, even though Jim had that phone call from Amanda, who wanted him to leak chapters of her book on the internet and stir up a social media frenzy. That's why he stole Penny's mourning veil after she took it off to drink her tea. It was all very clever, and of course, no one suspected Angus because he was an ex-cop."

"But what happened to poor Mina?" Mrs. Ellis leaned over to squeeze my hand.

"Amanda sent her an article about Penny Sledge, which made Penny look like the murderer. Amanda wanted to ruin both her husband and Penny to stir up a media frenzy before her erotic novel came out. That's why she leaked Danny's memoir to Beverly Ingram and gave her a ticket to the event."

"That nasty bitch!" Mrs. Ellis said, a hint of glee in her voice.

"Indeed." Morrie smiled. "Our lovely Mina was on her way to show the article to the police. Only Angus had got to the station first with free coffee and cronuts for all his ex-cop buddies, all laced with strong sedatives. Once he cleared the station he went downstairs, intending to hang Beverly in her cell with the leopard-print scarf and kill the last person who might realize he was the murderer. But then Mina bloody Wilde shows up with a purse full of dangerous insects and threatens to spoil the whole thing. And the rest you know."

"I'm so pleased you're all right," Mrs. Ellis gave me another hug, and a wet kiss on the cheek.

"We never would have found you if it hadn't been for Grimalkin. She sniffed me out outside Penny Sledge's house, and led me straight back to you. You were passed out. I was so scared that we were too late, but I found a faint pulse and called an ambulance. They arrived just in time." Morrie squeezed my hand. "I don't know what–"

"Yoo-hoo!" Mum's voice echoed down the hall. "I've been trying to get in to see you for nearly twenty minutes but some very rude nurse told me I wasn't allowed. I waited until she was called away and snuck past—" Mum tried to push the door open, but Heathcliff's bulk was in the way. He slid aside, smushing Morrie against the wall, and Mum stumbled into the room.

"Oh, hello, boys, Mrs. Ellis." Mum set down a bunch of

flowers on my bedside table, and leaned over to kiss me. "Mina, I'm so glad you're doing better. One more day and you can go home. I bet you're pleased."

I nodded. I was desperate to see the shop again. Heathcliff had been grumbling that ever since the police arrested Angus and let Beverly go, the shop had been wall-to-wall people. In fact, he'd been an hour late getting to the hospital this evening because he couldn't shove everyone out the door fast enough. The two romance authors who cancelled – Bethany Jadin and Marie Robinson – called to reschedule. They offered to run a reader party with lots of swag and booze and a couple of sexy male models. All the tickets to that had already sold out.

We were going to be able to pay the mortgage this month, with a bit leftover to save for the tagging system. It was going to be okay.

"I'm dying for some real food again," I croaked. "Maybe when I get out we can all go to the pub—"

"Oh, Mina, no. That food is so *unhealthy*. All that sugar and preservatives and saturated fat. I'm going to make sure you get all your vitamins and nutrients with my newest business venture." I groaned as Mum lifted an enormous object out of her tote bag and onto the bed. "It's a fruit snack machine. It's for people who want to be healthy but who can't stand the idea of eating fruit. You stick a whole apple or peach or fruit of your choice into this compartment, push the button, and the machine snap-dehydrates the fruit, slices it, covers it in salt, and spits it out here. They're fruit crisps – delicious *and* healthy. Isn't it remarkable?"

Remarkably disgusting. I tried to groan, but it hurt my chest. "It's… it's remarkable, all right. What happened to the Flourish patch?"

"Oh, I'm done with them. What a pack of scammers. Completely ridiculous. It's horrible how companies like that prey on the weak and uneducated," Mum said with a fierce scowl.

Morrie elbowed her in the side. "Tell her what happened, Helen."

Mum blushed. "Mina's had a traumatic experience. She doesn't want to hear about—"

Mischief glinted in Morrie's eye. "I know Mina. She will *definitely* want to hear this story."

"Tell me," I croaked.

"Fine." Mum sighed. "I had a little accident with my Mercedes."

My chest tightened painfully. "Are you okay? Were you hurt?"

"Oh, no, no. I'm fine. It's just..." Mum sighed again. "I was so excited about getting my Mercedes. I wanted to really see what it could do, you know? It wasn't much fun just popping down to the shops at a snail's pace. That car was built for the race-track, not for the speed bumps along the high street. I wanted to really put my foot down, enjoy my newfound wealth and freedom!"

"Mum, did you get caught speeding? You can't do that. You could get hurt, or you could cause an accident and hurt someone else—"

"No, no! I would never speed on the road. And the nearest racetrack is down in Barchester. I thought I'd find a nice open field. You know, one of the farms that backs on to the estate, just to really open her up and see what she can do."

"Oh, yes?" From the evil grin playing on Morrie's lips, I knew this was going to be good.

Mum's blush deepened. "It turns out that the field I'd chosen contained a small herd of prized Hereford cows. Of course I didn't see them because the field is so big! It shouldn't have been a problem. I was miles away from the cows when I let loose. Only, the grumpy farmer saw me barreling across the field toward his cattle, so he called the police!"

I let out a rasping laugh that stung my throat, but I didn't care. Morrie was already laughing. Beside me, Heathcliff let out a snort. Quoth covered his mouth with his hand, but I could tell from the way his eyes sparkled that he was laughing, too. Mum's face was beet red, but she continued. "The police come screaming around the corner, sirens blaring. Of course, I panic, and slam on the brakes. Except that now the wheels are so slick with cow dung that they're just spinning free. I can't get out. Everything I tried just buried the car deeper or splattered more dung around."

"The police had to tow the car out," Morrie gasped out between chortles. "One of the officers took a video and put it on Facebook. Do you want to see?"

"Hell yes."

"Mina! Morrie!" Mum looked horrified.

Morrie handed me his phone. Heathcliff, Quoth, and Mrs. Ellis crowded on the bed to watch. I hit PLAY and watched my mother waving her arms around, the Flourish logos visible even under the layers of crap.

"Mum!" I laughed. "You're going viral!"

"Mina, shhh!"

"You're famous. You'll be recognized everywhere in your Mercedes—"

"It's no good to me now," she snapped. "Of course, when the Flourish people saw the video, they decided I didn't have the right attitude to be a distributor for the company, so they revoked my membership."

Panic shot through me. "But what about the lease payments on the car? How are you able to afford—"

"It's fine," Morrie said. "I've sorted it."

Mum placed her arm around Morrie's shoulders and beamed. I noticed that he didn't look quite so jovial anymore. But I was too relieved to question him about it. That would come later, when we were back at the shop, when I was truly home again...

Heathcliff and Morrie continued bickering. Mrs. Ellis and Mum launched into a loud discussion about the various kinds of foods that could be made into crisps. Grimalkin slipped back into the room in her feline form and demanded to be let under the blankets to nuzzle against my legs. Quoth leaned over the bed and nuzzled my head with his.

"I'm so happy you're safe," he whispered.

But am I safe? Are any of us safe? We may have caught the murderer, but Count Dracula was still loose in the world, draining blood and building his power. And that wasn't even taking into account my grandmother being a shapeshifting feline water-nymph, my eyesight deteriorating, and Gary buying up the town and refusing to take no for an answer. I felt like the character in Poe's *The Pit and the Pendulum*, with a sword of Damocles waiting around every corner.

I glanced around the hospital room at all the people I loved most in the world, and a deep sense of trepidation settled in my gut. We might feel triumphant now, but an evil vampire and his plans for world domination could destroy everything and everyone I cared about.

"I don't want to be a downer," I whispered into Quoth's silky hair. "But I think our problems are just beginning."

CHAPTER THIRTY-FIVE

"*I* thought you weren't eating any of that hospital food," Heathcliff muttered as he staggered up the steps to Nevermore, holding me in his arms. "I thought you said it was, and I quote, 'so disgusting I'd rather drink Flourish smoothies'."

"I stand by that statement," I said, tightening my grip around his neck.

"Then why do you weigh more now than when you went in?"

"Hey! I resent that." I swatted his arm. "Blame Morrie. He's the one who kept sneaking in all those pork pies and Belgian chocolates."

Morrie took a bow. "I live to serve."

"I'm only kidding." Heathcliff's lips brushed my neck. "You're more beautiful than ever."

My heart swelled. Morrie dashed up the steps to hold the door open. Heathcliff carried me across the threshold. The scent of paper, old leather, dust, and cat fur permeated my pores. *Nevermore Bookshop.* It was so good to be back.

"Welcome home," Quoth smiled. It *was* my home now, in every possible way. In the hospital, the boys had asked me to move in with them again (actually, Heathcliff had demanded, and

Morrie had wheedled, and Quoth said nothing but smiled a tiny hopeful smile, and I was putty in their hands), and this time I couldn't refuse. Jo was awesome, but between the bugs and the crime scene reenactments and the refrigerator poison experiments, being her flatmate was a living nightmare.

For the first time, I, Mina Wilde, was moving in with my boyfriend. *Boyfriends*. That felt big and scary, but also perfect. I didn't know what the future held, but I knew I no longer cared what the world thought about me and my relationship. We were in love and proud of it, and if people had a problem with it, they could buy their reading material somewhere else.

Please don't buy reading material anywhere else.

"We've got something to show you," Morrie said, bounding up the stairs ahead of us. Quoth stayed by my side, as if I'd injured my legs instead of just my throat. Morrie dragged me to his room and flung open the door.

"I'm not sure now's the time for—" my words stopped in my throat.

The room had been completely transformed. Gone were the stark white walls and trendy industrial furniture. Instead of Morrie's pristine iron bed with the hospital corners, the clothing rack with rows of neatly paired brogues, and the rack of BDSM accoutrements, there was a brand new bed with a black iron frame, covered in a luxurious duvet and mountains of black and red pillows. On the wall behind the bed was an enormous iron sculpture painted in brushed silver – three panels, each one depicting a stylized scene from a novel – a grand rambling house on the moors, a two chairs sitting across from each other in front of a fireplace, a magnifying glass, gun, and pipe on the mantle, and a raven sitting on a bust.

"Quoth made that," Morrie said, as I stood on the bed to run my fingers over the metal.

"I thought you'd like something tactile," Quoth squeezed my hand. He looked concerned. I threw my arms around him.

"But... but..." I couldn't form words. It was all so, so perfect. "You gave up your room for me?"

"For us." Morrie slid his arms around Heathcliff and Quoth.

"But where will you sleep?"

"Oh, gorgeous, with you in the house, I don't intend to do any sleeping at all." Morrie's eyes glinted.

I wrapped him in my arms and drew him in for a deep, breathless kiss. "That was a serious question," I said as I came up for air.

"I've converted a storage room on the first floor into a bedroom," Morrie explained. "It's basically only large enough for a bed, but I'm storing my clothes and other items in Quoth's room. It's just temporary, until I can put the funds together to knock through these walls and create a large room for all of us. And we have one more surprise."

Morrie yanked me out into the hall and shoved the bathroom door. I turned my head away. "Don't open that! You don't know what horrors might spill out!"

"Stop being so dramatic," Heathcliff turned my head around. "It's not as bad as you think."

"Last time I opened te door it smelled like something died in there—"

I gasped. The once-grotty bathroom *gleamed*. Brand new marble tiles surrounded a beautiful roll-top copper bath and a pristine white basin. Fluffy cream towels hung from a copper rack, and a mattee-black storage cabinet in the corner held all sorts of delicious-looking bath products. Beside the basin was a skull-shaped toothbrush holder. It looked like a bathroom from a fancy hotel.

"It's amazing," I breathed. "But in a week it will be filled with mould and spiders..."

"Not if we stick to this," Quoth pointed to a chore-chart stuck to the back of the bathroom door. On it was a colour-coded cleaning schedule. The guys had already filled in their names.

Tears streamed down my cheeks as I embraced the guys. They'd done all this for me. *For us.* They were in this. How could I have ever doubted that they wouldn't want to be part of my harem? They wanted what we had to last forever, just like I did.

"I love you all so much," I whispered.

Heathcliff's mouth found mine, hot and needy. His broad chest pressed against mine. Behind me, Morrie brushed his lips against my ear, raking his teeth over my skin until I reacted with a shiver. Quoth laid a trail of light, fluttering kisses along my neck as he slid down my top, exposing my shoulder. We crashed out of the bathroom collapsed onto my brand new bed, the springs groaning under our weight as they rolled me over and...

Downstairs, the shop bell tingled.

"Fuck off!" Heathcliff yelled. I clapped my hand over his mouth.

I kissed them each in turn as I pulled down my top. "There's plenty of time for this later. We have customers!"

I bounded down the stairs, excited to see who had come in. Would it be someone trying to sell us a first edition Oscar Wilde, or another idiot confusing E. L. James and M. R. James? (not a mistake I'd want to make, personally.)

"Welcome to Nevermore Bookshop," I grinned as I rounded the staircase and spied a figure by the front door. "How can I help you today?"

The figure turned. Instantly, I recognized the stoic, grizzled face of Inspector Hayes. Behind him, DS Wilson stepped around the corner. "Hi, Inspector Hayes, can I help you find a book? We've got a pretty impressive true crime section—"

"I'm afraid I'm not here for a book, Mina." Hayes nodded to Wilson, who held up a pair of handcuffs and slapped them glee-fully over Morrie's wrists. "We're here to arrest James Moriarty on suspicion of murder."

TO BE CONTINUED

Morrie's been arrested on suspicion of murder. Mina knows the Napoleon of Crime is innocent, but how can she prove her favorite con-artist is being stitched-up? Find out in book 5 of the Nevermore Bookshop Mysteries, *Prose and Cons*.

Turn the page for an excerpt.

Can't get enough of Mina and her boys? Read a free alternative scene from Quoth's point-of-view along with other bonus scenes and extra stories when you sign up for the Steffanie Holmes newsletter.

FROM THE AUTHOR

I hope you enjoyed this mystery with Mina and her harem. I have a lot of fun writing this series and coming up with new murders.

The next murder mystery – *Prose and Cons* – is out now. I'm sorry for the delay, but I promise it was for a good cause. My husband and I celebrated ten years of marriage by returning to Wacken – the German heavy metal festival where we spent our honeymoon (we are NOT relaxing on the beach kind of people) – and going on an adventure of our own through Eastern Europe. I was conducting some important research for a new series that will be launching soon, as well as visiting some important sites related to Mina's arch nemesis – Count Dracula.

If you want to see some pictures from my travels and get fun updates about the series, then you can join my Facebook group Books That Bite or follow my Instagram.

And if you need something to read while you wait for more Nevermore Books, I've got you covered. Check out my Briar-wood Witches series – it's complete at 5 books, so that's 400,000+ words about a science nerd heroine who inherits a real English castle complete with great hall, turrets, and 5 hot English/Irish tenants. She also inherits some magical powers she can't control (also, there is MM). Grab the collection with a bonus scene. Turn the page for a teaser.

For something a little darker, try *Shunned*, book 1 of my Kings of Miskatonic Prep series. HP Lovecraft meets *Cruel Intentions* in a dark paranormal reverse harem bully romance about three broken bad boys and the girl who stood her ground. This is my most popular release EVER and readers are calling it, "The biggest mindfuck of 2019" so if you haven't read it already, I suggest you give it a try!

I'd like to thank my amazing family of writer buddies – aka, the Professional Perverts – for keeping me sane while finishing this book before my trip. Thanks Bri, Katya, Elaina, Kit, Jamie, and Emma for all the laughs and love. And to Amanda for the amazing cover art. You're a goddess.

And a big shout out to my adventure buddies – Gronk, Olya, Amy, Tony, Allan, Ian, Lee, Chrissy, Eli, Bree, and my amazing cantankerous drummer husband. I can't wait for more European shenanigans with you!

Until next time!

Steffanie

"I'm afraid I'm not here for a book, Mina." Hayes nodded to Wilson, who held up a pair of handcuffs and slapped them gleefully over Morrie's wrists. "We're here to arrest James Moriarty on suspicion of murder."

"What?" *That's... not possible.* "Murder?"

Morrie glanced between the two officers. The corner of his mouth tugged into a smirk that didn't reach his eyes. "I've got handcuffs in my room lined with velvet. They're so much more *sensual* than those old things. I'll wait here while you grab them, and then we—"

Sergeant Wilson shoved him toward the door. "James Moriarty, you do not have to say anything. But, it may harm your defense if you do not mention when questioned something which you later rely on in court—"

"Oooh, is the judge going to bang her gavel and tell me I've been a naughty boy?" Morrie purred. "Kinky."

"Don't say anything," I hissed at Morrie. Heathcliff, Quoth, and I barreled down the stairs and crowded into the hall. Heathcliff blocked the door while I threw my arms around Morrie and glared at Hayes (or the large, broad-shouldered blob I thought was Hayes. We hadn't turned on any lamps downstairs, so now that Heathcliff blocked the only light, all I could make out were shadows). "You have to tell us what's going on. We caught the garroter, so why—"

"This isn't about the garrotings." Hayes' voice was grave. "Mr. Moriarty is our lead suspect in the death of Kate Danvers."

"Who in the blazes is that?" Heathcliff's voice bellowed across the room. Tension rolled off his body – a palpable rage simmering in the room. I knew if we didn't get answers soon he'd go Full Metal Heathcliff and all that would be left of the inspectors would be bits of organs stuck to the ceiling.

"We don't have to explain ourselves to you." Wilson shoved Morrie toward the door. She tried to step around Heathcliff's bulk but ended up pressing Morrie into a shelf. Stacks of books cascaded down on us. "As much as you love to meddle in murders, *we're* the detectives here, and we say Mr. Moriarty's coming with us."

Heathcliff's shoulders tensed, and for a moment I seriously feared for all our lives. With a roar, he flung himself aside, giving Wilson a clear path. "He's innocent, and we'll fight this."

Heathcliff's words dripped with menace, and through my fear, I felt a jolt of hope. Ever since their fraught kiss, Heathcliff had distanced himself from Morrie. I knew Heathcliff felt something for Morrie, but his Heathcliff-ness meant he wouldn't acknowledge or give into it. Instead, he raged and sulked and became a complete shit until he drove Morrie away so then he wouldn't have to deal with it.

But right now, he was ready to fight *for* Morrie. He might not be able to articulate his feelings, but he was a slave to them. Heathcliff didn't know a thing about control, about hiding things that were ugly or scary or uncomfortable. He just *was*. And right now he was ready for a homicidal rampage on Morrie's behalf, and that *said* more than all the sweet nothings he might've whispered in Morrie's ear.

But it wasn't enough. We weren't at *Wuthering Heights*. This was the real world. The police were taking Morrie away, and we couldn't do a thing about it. A shiver ran down my spine. *Why are they taking Morrie? Why are they so certain he killed this Kate woman?*

I watched Morrie's face as Wilson shoved him outside. Flaccid British sunlight poked through the converging storm clouds, illuminating his sharp, chiseled features and the haughty tilt of his chin. Morrie's eyes sought mine, and he flashed me a reassuring grin that was all teeth and bravado.

A grin that I might have believed, if not for the fact it didn't reach his eyes. Morrie's ice-blue eyes were wide, darkened with shadows.

Resigned.

Not surprised.

"I'm sure it's a misunderstanding, gorgeous," Morrie called out as he scuffed the chipped stone steps with his brogues. "Don't worry your pretty head about me."

But that look in Morrie's eyes said otherwise. Whoever this Kate Danvers was, he knew her, and he already knew she was dead.

Why doesn't he look surprised?

My mind whirred with memories from the past couple of months. Morrie frowning at his phone, having his assets frozen, working on an algorithm to track Dracula's movements and making *certain* I knew how to use it. I worried about him, of course, but between figuring out who garroted Danny Sledge, discovering the shop cat Grimalkin was really an ancient Greek nymph named Critheïs *and* my grandmother, and hunting for a blood-crazed vampire intent on enslaving the world, I hadn't had time to get to the bottom of his odd behavior, and now…

… now he's gone and done something stupid.

Wilson pushed Morrie down the steps, tearing his gaze from mine. Heathcliff reached out to hold me back, but I slipped under his fingers and followed the detectives along Butcher Street to the town green, where a squad car waited, door open, ready to whisk Morrie away from me. Hayes placed a hand on Morrie's neck and directed him into the backseat.

"I'm going with him." I dashed around to the other door and slid inside before Wilson could stop me.

Hayes sighed. He was used to me by now. "Fine. We'll see you at the station. If James has his mobile on him, I recommend he contact his lawyer."

The officer behind the wheel nodded at Hayes and pulled away from the curb. He flicked on the radio, and loud violin music pumped through the speakers, so loud it shook the vehicle.

The seats reeked of sweat and urine, a fact I first noticed when the police arrested me on suspicion of murdering my ex-best friend, Ashley. It was hard to believe it was only a few months ago that I'd been sitting in this exact same position, wringing my hands and panicking about what would happen next. it felt like another time, and I was a different person now.

The new Mina – the one sitting across from her boyfriend, the Napoleon of Crime – this Mina wasn't afraid. She was *pissed as fuck*.

"What the bloody hell is going on?" I yelled over the music, leaning over to punch Morrie in the arm. "Who's Kate Danvers, and why do they think you killed her?"

Morrie rubbed his bicep. "Because I did kill her."

"Shhhh." My gaze flicked back to the officer, but he waved his arm about like a conductor, completely oblivious to Morrie's confession. "Don't say things like that. Didn't you listen when they cautioned you?"

"Relax, gorgeous. He can't hear a word over his Vivaldi. I'm more a fan of the Russian composers myself. No sense of melody whatsoever, but they embraced chaos—"

"Stop talking for a second so I can think." I sucked in a deep breath. My hand sought the comfort of Morrie's long fingers. "It's okay. It's going to be okay. Jo's our friend. She'll go over that body fifty times, *a hundred times*, until she finds the evidence to exonerate you. Is your phone in your pocket? I bet you've got some fancy lawyer friend down in London on speed dial. We'll call him and..."

My words trailed off as I noticed Morrie wasn't listening to me. His gaze was glued to his window, where houses and rolling fields whizzed past at top speed. The corner of his mouth tugged upward, but I couldn't tell if it was a smirk or a grimace.

That's odd. We should have reached the police station by now. It was only a few blocks across the village of Argleton. Instead, the oaks of Kings Copse Wood loomed over us as the squad car snaked out of the village, past quaint farm buildings and towering hedgerows, toward the wild peaks of the Barsetshire Fells.

"Morrie..." I poked him in the ribcage. "Why aren't we going to the police station?"

"I haven't the foggiest idea."

"Hey!" I banged on the cage separating us from the uniformed officer. "Where are you taking us? What's going on?"

In response, the officer turned the music up louder. I yelled and shook the cage. Morrie joined in, but neither of us could elicit even a nod of acknowledgment from the officer.

Fear clutched at my stomach. *This doesn't make any sense. Hayes would have told us if we were being taken somewhere else. What's going on?*

"What should we do?" I asked Morrie.

"I don't have my phone on me," Morrie patted his pockets. "I left it beside the bed. I do have a Montblanc pen I might be able to fashion into some sort of weapon—"

"It may come to that." I pulled my own phone from my pocket and dialed Quoth. When I raised it to my head, a weird hissing noise assaulted my eardrum, followed by a series of beeps. "What's that? Quoth? Can you hear me?"

Morrie took the phone from me and tried another call. "It's

not connecting. The cop's got some sort of jamming device in front. We're not getting through to anyone."

I stared at the picture of a litter of guide dog puppies on my phone's lock screen. My vision blurred until the puppies became a blob. "Okay, I'm officially scared now."

Morrie reached over and tried the door and window. Both were locked. He glanced back to me, but didn't say a thing, which only made my chest constrict more. Morrie always had a smartarse comment for every situation.

He laced his fingers in mine and squeezed. That squeeze told me more than words ever could – the indomitable James Moriarty was just as scared as I was.

We drove for what seemed like hours through increasingly barren dales. Limestone outcrops jutted through tufts of heather bent double in the wind. We wound through narrow roads up into what passed for mountains in the UK (an 'arduous hill' in any country with actual wilderness). We passed a small village named Barset Reach – just a collection of stone cottages, a pub, and a petrol station – and turned off the road onto a forest track.

Trees bent over the road, swiping at the sides and roof of the car – the fingers of a forest witch threatening to drag us away to a gingerbread house. Darkness swept my vision as the trees obscured the light, and my temples flared with a migraine as my eyes strained to make out shapes and shadows.

We came to a fork in the road. As the car swung right, Morrie leaned over and read out the sign. "It says, WILD OATS WILDERNESS SURVIVAL SCHOOL,' but it's pointing left." He frowned. "I recognize that name."

"Why are you frowning like that? Did you go there on a company team-building day and they make you eat cockroaches?"

"That's where Kate Danvers' body was found."

Shite. So why has the cop brought us back to the crime scene without telling Hayes? I squeezed Morrie's hand as the sharp stab of my migraine pierced my skull. Fluorescent green and orange lights danced in front of my eyes. Nothing like sheer terror to make vision loss worse.

We drove away from Wild Oats, away from the last sign of civilization, and bumped our way along a deteriorating path until we came to a clearing in the trees. The officer shut off the car and picked up his gun from the seat. The doors made a clicking noise as he released the lock.

"Get out of the car," he growled, tugging his peaked cap low over his face to hide his eyes in shadow.

My fingers trembled so hard it took me three tries to push the handle to open the door. Morrie was already around the side of the car, tugging me into his arms. He steadied me with his possessive grip, and I noticed he angled himself so he was between me and the constable, who I was now certain was not a real officer of the law. "I am a rich man. Whoever is paying you to do this, I'll double it. If you let Mina go, we can talk terms."

"Typical." The officer's voice dripped with derision. "You assume I am as corruptible as you. Girl, hand me your phone."

I thought about pretending I didn't have my phone with me, but I couldn't stop staring at the barrel of that gun. I drew my phone out of my pocket and held it out. The officer leaned forward to grab it from me. His fingers brushed mine and, for a moment, a sickly heat crackled on my skin. I itched to slap him, to scratch his eyes out, *anything* other than standing here like a useless fool.

The officer tossed my phone into a puddle, where it fizzed and sparked. The screen went blank as the puppies disappeared under the brackish water.

We're alone out here with this madman.

Morrie gripped me tighter, and I drew comfort from his presence. It would take a fellow madman to get us out of this mess, but that was exactly what Morrie was. Morrie didn't rage like Heathcliff – instead, he used his considerable intellect to think his way out of every jam. I could already see the cogs moving in his mind, his eyes flicking into the trees and then back at the gun as he considered our options. He tried again. "I can help you. I can give you the money and the means to disappear forever, and no one need know what happened here today."

The officer jabbed his gun in the direction of a narrow path winding up the side of the peak. "Walk. Don't make me ask twice."

Morrie's been arrested on suspicion of murder. Mina knows the Napoleon of Crime is innocent, but how can she prove her favorite con-artist is being stitched-up? Find out in book 5 of the Nevermore Bookshop Mysteries, *Prose and Cons*.

Morrie's been arrested on suspicion of murder. Mina knows the Napoleon of Crime is innocent, but how can she prove her favorite con-artist is being stitched-up?

Being the spider in the center of a vast criminal web has left Morrie in hot water. His list of enemies is long... too long for Mina and her men to unravel. Mina doesn't have a clue to stand on when a shadow from Morrie's past shows up and threatens to destroy everything she's fought for.

If Morrie's ex solves the murder before them it could mean the end of Nevermore Bookshop. But is Mina ready to pit her sleuthing skills against literature's foremost consulting detective?

Add a rambunctious puppy, a meddling mother, a cockroach cookery lesson, and their ultimate enemy closing in, and Mina's on her toughest case yet. There's only way to get the answers they need, but are Heathcliff and Quoth prepared to make the ultimate sacrifice to save their friend?

The Nevermore Bookshop Mysteries are what you get when all your book boyfriends come to life. Join a brooding antihero, a master criminal, a cheeky raven, and a heroine with a big heart (and an even bigger book collection) in book 5 of this steamy reverse harem paranormal mystery series by *USA Today* best-selling author Steffanie Holmes.

Read Prose and Cons now.

Dear Fae,

Don't even THINK about attacking my castle.

This science geek witch and her four magic-wielding men are about to get medieval on your ass.

I'm Maeve Crawford. For years I've had my future mathematically calculated down to the last detail; Leave my podunk Arizona town, graduate MIT, get into the space program, be the first woman on Mars, get a cat (not necessarily in this order).

Then fairies killed my parents and shot the whole plan to hell.

I've inherited a real, honest-to-goodness English castle – complete with turrets, ramparts, and four gorgeous male tenants, who I'm totally *not* in love with.

Not at all.

It would be crazy to fall for four guys at once, even though they're totally gorgeous and amazing and wonderful and kind.

But not as crazy as finding out I'm a witch. A week ago, I didn't even believe magic existed, and now I'm up to my ears in spells and prophetic dreams and messages from the dead.

When we're together – and I'm talking in the Biblical sense – the five of us wield a powerful magic that can banish the fae forever. They intend to stop us by killing us all.

I can't science my way out of this mess.

Forget NASA, it's going to take all my smarts just to survive Briarwood Castle.

The Castle of Earth and Embers is the first in a brand new steamy reverse harem romance by *USA Today* bestselling author, Steffanie Holmes. This full-length book glitters with love, heartache, hope, grief, dark magic, fairy trickery, steamy scenes, British slang, meat pies, second chances, and the healing powers of a good cup of tea. Read on only if you believe one just isn't enough.

Available from Amazon and in KU.

THE CASTLE OF EARTH AND EMBERS

*R*owan showed Maeve around the kitchen, pointing out the spice racks and explaining his stupidly complicated fridge-stacking system. Maeve listened attentively, and she didn't laugh or poke fun of any of Rowan's OCD tendencies. The tension slipped from his shoulders. She was affecting even him.

"What are you making here?" Maeve peered into the baskets of produce and empty preserving jars on the island.

Rowan's face reddened and his shoulders hunched back up again. I winced. That didn't last long. Maeve looked at Rowan's face as his jaw locked. He stared at his feet and twirled the end of a dreadlock around his finger.

"Rowan, is something wrong?" Maeve's voice tightened with concern. She reached out a hand to him, but he stepped back, leaving her arm hanging in the air. The awkward tension in the air ratcheted up a notch.

Time to save this situation. I stepped forward and grabbed Maeve's arm, doing my best to ignore the tingle of energy that shot through me when our skin touched. I'd have to get used to ignoring it. I dragged her across the room.

"This is really cool," I said, opening a door at the back of the kitchen to reveal a narrow staircase. "This was installed when the castle was a grand stately home so the servants could rush meals up to the bedrooms without being seen in the main part of the house. It comes up near the staircase that goes up to your bedroom, so it's a good shortcut down to the kitchen if you fancy a nightcap."

"Duly noted." Maeve sashayed across the room and peered up the narrow staircase. "Are the bedrooms upstairs? Can I see?"

At the word *bedroom* passing through her red, pursed lips, my cock tightened in protest. *Don't think about it.* But that was like telling Obelix – the pudgy castle cat – not to think about all the delicious birds sitting in the tree outside the window.

"Sure." I gestured to the staircase. "After you."

Maeve started up the narrow steps, her gorgeous arse hovering inches from my face. I made to follow her, but something heavy slammed into my side, knocking me against the wall. I cursed as my elbow scraped against the rough stone of the wall.

"Sorry mate," Flynn flashed me his devil's grin as he leapt past me and followed Maeve up the stairs. "I didn't see you there."

"I believe you," I mumbled as I followed them up. "Millions wouldn't."

At the top of the stairs, Maeve pressed her hands against the wood panel. "How do you get this open?"

Flynn tried to reach around her to unlock the clasp at the top of the door, but this time, I beat him to it. As I reached around Maeve, she turned slightly to press her back against the wall and her breasts brushed against my shirt, setting off a fire beneath my skin.

Her lips formed an O of surprise, and I couldn't help but mentally fill in that O with the shaft of my cock. I blinked, trying to stop thinking about her like that, trying to remember that it was the magic making me into this *animal*.

The air between us thinned, and an invisible force drew my

body forward, my arm brushing hers. A few inches more, and my lips would be pressed against hers—

No. You can't do this. You can't encourage her to choose you.

"Well, isn't this intimate?" Flynn shimmied his way through the gap so that he had his back against the opposite wall, his hands falling against Maeve's hips. If he wanted, he could slide her back so her arse rubbed against his cock, and even though that was totally cheating, I wouldn't even blame him. I was cheating just as bad – my face in hers, my eyes begging for her touch. All I'd have to do was lean forward, press my lips to hers, and it would all be over…

Want to find out what happens next – Start The Briarwood Witches series today.

OTHER BOOKS BY STEFFANIE HOLMES

This list is in recommended reading order, although each couple's story can be enjoyed as a standalone.

Nevermore Bookshop Mysteries

A Dead and Stormy Night

Of Mice and Murder

Pride and Premeditation

How Heathcliff Stole Christmas

Memoirs of a Garroter

Prose and Cons

A Novel Way to Die

Kings of Miskatonic Prep

Shunned

Initiated

Possessed

Ignited

Broken Muses of Manderley Academy

Ghosted

Haunted

Briarwood Reverse Harem series

The Castle of Earth and Embers

The Castle of Fire and Fable

The Castle of Water and Woe

The Castle of Wind and Whispers

The Castle of Spirit and Sorrow

Crookshollow Gothic Romance series

Art of Cunning (Alex & Ryan)

Art of the Hunt (Alex & Ryan)

Art of Temptation (Alex & Ryan)

The Man in Black (Elinor & Eric)

Watcher (Belinda & Cole)

Reaper (Belinda & Cole)

Wolves of Crookshollow series

Digging the Wolf (Anna & Luke)

Writing the Wolf (Rosa & Caleb)

Inking the Wolf (Bianca & Robbie)

Wedding the Wolf (Willow & Irvine)

Want to be informed when the next Steffanie Holmes paranormal romance story goes live? Sign up for the newsletter at www.steffanieholmes.com/newsletter to get the scoop, and score a free collection of bonus scenes and stories to enjoy!

ABOUT THE AUTHOR

Steffanie Holmes is the author of steamy historical and paranormal romance. Her books feature clever, witty heroines, wild shifters, cunning witches and alpha males who *always* get what they want.

Before becoming a writer, Steffanie worked as an archaeologist and museum curator. She loves to explore historical settings and ancient conceptions of love and possession. From Dark Age Europe to crumbling gothic estates, Steffanie is fascinated with how love can blossom between the most unlikely characters. She also writes dark fantasy / science fiction under S. C. Green.

Steffanie lives in New Zealand with her husband and a horde of cantankerous cats.

STEFFANIE HOLMES VIP LIST

Can't get enough of Mina and her boys? Read a free alternative scene from Quoth's point-of-view along with other bonus scenes and extra stories when you sign up for the Steffanie Holmes newsletter.

Come hang with Steffanie
www.steffanieholmes.com
hello@steffanieholmes.com

Milton Keynes UK
Ingram Content Group UK Ltd.
UKHW040032061123
432037UK00001B/11